Droplet's Journey Life in the Flow

Ishara Kassirer

MISCHIEVOUS MUSE PRESS   WORLD NOUVEAU PUBLISHING

World Nouveau

Droplet's Journey: Life in the Flow
A Mischievous Muse Book / May 2016

Published by Mischievous Muse Press
An imprint of World Nouveau, Inc.
Los Angeles County, California

Cover design by Gineve Lynnara

Library of Congress Cataloging-in-Publication Data
Kassirer, Ishara.
Droplet's Journey / Ishara Kassirer
spiritual fiction / speculative fiction
Droplet's Journey/ Ishara Kassirer

Mischievous Muse Press/ World Nouveau Publishing
ISBN: 978-1-9382081-9-5
Printed in the United States of America

10 9 8 7 6 5 4 3 2 1
BVG

Mischievous Muse Press
A Subsidiary of The World Nouveau Company
WWW.WORLDNOUVEAU.COM

Dedication

To the fateful attraction of hydrogen and oxygen, and to their fluid love-child. To that which resides in our cells, circulates within us, and without which we could not live.

To that which flows under our floors and behind our walls, letting us cleanse our bodies, our clothing, our households, while carrying away our wastes and asking nothing in return.

To life-giving moisture, willingly sharing itself with all plants, creatures and Beings.

To drops that fall from the sky, springs that bubble-up, currents that flow. To that world-building substance which is home itself to myriad creatures.

To that which separates territories and creates continents. To that which always finds the way of least resistance.

To that which constantly changes while staying the same. To that which reflects our spiritual nature, and so much more.
To water.

Praise for *Droplet's Journey: Life in the Flow*

"Ishara Kassirer has given us in *Droplet's Journey*, a **wonderful parable of the development of consciousness** and its expansion into a universe of wonderment and life. That she does this using a droplet of water as her protagonist is **a remarkable feat of imagination**, while her storytelling talent brings Droplet and all his companions and their **adventures** alive, making us care for them. Droplet's world may seem far from our own, but in fact, we, too, are part of a larger Flow. In understanding *Droplet's Journey*, we gain **rich insights** into our own."

> -David Spangler
> Author of *Journey into Fire* and *Apprenticed to Spirit*

"In this day and age, it's rare to find something wholly and completely original. And to discover a book that is not only **wonderfully unique,** but also **deeply moving, thoroughly engaging,** and beautiful to its core, is an utter gift in this world. *Droplet's Journey* is just such a book. What a pleasure it has been to immerse myself in Kassirer's liquid realms, and take this **extraordinary journey into consciousness** with such a wise (and surprisingly entertaining) guide."

> -Elayne G. James
> Author of *The LightBridge Legacy Series* and *The Saint of Carrington*, a Holiday Novel

Droplet's Journey

Prelude

The wise and very ancient Being settled in to wait. He had secreted himself at the bottom of the creek among the knobby roots of a great evergreen, across from a mossy bank the woman frequented. He judged the conditions to be just right—the season, the time of day, the sun's warmth—and had to set aside his rising expectation several times as he waited. What would be, would be, he reminded himself. He needed to be as calm a presence as possible, for the woman, if she came, had sensitivities far beyond most of her kind.

He must have dozed off, for suddenly she appeared on the other bank, dressed in her sturdy work clothes, wiping moisture from her brow. She bent to seat herself on the shade-dappled bank of the creek with a familiar economy of movement. He knew she belonged to the seventh generation of women to work this farm, and like those before her, she worked her land hard and cherished these brief periods of relaxation and renewal.

The woman settled herself physically, took a couple of deep breaths, and began a series of visualizations and inner exercises which allowed her to enter a calm, meditative state. Her experienced Watcher also moved through a similar series of mental exercises designed to match her inner progression. Finally, he could begin the delicate process of linking with her mind, and as he made the final shift, her thoughts flooded through him in a familiar, though not particularly comfortable, way. The intense sensory data he received could be unsettling; through her awareness he heard the calls of birds and humming insects, the sound of the wind's passing, and the lively burbling of the creek itself. He also received her perception of the rich fragrances surrounding her, along with her bodily sensations of fatigue and several tiny injuries she had sustained while working. Fortunately, by the time he completed the link, her eyes were closed so he didn't have to try to integrate her complex visual abilities. After a few moments of adjustment, he could observe her through multiple levels—her physical presence, her spiritual essence, and her deepening thoughts and inner experience.

He heard her tender self-encouragement: *Let it go now, Millie, let it all go. Feel the softness of the earth as it gently holds your tired body, and let everything else go.*

Merged with the woman's mind, he followed her thoughts as they moved in deepening currents, meandering through graceful landscapes of love and gratitude for all of life. Beneath her thoughts, in the subtlest current of all, he discerned the sweet, steady call of her heart to Source—an attraction he recognized as the foundation of his own Being as well.

With a sigh, the woman released the tension in her body and moved into an easy meditative state, envisioning each of her cells imbued with love, shining with consciousness.

A birdcall roused her and without opening her eyes, she casually leaned over and dipped her right hand into the creek. She lifted a shallow handful of water, and touched her cheeks and forehead with its coolness. Then she eased back onto the moss with her arms out-stretched, her left hand resting on a smooth rock, her right hand hanging over the edge of the bank.

The attention of her Watcher imperceptibly quickened.

Several drops, left over from water she'd used to cool herself, slowly rolled down her palm and onto the outer edge of her relaxed hand. At the tip of her littlest finger, they gradually came together to form a single, quavering drop.

The rounded edge of the drop caught the sunlight as the leafy canopy above it swayed in the freshening breeze. In an instant, radiant brilliance penetrated it. Fully saturated with light, it aligned in subtle alchemy with the timeless compassion and intention of the Watcher, and then with the strong, clear love and consciousness emanating from the woman.

A few moments later, the drop elongated pendulously and began to fall away from the woman's finger.

The Watcher respectfully and very skillfully released his connection with the woman, and followed the drop with his full attention. He observed the flexible, micro-thin covering which formed around it as it started its fall, and knew that when the drop entered the creek this covering would keep it from dissolving. He also knew that this resilient casing would make the drop a little heavier than the fluid surrounding it and give it a slight opacity. Most importantly, it would foster a focal point for consciousness.

With a small, gratifying splash, the Watcher saw/felt the drop enter the creek.

Its formation complete, the new and rare, but not entirely unique, Being slowly descended until it came to rest on the sandy creek bottom.

The Watcher added his own quick blessing of joyful welcome to the little droplet, which was softly pulsing with vibrancy, and then departed to pass the word.

A short time later, the woman, unaware of the special outcome of her meditative repose, arose deeply refreshed and returned to finish her work for the day.

One

*In the fine sand of the creek bottom, the first flickers
of a tiny consciousness stirred . . .*

Drifty, vague awareness reigned. With no ability
to control or focus this sentience, the droplet
observed its surroundings with blurry interest.
Toward the end of the day, in a slow in-turning of
consciousness, the droplet became cognizant of its physical
form for the first time. It explored this new awareness;
detecting tension on its upper form, and pressure on its lower
form. It somehow 'pushed out' on this boundary and
discovered it to be both finite and resilient.

While investigating the qualities of its form, it experienced
a second perceptual shift: the clear contrasting of *inside* from
outside. Now for the first time, it discerned its surroundings
as separate from itself—a subtle, but significant
achievement—for from the seeds of this distinction blossomed
the birth of a sense of identity. This emerging singularity
offered, as one of its many gifts, a consistent point of
reference.

The droplet now observed discrete shapes and forms
around him in the fading light. He saw large and small
objects, some still, many moving; soft brightness and deep
shadow; things soaring above him, and big, stationary objects
nearer him. It was a gala of visual stimuli, and he experienced
it all with a growing sense of *self*.

In the early rhythms of evening, the tired droplet made the
final discovery of a very full day. He was moving. Yes, there
was a subtle movement, a gentle rocking of his form. He
relaxed and stayed with this simple motion until his
awareness faded into somnolence.

That night, storm clouds moved into the foothills above the
creek where the droplet lay. The rain they released soaked the
thirsty earth and then formed rivulets, which entered the
creek at several points. The enlivened current, bearing an

1

array of twigs, dust and leaves, captured the unaware droplet and carried him far downstream from his point of origin. Toward morning it deposited him in a silty recess near a thick root in a larger, deeper creek.

Light again, but much dimmer now. All he could perceive was a shadowy haze, which he quickly lost interest in. With an intensified sense of presence, he focused again on his form.

He noticed his rocking had stopped so he studied this. Could he start moving again? Could he change his direction or turn himself? He tried everything he could imagine doing, but all of his attempts were fruitless. Unable to achieve volitional movement, he then tried to alter his view. At this, he was equally unsuccessful.

After thoroughly exploring his limits (many) and his abilities (few), he shifted his awareness beyond himself again and noticed that the murkiness around him had lessened. Although the forms were not as clear as they'd been before, he could once again make out large and small objects. He discovered his immediate environment had changed too; now he was quite near a dark, solid object which towered over him and, sadly, blocked much of his view.

He watched his way through the long span of light. Everything of interest flowed above him and then quickly moved beyond his field of vision. Now and then, a new sight would thrill him, but most of what he observed he'd seen before, and his inability to move or change his view in any way tempered his enthusiasm.

By the middle of his third day of sameness, lassitude had capsized his ability to focus his attention. No longer engaged and shrouded in dimness, his awareness slipped in and out of billowy dream-states.

The exquisite link with his increasingly transparent corporeal form began to tatter and fray.

As with the newly-born of any species, this tiny life-form required contact, nurturing, and guidance to survive. The circumstances of his birth, the coming together of Love and Light guided by the wisdom of shared Mind, gave this particular sentience tremendous potential. To keep his individual awareness from slipping away entirely, as so often happens at this stage of emerging consciousness in water, one thing was absolutely essential.

He must be found.

Upstream, the two Finders were frustrated. They had searched and cross-searched the most likely areas of the creek bottom for several days, but they'd been unable to locate the tiny spark of awareness it was their job to find. Tired and close to quitting, they traveled back downstream, giving it a final sweep.

"I *know* I felt something near here," Lemsel sent via focused energy to his partner.

"Well, you're the best there is, Lem. If you've sensed a potential foundling around here, we'll just have to search till we find it."

Lemsel felt revitalized by Boklin's confidence in him. "Okay, let's search the other bank again."

The two finders, long partners, moved together across the creek bottom toward the hither bank, searching as they went.

"Wait, what was that? Do you sense something here, Bok?" Finder Lem had zeroed in on a silty patch near a large root.

Boklin, who was right next to him, responded with, "Huh. It might be an awareness, but it's very faint."

The two finders eased their corpuscular shapes down into the silt and worked together to ruffle it up a bit. "I think it's just here," sent Lem. Then, "Ah, here we are."

As gently as they could, the Finders uncovered the small droplet, who appeared transparent and somewhat flattened, with a weakly fluttering spark of awareness.

"He's in a bad way, Lem." Boklin started pulling back, in the belief that they were too late.

"Wait. Stay near, Bok. We'll send him an energy charge together—very gently. Ready?"

Finder Lemsel received the gentle electrical charge from his partner, and directed it into the floundering foundling. They waited briefly and tried again.

"No response, Lem. We can't always find them in time, and this bit of consciousness seems too faint and scattered to be a true foundling. Let's just go back now."

"No. There's something about this little . . ."

3

Finder Lemsel quickly swept his perception through its whole range. "We can't give up on him Bok, I can still sense his *esse*. Hmm . . . Wise Elder is still visiting, isn't he? Go get him Bok, while I stay here and try to keep the foundling conscious with energy bursts. Hurry!"

A short time later, Finder Boklin returned with the venerated traveler known as Wise Elder.

"Here, let me see what you've got there, Finder Lemsel." Wise Elder moved next to Lem and pushed gently against the limp droplet.

"Hmm yes," he agreed, "the consciousness is very faint." Wise Elder deepened his perception and with a thrill of excitement encountered the foundling's somewhat dispersed, but surprisingly strong *esse*. "But there is a very strong *esse* here," he sent to the finders next to him. "Let's see if we can revive him."

With that, Wise Elder skillfully sent a potent questing current into the little droplet.

The foundling droplet, whose awareness was almost completely diffused, felt a curious stirring; something distinct occurring in the field of undifferentiated awareness in which he hovered. He focused listlessly on the slight commotion.

Suddenly, there was a flare of light *inside* him, where only dimness had been. This surprise was quickly surpassed by the appealing nature of the light itself. It was focused and intense, but also alluring. Fully roused, the droplet became enticed with the quality of light now filling his inner awareness.

From within, Wise Elder noticed this reaction and altered his intention. He modified his *esse* until the stream of light-awareness engaged thoroughly and safely with the foundling's more delicate consciousness. Their two points of awareness started circling one another. Next, Wise Elder increased the attractive quality of his light.

Their connection strengthened and stabilized.

Then, with great care, Wise Elder guided the foundling's fragile consciousness back into the world of form.

With a jolt, the droplet became aware of his physical

surroundings again. In the relative brightness he could perceive—in an unfocused sort of way—three softly-lit spheres quite close to him.

Without volition, his perception abruptly sharpened. Now he could clearly discern two of the globes flickering faintly, and another pulsating brightly. He then felt the subtle arrival of his first emotions; relief and gladness, and sensed they came from the brightest globe touching him.

Light here contacting me, was the foundling-droplet's first complete thought of self-awareness.

With great sensitivity, Wise Elder received the foundling's tenuous thought, and responded by strengthening his own *esse,* and adding the simple energy sending of, "Welcome, Little One."

The foundling quickly oriented on the sending, but lacked the experience to understand it. Intrigued, he brought his total awareness to the task.

Impressive, thought Wise Elder to himself. Then he sent to the two finders who were observing closely, "Ah, and now we see some of this little foundling's potential."

At this point, the finders agreed with what Wise Elder had become certain of: before them was a true foundling, one like them, with an *esse,* and a mind capable of conscious thought and self-awareness.

"Well done, Finders Lemsel and Boklin. I know that this was a difficult finding, but I believe this little one will be well worth it. I sense real promise in him, along with some unique abilities for one of our kind. Now let's get him back to the Others, so he can be nurtured and taught."

With that, the three globes carefully slipped beneath the foundling, who was both smaller and somewhat lighter than they were. Then, generating a simple attractor-charge, they lifted the little foundling, and slowly carried him out into the current.

This journey, the foundling's first with awareness, was wondrous. He felt completely engaged with what was going on, and very interested in everything he could perceive. Soon, the four of them moved out of the shadows and into the full light of something very bright, which enhanced the appearance of everything. Now instead of vague shapes he could see defined objects, and much more movement! There were big and little objects flitting and moving all around them, almost all going in the same direction they were. The foundling found all of this activity enticing.

After a long while, they came to a stop near something large and stationary. The softly glowing globes surrounding him eased him into a shallow depression and then moved slightly away. The foundling could feel electrical pulses near him again, and then the brightest globe—the one he'd felt such a strong affinity with—departed. The other two were a calming presence though, and with the arrival of dusk, drowsiness ensued.

The foundling had a vague sense of fulfillment and rightness as he drifted into the sleep of true innocence.

When the foundling returned to consciousness, darkness was gradually dissolving into brightness. He realized much had changed as he watched the details of his new location emerge in the slowly increasing light. He was quietly delighted with his situation, especially his increased ability to perceive his surroundings.

Eventually he focused his awareness on his physical form. He was still between the two familiar globes, at least one of which seemed to be conscious of him.

Finder Lemsel observed the foundling carefully. Before he left, Wise Elder had told them that they would need to care-take the foundling until the nearest available mentor could be notified. Wise Elder believed the closest unattached mentor was Mentor Sootan, and if so, it would likely take him a couple of days to get to them. Wise Elder told them he would contact Mentor Sootan immediately, and was confident they would do just fine with the foundling, who was now very alert.

But they were *finders* and their responsibility usually ended with a successful finding. What did they know about the caretaking of foundlings? What were they supposed to do with one who couldn't move or even communicate? Both finders knew it took someone skilled in teaching foundlings to help them grow and mature properly. There were enough tales of foundlings losing awareness, going *wavy*, or being otherwise damaged to the extent they were unable to have a normal existence, to earn mentors ample respect for what they did. For what they were carefully *trained* to do.

When his partner finally awoke, Lem calmly moved over next to him, all the while maintaining contact with the foundling—at least he knew that much—and unloaded all of his thoughts and concerns in a tight sending.

"*Swirling flumett*, Lem! What are you going on about? So we have to do a bit of caretaking. How hard can it be?"

The answer to that question revealed itself over the next two days.

"I think he's bored, Bok," Lem sent quietly. After an uneventful first morning of constant but very quiet contact, the foundling's awareness was starting to waver.

"Naw, he's probably just tired. Think we should try something to keep him engaged, or let him drift off?"

"I have no idea."

"Oops—he's starting to rally. Do you think he can sense our sendings?"

"Maybe."

But it was the large flasher, swimming near the center of The Flow that had caught the foundling's interest. Both finders could sense the foundling's increased intensity. They could also sense his difficulty in focusing on the flasher.

"That's strange. He can't really focus very well, can he? Maybe we can help."

"I don't know Bok, I don't think we should interfere with him."

"I'm not talking about interfering; I'm talking about helping him perceive—what is more basic than that?"

Lemsel thought about it and then sent, "Well, I guess we could try—but I think we need to be very gentle. What did you have in mind?"

"Let's see if we can engage his *esse*, first. Then we'll know if we can help him or not. Okay?"

"Yes, but if it doesn't work we need to leave him alone."

In agreement, the two finders focused their *esse-sight* on the little foundling, who gradually responded. Through the power of their combined concentration, the foundling's

7

perception grew abundantly more clear. His immediate surge of interest/attention communicated this to them perfectly. By linking with his awareness even more, the finders were able to show him how to change perceptual focal lengths. Over and over they helped him switch from up-close, to medium distance, and then to far distance, until the foundling could do it on his own.

When the 'lesson' spontaneously concluded, they all shared a sense of tired satisfaction. The rest of that day and night passed quietly as the foundling worked on *perceiving*.

Early the next morning the foundling was awake, and again practicing his new skills. Where before he could only make out the basic shape of objects around him, now he could discern clean edges, depth, and texture in the things both close to him and far away.

By tightening his focus, he was also able to detect small differences in his two companions: one was slightly larger than the other and had an uneven texture. The other was smoother and had a small dip near the top of its surface. Both were nearly perfectly round and were gently pressing against him. Adjusting his focus even more, the foundling discerned a bright glow deep within each of them that gradually became harder to see as the day brightened around him.

There was a sudden dimming of light and the foundling looked up to see a large angled shape gliding over him. He had seen other shapes like this one, but this one was bigger. As it moved away he had a strong urge to follow it, but try as he might, he was still unable to move in any way.

The finders had been awake for a while, observing their charge covertly. They had noticed the foundling's attention shift to the large flasher above them, and had also detected his impulse to move.

After thinking about this for a bit, Bok made a decision. "I think we should show him how to move, Lem. If we did it very gradually, I'm sure it would be all right. What do you think?"

Lem received Bok's tight-band sending, designed to go unnoticed by the foundling between them, but didn't answer right away. He was pretty sure they shouldn't attempt it, but he had trouble imagining spending the whole day doing nothing, because their little foundling was incapable of doing *anything*.

"Okay. Maybe we could start by rolling him a bit. I'll move him to the top of the hollow and then let him roll down on his own. You nab him when he gets to the bottom. That way he'll almost always be in contact with one of us."

"Great idea. Let's do it."

Using an attractor-charge, Lem easily moved himself to the outer edge of the shallow depression.   used a softer, wide-beam attractor-charge to draw the foundling to him. Lem waited until the foundling oriented on him, and then gently withdrew the charge. The foundling rolled to the bottom of the hollow, his *esse* spinning wildly, where Bok snagged him with an attractor-charge. They watched carefully as his *esse* slowly came to a stop.

"Well that was a surprise." Bok drolly distance-sent to an amused Lem, who was still at the hollow's edge. "I didn't imagine his *esse* would spin like that. How in The Flow are we going to teach him to hold his *esse* steady while his form moves?"

"Once again, Finder Boklin, I have no idea."

After a pause Bok suggested, "Let's try it again and see if he figures it out on his own."

Several tries later they had a seriously dizzy, but otherwise unharmed and obviously still eager, foundling. Even taking a turn rolling around the foundling themselves—while holding their own *esses* steady—hadn't inspired him.

"So, he's not figuring it out very well, is he?" All three of them were together at the bottom of the hollow pondering the situation in their own ways.

"At this point, I don't imagine anything short of making a direct connection with his *esse*, and holding it steady for him as he rolls, would work."

The two finders looked at each other.

"All right. Lem, you've got the more sensitive *esse*. You do a simple bond with him, and I'll roll him a bit until he gets it. Shall we try it?"

The foundling had been very intrigued by all of the motion he was experiencing. He knew *he* wasn't making it happen, but he really did like moving and he'd been observing the others carefully.

Eventually he even understood what they were trying to show him—to keep part of him still while the rest of him moved—but he hadn't a clue how to do this. He had no awareness of any differences inside of him, and no way to make the distinction. That is, until one of the others made an *inside* connection with him, like what they did to help him learn to see better. Then, while this one held his inside part steady, the other one moved him around. All at once he understood! There *was* a difference between the part being held steady inside of him, and the part of him that was moving. As soon as he realized this, the one holding him steady retreated and let him manage on his own. Finally he could roll without spinning inside! This brought a surge of satisfaction.

Lem could easily sense the foundling's strong emotion even though he had broken the *esse-contact*. He didn't believe all foundlings had such a strong presence only a few days after being found, but this one certainly did. And now the little droplet was slightly bobbing his *esse* up and down—showing his new ability, and clearly ready to be rolled again.

After they'd rolled most of the morning away, they moved on to bouncing the delighted foundling between them as they gradually moved further apart.

It wasn't until mid-afternoon, after they had become very proficient with this activity, that Mentor Sootan finally arrived.

Mentor Sootan had been traveling at his top speed. He well knew the first days of a foundling's training were crucial to its development. And of course a foundling's early development was his responsibility, a responsibility he took very seriously.

As he came up over the edge of the small hollow where he expected them to be waiting, he was quite shocked to see the two lumbering finders—Lemsel and Boklin, he noted—at either end of the hollow *bouncing* the little foundling back and forth between them. He paused briefly to try to calm his incredulousness—*you just can't trust finders with anything but finding!*—then he bustled into the hollow to take charge.

"Great Wave! What do you think you are doing?" His strong distance-sending brought the activity in the hollow to an abrupt halt. The foundling was carefully contained and then lowered to the ground by a chagrined Boklin, as Mentor Sootan approached them bristling with agitation.

Lemsel, always the quicker one, responded calmly. "Ah, Mentor Sootan, you've arrived. We were merely helping the foundling learn about movement."

"Like that? That is far from an approved method—there are protocols to be followed. You could have harmed him!"

"We were actually very careful with him, Mentor Sootan. He's fine. Now that you've arrived, we'll just be on our way."

Boklin gently rolled the alert but subdued foundling over to Mentor Sootan and detached from him. Both finders watched as Mentor Sootan did a quick scan of the little foundling and then turned back to them.

"Well, he seems to be all right," he acknowledged. "But I strongly recommend you never do anything remotely like that again. I'm serious about the potential for harming foundlings. As you should well know, they require constant contact, and gentle guidance and care."

"Yes, we do know that." Boklin finally felt ready to enter the conversation. "We started out very slowly with him before we worked up to what you just saw. And he really seemed to like it. I'm sure if you just—"

"Yes, *thank you,* Finder Boklin," Mentor Sootan cut in sharply. "I will take over from here. I'm quite certain your services are needed elsewhere."

"Yes, they probably are." After responding to the mentor's obvious dismissal, Lemsel sent a tight-beamed message to his partner, and the two of them rolled to the edge of the little hollow. Before they moved beyond it, they both turned to see Mentor Sootan gently nudging the tired-looking foundling.

"He'll do fine," sent Bok calmly as they headed downstream together and picked up speed.

"I know. I just wonder how he'll get on with Sootan."

Two

Mentor Sootan knew himself to be tired from his journey and not as alert as he needed to be. As soon as the two finders left, the mentor used a soft attractor-charge to move the foundling into an indentation at the bottom of the teaching hollow, where he could rest without needing to use a charge to maintain contact. Once they were situated, he surrounded the little foundling with a gentle calming charge.

As soon as the foundling, who appeared to be exhausted, had completely relaxed, Mentor Sootan let his awareness drift into an unfocused and deeply restful state.

The foundling awoke first. In the dimming light he noticed that the two larger beings were still gone, and that he was being touched by the new and unfamiliar presence next to him.

He practiced his perceptual skills until it grew completely dark; then he wanted some interaction. He attempted to get the newcomer's attention, but he could not. He tried building-up a charge the way he had observed the others doing, but nothing happened. When he tried to nudge or bump the being next to him, he discovered he still couldn't move on his own. As nothing he tried worked, his *esse* began to flutter, and he experienced an unpleasant sensation.

Finally, the being next to him stirred, its inner glow brightening. When the being focused its awareness on him, it quickly sent him a gentle charge which calmed him.

The foundling stilled and gathered his attention.

Then something completely unexpected happened. The new being sent him a peculiar charge which caused images to form in his awareness. This felt very different from the kind of interaction he'd shared with his first two companions. Thought-images of brightness and safety seemed to invade his awareness in a way that was not entirely comfortable. The soothing content of the *sendings* seemed at odds with his experience of receiving them. When he tried to form a direct link with their sender, the steady glow he could perceive in the being would recede, avoiding contact.

After receiving several of these sendings, and surprised by the other's avoidance of direct inner contact, he felt increasingly unsettled. A sense of pressure and urgency began to mount inside of him; he wanted to resist, to alter the experience, or to reciprocate in some way, but how?

All of this thought and urgency built in him until it created an electrical charge which suddenly traversed the thin barrier between them and dissipated. When this occurred, he instantly felt a lessening of pressure, along with a subtle sense of relief.

Just as he began to wonder what had happened, an answering charge came to him from the other. The brightness of this charge and its playful message of invitation completely captured his attention and dissolved his discomfort.

Again and again, the energy charges moved between them, mostly comforting or encouraging, sometimes with little variations which were always initiated by the being next to him. Very quickly he learned to exactly mimic what he received, and send it back.

Then, at one point, he intentionally changed the charge before sending it back. He was quite pleased to instantly receive a new and completely different sending from the being touching him as well. With this charge, came the image of a circle of many globes touching one another, and the thought-feeling of achievement and acceptance.

Pleased, and suddenly exhausted, his awareness drifted away.

Mentor Sootan felt the foundling's awareness ebb, and gently detached himself. In all his time of working with foundlings, Sootan had seen many personalities emerge. He was pleased to discover this foundling's bright and curious mind, along with his eagerness to communicate. But he'd had to work hard to discourage the foundling's persistent attempts to link *esses* with him, and instead encourage *sending*—the common and proper form of communication between Others of his kind. *Esse-bonding with newly emerged foundlings! What were those two finders thinking? They certainly didn't make my job any easier, but at least they didn't harm him, as far as I can tell.*

Sootan briefly and automatically probed the foundling next to him, and found him moving into a deeper sleep pattern. *Good.* While still longing for sleep himself, Sootan took this opportunity to gather his thoughts and customize his lesson plans based on what he'd learned of his new pupil so far.

The education of foundlings centered around two precepts: the first was that they work with one mentor until a sufficient connection formed to allow them to trust and to learn. The second was that they remain isolated from the rest of their kind until they'd mastered basic communication skills, could move independently, understood common social structure, and had *crested* developmentally.

Once a foundling could initiate and respond to sendings, Mentor Sootan liked to introduce a matching game. This exercise helped to shape a foundling's thought processes, and gave him experience in matching thought-pictures to actual objects in The Flow.

Mentor Sootan, who had kept a tendril of his awareness connected to the foundling throughout the night, awoke just as the foundling became alert. The surface of The Flow had barely started to reflect the coming dawn, and their hollow was still in deep shadow.

Although he could sense the eagerness in the foundling next to him, he knew they needed to wait for the full light of day before beginning the matching game. He quietly held the foundling close with a soothing attractor-charge.

The foundling had rested deeply and felt eager for something new. The being next to him, though, was calm and still, and after a moment he settled as well.

Very slowly, all around him objects were becoming clear. He couldn't understand the process of darkness giving way to light, but he felt a spontaneous appreciation for the increased clarity and possibilities of daylight.

Just as he began to lose his focus, he received a sending

from the other next to him and returned it immediately, hopefully indicating his readiness for something new.

Mentor Sootan used a focused attractor-charge to pull the foundling to the edge of the hollow on the aft side of the creek. He brought them to a stop near a pale, flat stick wedged under a dark rock. He waited until he had the foundling's full attention and sent the thought-images for *stick* and *rock*.

The foundling received the thought-images, but didn't know what they meant. After receiving them two more times in a different order, along with a little nudge toward the objects near him, he suddenly understood. The thought-pictures looked similar to what he perceived in front of him, so he sent them back along with his excitement at understanding something new.

From there, they explored the entire rim of the teaching hollow while he identified each object after receiving the thought-image for it from his guide. This required his full attention and he liked that.

After taking a short break, his guide moved them next to a specific object and he would have to recall the thought-picture he'd learned earlier and send it correctly. He made a few mistakes, but was always encouraged to continue until he got it right.

By mid-day he'd successfully matched thought-images to many nearby objects including *plants, stalks, sand, mud, silt, hollow, rim,* and several types of *rocks,* including *larger stones* and *pebbles.* He'd also mastered *surface, current, bank, moss, tree, roots,* and floating objects like *leaves, bark,* and *foam.* Finally, he'd learned the trickier terms that described parts of objects, like *top, bottom, up, down, inside, outside, front* and *back;* as well as moving terms including *coming, going, in, out, rolling, floating, bounce, travel, explore, upstream* and *downstream.*

When he received the thought-picture for *bouncing* he was immediately reminded of the two others who had been with him. He had the impulse to ask where they were, but didn't know how.

Everything the foundling saw and learned brought him a sense of satisfaction. He liked learning about his surroundings almost as much as he enjoyed just being aware of the amazing things around him without thinking at all.

Mentor Sootan was pleased with the foundling's progress. He had just returned them to the bottom of the teaching hollow for a rest, when two large shapes passed over them, putting them briefly into shadow.

"Those are *creatures* called *flashers,*" he sent to his pupil, who had noticed the shadow and looked up at the movement.

Flashers, his pupil replied in what was now a well-practiced ritual.

Then Mentor Sootan took them to the next level by sending the complex thought-images, *"Flashers swimming upstream."*

To the foundling, tired as he was, the *flashers* were a wonder. Until he had seen the sleek shapes *moving* above him, he had focused on learning the terms for fixed objects. And before clearly observing the flashers, he hadn't seen anything that moved *upstream* on its own. He watched them recede into the distance until they were gone. Then, quite unexpectedly, his awareness faltered and exhaustion claimed him.

Late that day, as twilight turned the surface above them silvery and daylight ebbed away, Mentor Sootan taught his pupil the thought-images for *light, dark, day, night, dawn, morning, mid-day, twilight or evening*, and the most common thought-images for *sol or sun*, and *moon or orb*.

Then they practiced stringing the thought-images together into phrases and sending them back and forth, like, *sol shines in day*, and *orb lights the night*.

For the final lesson of their very productive day, Mentor Sootan sent, "This, all around us, is *The Flow*."

"*The Flow*." His tired pupil returned the complex thought-image slowly.

"Yes, we are inside The Flow; it is where we exist."

"Inside The Flow," his pupil responded dreamily.

Aware that they both needed a full night's rest he sent, "Yes. Rest now, more tomorrow."

Three

The foundling awoke as first light gradually brightened his surroundings. *The Flow*, he remembered, as he watched the currents ripple the surface above him. He intuitively felt connected to what he was seeing in a deep way. By relaxing something inside of him, his awareness expanded until it seemed to fill all of The Flow around him. This experience, though delicate and quite brief, brought him a sense of peace.

A short while later, when his companion awoke, his focused learning continued.

Mentor Sootan took them to a little ledge just beyond the rim of the teaching hollow. Then he introduced the thought-images for self and other to his very alert pupil.

"*Self?*"

"Yes, your *form* and *awareness* make you a *self*. Both *you* and *I* are *selves*." He made the thought-images as simple as possible to help facilitate the shift to more abstract concepts.

"*Self* in Flow?"

"Yes, *self* is in *The* Flow," he corrected. "And there are many more selves; these are *Others*, as in *Others-of-our-kind*." The thought-picture for Others was very clear—a cluster of softly luminous globes. This supported the concept of self as one among Others.

The foundling took this in quietly. Then he sent, "I am self, you are self, others are self?"

Pleased with the foundling's quick understanding, he sent back, "Yes, each of us is a self; *all* of us are *selves* within The Flow. We often form *groupings* together—as a way to get to know one another and share experiences."

The thought-image for *groupings* resembled that for *Others*, but included a soft light surrounding them as a whole.

17

After a long pause, the foundling sent, "See more The Flow now?"

Mentor Sootan lowered them back to the edge of the hollow, and allowed them to roll separately down the outer slope toward the base of some nearby plants.

The foundling remembered how much he enjoyed rolling. "Learn roll, *me*," he sent his attentive companion.

"Yes, I can teach you how to roll *on your own*. First you focus your attention on the upper part of your form, like this." His companion helped him get his attention focused. "Then you focus on the lower portion of your form and *lean* forward with your *intent*."

The foundling had no idea what these thought-images meant, but he felt very determined to learn to roll on his own. After many tries, and lots of encouragement, he finally mastered it. He demonstrated his ability by rolling straight toward the plants.

"Well done," came the feeling-toned response he'd expected. "As long as there is no current and the area is flat, you should do fine. Now see if you can roll *among* the plants, here."

The foundling rolled up to the first plant stalk, bumped it lightly, and came to a stop. He tried several things, but he couldn't seem to roll around or even away from it.

After a moment, his companion showed him how to use his focus and intention to roll *backward* and then *change direction*.

Once he'd mastered these refinements, he entered the small cluster of plants on his own.

The first thing he noticed was the muted light at the base of the stalks. He felt a deep stillness in The Flow here; it felt interesting and a little strange to be alone in such a different environment. As he rested for a moment against a smooth stalk, he felt small shaking movements. He looked for the source of the movement, but The Flow around him remained still. It wasn't until he looked up that he discovered the relationship between the movement he sensed and the noticeable tug of the current on the plant's upper portion.

He continued exploring by rolling to the far edge of the cluster where he discovered two small flashers, nearly motionless and hidden among the fronds of the largest plants. Fascinated to be this close to such intriguing creatures, he stayed and watched their tiny motions until his companion approached and suggested they continue learning.

Mentor Sootan had observed his pupil exploring the plants and felt pleased with both his curiosity and his growing ability to *think* about what he experienced. When the foundling was ready to resume, he decided to introduce the topics of personal names, social interaction and titles.

"Each of us, each self has a *name*. My name is *Sootan*." He sent the thought-images for his name, *Soo-tan*.

"*Soo-tan*. My self has name?"

"Yes, a name which you will *choose*."

After *choosing* was explained, his pupil surprised him by sending, "My name I know—*Droplet*." The thought-image was quite clear.

"You know your name is *Droplet*?" In his experience it was uncommon for a foundling to know his name, but it did happen, and it eliminated the often lengthy process of choosing one.

"Yes, Droplet."

"All right then, Droplet it is."

Next he taught his pupil, Droplet, what he called the *social courtesies*. These included forms of *greeting* Others, *introducing* oneself, and of *leaving*. They also discussed how and why to defer to *elders*, and how to show respect to anyone by your choice of sending and *attitude*.

They practiced all of the forms together until Droplet was proficient. For some reason, his pupil found the common introduction, "Hello, my name is Droplet" a very funny sending. His mirth affected his ability to send it clearly, and this made it quite humorous to them both.

After a short break, Mentor Sootan explained the concept of titles. "Because I *teach* Others, my title is *mentor*. This thought-image *precedes* my name like this: *Mentor* Sootan."

"*Mentor Sootan*." Then came the expected question, "What my title?"

"What *is* my title? You are called a *foundling*, because we recently found you. You are also my *pupil* because I teach you, but you don't have a title yet."

"Why?"

"A title is *acquired* or *earned* over *time*," sent Mentor Sootan, slowly building the appropriate thought-images. "It has to do with one's *interests* and *attributes*; what one enjoys doing. But a *use-name*, such as Droplet, is chosen by the individual. It often includes the first two letters one's *Grouping*. For example, I am of the *Sonnfork* Grouping, so my name begins with 's-o'."

"What is *Sonnfork* Grouping?"

"It is the grouping with which I *reside*. It is the place I go to be close to the Others I most like to be near." He added the feeling-tones of comfort and closeness to the thought-images in this sending, and then waited patiently for Droplet's response.

Droplet received the thought-images and wondered at the other information he could sense in the sending. He remembered getting something like this from his mentor very early on. Finally he asked, "What you send?"

"Good, I knew you would notice," came the immediate reply. "I added basic *feeling-tones* to the thought-images. By adding feeling-tones to a sending we're able to increase or *refine* the meaning it conveys."

Droplet thought about this. He did get more information from the feeling-tones; the sending felt richer or fuller somehow. He also realized he understood the feeling-tones— no, he *felt* them—without having to learn what each one meant. But when he tried to add a feeling-tone to his response, he found he couldn't.

"How do you add feeling-tone?"

"The easiest way is by feeling them yourself, Droplet. Think of something that makes you feel happy and then add that feeling-tone to your sending."

Droplet thought of how The Flow looked just after dawn, added the way it made him *feel*, and sent, "I like early morning."

"Yes, well done! I received that perfectly."

He easily incorporated his pleasure at receiving this praise into his next several sendings.

Toward the end of the day Mentor Sootan sent, "Now let's change our focus and work on counting."

Droplet quickly learned to count in *twelves*, as instructed. He spent the early evening counting everything he could see, until darkness rendered countable objects invisible.

The next morning, Mentor Sootan used a simple attractor-charge to roll him downstream to a flat area full of pebbles. Droplet paid close attention to the attractor-charge, but he couldn't determine how it worked.

"Want to learn that," he sent along with a thought-image of being pulled.

"Work on counting first. Later I will teach you more about moving."

Surprised at his mentor's response, Droplet looked around at the dark, shiny pebbles, and then started counting. He quickly discovered there were more than twelve.

"Can't count all. Too many," he sent his mentor.

"Yes. When there are more than twelve, we consider each *unit of twelve* and count that: *two-twelves, three-twelves*, etc. When there are more than *twelve-twelves* we say there are *many* twelves, or too many to count. So how many pebbles can you count here, Droplet?"

Droplet discovered he had to hold the awareness of each unit of twelve separately in his mind from those he was continuing to count. At first this was challenging and he would lose his count. After several tries, though, he mastered it.

"Seven-twelves, with more," he finally sent, quite pleased with himself.

"Very good, Droplet. When you find that there are extras you can either leave them out of your count, or you can call it a *partial twelve*."

"Okay." Droplet had noticed several spotted flashers down-flow coming toward them. He spent the next few minutes trying to count them as they darted and flashed around the edges of The Flow.

Eventually frustrated, he sent, "Hard to count."

Mentor Sootan, who had been watching, showed him how to wait until a moving object passed a fixed object to count it.

Of course, they both agreed it was harder with flashers who might pass the same fixed object several times.

After practicing on his own for a while, his bright pupil sent, "Want to see more Flow now."

"Yes, you've done well, Droplet. *We* can explore more *of* The Flow now."

Two mornings later Droplet awoke again at daybreak. Without disturbing his sleeping mentor, he tipped back to watch the rippling surface above. He felt his awareness expand as he softened his gaze. The steady current at the center of The Flow moved small objects toward, near, and past him. For a moment he almost felt like he was moving instead of the current. He relaxed more and opened his range of view to include both banks and all of the large, stationary things beyond The Flow. *So beautiful*, he mused as the increasing light illuminated each detail.

When his mentor finally roused, Droplet felt relaxed and ready for another day of learning.

Using intermittent attractor-charges to pull the foundling upstream to a group of mixed rocks on the hither side of The Flow, Mentor Sootan began explaining the importance of locator terms.

"There will be times when you will need to refer to the location of something with great accuracy."

"Don't understand," sent the foundling while peering into a cleft between the two tallest rocks.

"Pay attention now, because this is important. You need to learn the terms for The Flow's different characteristics, how to tell which side of a river or creek you're on, and how to describe what you see in detail."

Sensing the coming of a challenge, the foundling channeled his full awareness to his mentor's sending.

"So, I want you to explore these rocks, paying very close attention to as many details as you can. And then come back and explain what you've seen."

Droplet rolled among the large and small rocks and stones. He noticed some of the rocks had different textures, and their sizes and shapes were different too. When he returned to

Mentor Sootan, he used image thoughts to convey what he'd seen as accurately as possible.

"Good. But let me show you something," sent his mentor as he pulled him around behind the rocks.

"How accurate were the images you sent me when viewing the rocks from this side?"

Droplet could easily see the images he'd sent didn't look at all like what he saw now. His mentor pulled him between the two tallest rocks and had him look up, and then took him to the upper surface of one of the rocks, and had him look down. Each of these positions created a completely different view.

"Not only does each view give a different appearance, Droplet, each of us might see the same view differently based on our exact location, whether we're moving or not, and even how familiar we are with the area."

Mentor Sootan encouraged him roll out of the rocks and onto a sandy spot. "Now I will teach you how to describe what you see using locator and descriptive terms."

"First of all, in a river or creek with two banks such as this, the current is always streaming or flowing in one general direction. We use the terms *upstream* or *up-flow* to indicate the part of The Flow that is moving toward us, and *downstream* or *down-flow* to refer to the current that is moving away from us when we are stationary. So which term describes the location of these rocks compared to where the teaching hollow is?"

He studied this for a moment and then sent, "Teaching hollow is downstream."

"Yes, very good. We could also say that we are upstream of the teaching hollow. Both would be accurate." Mentor Sootan paused briefly and then sent, "Here we are closer to one side of The Flow, or to one *bank* than to the other. We have terms for this as well. This group of rocks is on the *hither* side of The Flow, while our teaching hollow is on the *aft* side. To identify the correct term we always turn downstream. When looking downstream, the hither bank is always this side, and the aft bank is always that side."

Droplet looked at the far, *aft* bank and then turned to look up and then downstream. "Why look downstream? Aren't sides always same?"

"That's a very good question. Yes, the sides don't change,

but in order to describe which side, we use the terms *aft* and *hither*, and so that everyone always uses these terms in the same way, we've agreed that this side is always *hither* and that side is always *aft*, as we *look downstream*. Now let's work on all of the ways to describe this group of rocks."

Droplet learned that the rocks near them, called *mixed stone*, included *domes* and *mounds*—partly buried stones, *flats*, *angulars*, and *tilts*—rocks that leaned against other rocks. He discovered that some plants—mosses and lichens—don't always look like a plant with a stalk or fronds. He was shown *twinkle moss, spangle lichen, tangle moss, blotch lichen* and *ripple lichen* on the stones and bank nearby.

When they finished, he had to give a detailed description of the area they'd explored together. After being corrected a few times, he thought hard and then sent: "Mixed group of rocks near the hither bank of The Flow. Has three mounds, some flats and angulars, and one tilt. Three angulars have spangle lichen and one mound has twinkle moss at its base."

"And which side of the angulars have the spangle lichen?"

"Um." He looked at the rocks and to each bank and then remembered to include the direction of the current. "The upstream, hither side of the angulars."

"Yes, very good. Let's have you explore on your own a bit and then we'll head back to the teaching hollow, which is...?" his mentor prompted.

"Downstream near aft bank."

"Just so." Droplet received the affirmative with a distinct sense of accomplishment.

After exploring more of the hither bank, they crossed to the aft bank and rolled together back to the familiar, but increasingly less interesting, teaching hollow. This time when his Mentor used an attractor-charge to pull him up the outer side of the hollow, Droplet focused carefully on it. Just as they got to the rim, he made a discovery. *Oh. It's a kind of sending, but with force instead of information. So if I adjust this and send it back . . .*

Suddenly, Droplet repelled away from his mentor.

Before his mentor could react, Droplet shot toward the surface at an angle and was instantly whisked away by the current.

Four

It took Droplet a few seconds to recover from his shock and adjust to being *in* the current rather than watching it. He was moving very fast, and he couldn't stop rolling or spinning! During one of his revolutions he noticed he was getting close to the surface but staying away from both banks, which appeared to be moving steadily by him. After some quick experimentation, he found he could not alter his circumstance in any way—he couldn't stop spinning, he couldn't roll or bounce out of the current, and even if he had been able to summon an attractor-charge, there was nothing nearby to attach to.

He had only tried to understand his mentor's attractor-charge, but now he was caught in the current, tumbling down-flow. He couldn't believe how fast everything had changed and his reaction shifted from surprise to distress.

Just then Mentor Sootan reached him and soundly nudged him out of the current. Droplet, much relieved, watched as his mentor skillfully used multiple attractor-charges to pull them both toward the now unfamiliar bank.

Once they were stationary, Droplet could sense high emotion coming from his mentor.

"Um, thank you for helping me," he sent, glad to be back on solid ground and pleased to have an opportunity to use one of the social courtesies he'd learned.

Next to him, Mentor Sootan seemed very controlled, but his *esse* flared and pulsed in a way Droplet found disturbing.

"I didn't just help you, I r*escued* you!" He turned away, then whirled back and latched onto him with a very strong charge.

"That was both impressive and very alarming, Droplet," he finally sent. "What would you have done if I hadn't been able to get you out of the current?"

"I, um…" The intense feeling-tones of this sending rocked him.

"You could have been lost."

"*Lost?*"

"Lost—*swept away* by the current. Gone before you'd learned all the things you need to learn." Mentor Sootan seemed to be regaining his composure, but his emotions were still sharp.

Droplet took this in silently.

After a little while, he sensed a shift in his mentor who looked around and sent, "It's going to take us the rest of the afternoon to return to the teaching hollow. I don't want you to try anything like that again—at least not until you know how to control it, agreed?"

"Yes," he agreed.

With that, his mentor locked onto him with a firm attractor-charge and then skillfully used alternating attractor- and repulsion-charges to pull and push them upstream. Droplet studied the charges and the way his mentor used them very carefully. He admired his mentor's skill, but wasn't even tempted to try it himself.

It turned out Mentor Sootan was right, they didn't actually reach the teaching hollow until early evening. They were both exhausted and there were no more lessons that day.

Droplet had the whole evening to think about what he'd learned. For the first time he understood that there were things he shouldn't do and experiences he wasn't ready for.

As the night deepened, he felt a new appreciation for his mentor, someone who was teaching him things, but who also cared about what happened to him.

Finally dipping toward sleep, his thoughts veered into the remarkable feeling of being snatched away from everything familiar. A secret part of him thrilled at the whole strange adventure.

Droplet awoke with the increasing light, *dawn*, he remembered sleepily. He allowed his awareness to move in and out of focus; sometimes he was aware of the lone pebble stuck into the edge of the teaching hollow near him, sometimes he was aware of everything above and around him all at once. *Moving*, he thought with new savor, *The Flow is always moving.*

When his mentor awoke and oriented on him a short time later, he felt no trace of the strong emotions of yesterday. They easily moved into a more philosophical discussion of the nature of The Flow; a *fluid*, capable of constant movement. Then he learned about the fascinating relationship between movement and change.

"Almost everything in The Flow happens in repeating patterns called *cycles*, Droplet. As you know, there are alternating day and night cycles corresponding to the movement of the sun, or sol. Each day and night cycle brings its own creatures, activities, and rest periods. There are longer cycles of few and many flashers, and other creatures. The greatest cycles in The Flow, called *seasons*, regularly change between seven-twelves and nine-twelves of days.

"It's important to stay aware of these greater cycles, because they often change The Flow itself for many days at a time—making it fuller or shallower, muddy or clear, giving it a much stronger or weaker current, along with other changes as well."

As Droplet took in all of these thought-images, he got an inkling of just how vast The Flow really was. Before he could ask more about this, his mentor challenged him to see how many cycles he could observe.

Droplet spent the morning rolling around looking for cycles. He thought he noticed patterns in the shifting light of sol, repeating flickers of the leaves on nearby trees, subtle changes in the currents he could see, and the movements of creatures in and beyond The Flow. His mentor taught him to distinguish between movement, patterns and cycles, and reminded him that cycles usually occur slowly and often comprise several patterns.

"So how I see cycles now?"

"Good question," sent his mentor with a reassuring feeling-tone, "you have realized you can only see cycles over longer periods of repeated observation."

Droplet felt pleased with his increasing ability to *think things through*, as his mentor had taught him. Then he sent the question he really wanted to ask, "Now teach me how *you* move?"

"Hmmm," came the reply, as his mentor observed him closely. "Although it is a bit soon, you do seem just about ready, and after yesterday's antics it is probably safer to teach you than not."

After another inexplicable pause, he gave Droplet the answer he was hoping for.

"Yes, I will teach you, but you must do exactly as I show you and absolutely nothing more."

"I agree," he replied, enthusiastically.

Mentor Sootan knew that his pupil had barely mastered the inner focus required to learn the more complex forms of movement, but he obviously had the interest and will-power, and he believed they had established enough trust to proceed.

Over the course of mentoring many foundlings, Sootan had learned that teaching self-propulsion skills too soon could overwhelm even the most eager of pupils. Also, acquiring self-propulsion skills fostered a greater sense of independence, and if this happened too soon the relationship could be severed before *cresting* occurred, which was disastrous.

He took his pupil to a sandy bar well upstream of the teaching hollow and carefully taught him the multi-layered form of sending which created attractor- and repulsion-charges.

Droplet quickly learned that reversing someone else's attractor-charge was a whole lot easier than generating his own. No matter how hard he tried, he could only form the weakest of charges. His frustration grew into an obstacle.

"No, you're actually doing just fine, Droplet," sent his mentor encouragingly. "Learning this takes time and a lot of practice. Now let go of all the effort and visualize the *rock-on-stick* at the edge of our hollow. "

With an inner huff, he released the struggle he'd been feeling and visualized the *rock-on-stick* he'd used during their early exercises on controlling his awareness. When he could see it clearly within his mind, he finally relaxed.

"Good. That's better. You can always use the *rock-on-stick* image to help you shift your focus. Now, remember, it is *force* you want to send rather than information, and you need to let the charge build-up before you try to direct it."

After working most of the rest of that day on building and focusing an attractor-charge, Droplet could barely send a strong enough charge to give him a little tug.

"Not bad. Are you too tired to try sending a repulsion-charge?"

Droplet responded that he wanted to try. He paid close attention to how his mentor slowly fashioned a repulsion-charge and then directed it toward a solid object. To his delighted surprise, he was able to actually push himself away from a rock on his second try.

"I can do it!"

"Yes, repulsion-charges often come more easily after working on attractor-charges for a while. Let's head back now, shall we?"

Droplet found it was a relief to let the soft current help roll him downstream back to the teaching hollow where he fell into a deep sleep before it even got dark.

The next day, his mentor suggested they take a break from focused learning, so they traveled downstream toward an area of flat, smooth stones further along the aft bank. Droplet remembered being dragged briskly through these stones by his mentor after he'd been rescued from the current.

As they got closer to their destination, he noticed that the stones ahead were moving. *That's odd.* In his experience, rocks and stones didn't move.

At his mentor's suggestion, he carefully approached the wavering stones. When he got close to them, he discovered he was surrounded by dazzling *beams* of sunlight. The surprising brightness distracted him for a moment. Although he had observed sunlight illuminating other places in The Flow, he'd rarely been in such bright light himself. For an instant, he almost remembered another time of intense brightness, then the memory faded.

He reoriented on his surroundings and peered into the shimmering light. Just then, the brightness abruptly diminished and the objects around him appeared flat and stationary. In the very next instant, the brilliance returned, and the mounds were rippling again. *So, it must be the bright light.* He turned to his mentor to share this observation and got another surprise. In the midst of the sunbeams his mentor was nearly invisible.

"Mentor . . . ?" he directed his sending toward his mentor's thin, transparent outline.

"Yes, I'm here. In strong light we're hard to see. This is why we usually stay out of brightly lit areas of The Flow."

Oh.

After getting used to the experience of seeing *through* his mentor, Droplet turned his attention back to the moving stones. *Was it just an appearance, or did the light somehow cause the stones to move?* He rolled toward the nearest stone, a low mound with a smooth surface, which definitely appeared to be undulating. Approaching slowly, and ready to spin out of there if necessary, Droplet rolled into a dip on the mound's flickering surface.

It felt completely solid and still.

The next stone he tried felt still as well. Just then, the intense light unexpectedly ceased again. He looked up and saw a long, dark branch beyond the surface swaying back and forth—blocking or allowing the light to shine into The Flow around him. *So it is only an appearance.*

Mentor Sootan, who had stayed close, explained some of the more interesting features of light, shadow, and the attributes of *perspective* and *visual illusions.* Then he suggested they return to their hollow.

They took their time on the way back, so that Droplet could practice generating his own attractor-charges to augment his progress. A little more than half of his attempts were successful in some fashion.

When they got near the hollow, Mentor Sootan took them directly to the nearby plants where he practiced some more. He found it easier to generate either kind of charge when he was stationary, and pulling himself from stalk to stalk got easier as he worked at it. But even after a lot more training, quickly alternating between attractor-charges and repulsion-charges as his mentor did remained beyond him.

While he focused all of his energies on moving about, his mentor, resting nearby, made suggestions using a technique he called *distance-sending.* Droplet looked forward to acquiring this skill as well. But even when he gave it his full attention, he could receive, but not send, from a distance.

By the end of the day, Droplet was pleased with his adventure, and with his slow but determined progress in learning self-propulsion.

That evening, just after twilight, a bright, curved light gradually came into view above The Flow. Droplet found the way it illuminated some objects, and made others look shadowed and flat, fascinating. *Light is very interesting,* he thought to himself drowsily.

"That light, called the moon or orb, has a very predictable cycle of change. It gradually gets larger for a little over twelve nights and then smaller for the same number of nights. For a few nights it disappears from view, and then it starts increasing in size again. In a much larger cycle, it also changes position relative to The Flow; sometimes higher, sometimes much lower."

"Why?"

"There is no reason that we know, it just does this and always has."

Droplet watched the orb slowly travel higher above The Flow for as long as he could; then fatigue overcame him and he slipped into sleep.

Three full days of practice later, Droplet could effectively use attractor-and-repulsion-charges to propel himself through The Flow as long as the current wasn't too strong, and there were large objects nearby that he could pull himself toward or repel from.

He was immensely pleased with himself.

While spending that morning practicing his new skills, Droplet discovered some flat, round-ish creatures with thin, pointy parts—*legs*—scampering about in the dark stones he had counted earlier. Mentor Sootan explained some of the more peculiar traits of *creatures*, which Droplet found quite bewildering. But before he could ask more about creatures in general, his mentor indicated an angular rock embedded about half way up the bank and challenged Droplet to get himself there.

After working at it for most of the afternoon, he finally mastered the pull-stabilize-push-stabilize-pull technique needed to gain the high perch. And the view it afforded was worth it. His mentor quickly joined him and they watched together as sol's slanted rays briefly illuminated The Flow before it surrendered to the shimmer of early evening.

In the deepening shadows, Droplet thought he saw something glowing on the far bank.

"What glowing on hither bank?"

"What *is* glowing, Droplet. That glow is the nearest grouping of Others to our teaching hallow. They call themselves the *Boktow Grouping.*"

Oh, Others! As the night deepened, Droplet thought he could make out many softly glowing Others very close together.

"How many Others in Boktow Grouping?"

"See how many individuals you can count from here," his mentor challenged in a now familiar way. Then he added, "But I can tell you that a grouping always has at least twelve *members.*"

"Grouping always twelve members?"

"No. Groupings always have at *least* twelve members, because twelve is the minimum number required to form a complete grouping. Some groupings have many more than twelve members."

He studied the shining grouping carefully and then sent, "Too close together to count. Can we go see?"

"No, Droplet," replied his Mentor firmly. "I wanted to show you they are there, but you and I have more work to do before you're ready to have contact with Others of our kind. Now, let's go down to the hollow before it gets completely dark."

What work? he wondered, as they descended the bank— which also required considerable skill—and returned to the teaching hollow.

Late that night while his mentor slept, Droplet watched the increasingly round-ish orb rise high above The Flow. Light from the orb, so much gentler than sol's light, seemed to fall toward him in wavy streams.

When the soft light touched the surface of The Flow, it released flickering sparkles which shimmered downward—

almost, but not quite, reaching him. He watched quietly for a long time, noticing how the orb's gradual movement changed his perception of familiar objects and the shadowed Flow itself. Finally it disappeared from direct view, but Droplet could still see the effects of its radiance on the large objects beyond The Flow.

I wonder if the Others see this too, he thought, as he gently drifted into sleep.

The following morning, Droplet again awoke before his mentor, and decided to have some fun. Taking extra care, he very gently rolled to the edge of the teaching hollow and looked around. Then, using his newest skills, he climbed the steep bank and returned to the ledge on which they had perched the previous evening.

Most of The Flow was still quite dark, although the surface was starting to lighten. Above the surface, he could just make out the faint stirrings of creatures he'd learned were called *flyers*. Droplet enjoyed watching them *soar* high above The Flow, and now he watched their quick little movements in the *bushes* and trees along the bank above him. Everything else beyond the Flow was completely still.

Even The Flow itself seemed subdued. *Lovely, and very peaceful.*

Through many days of observation, Droplet had noticed that the light within The Flow always increased more slowly than the light beyond The Flow at the start of the day. It also darkened more quickly at day's end. He had no idea why this happened, and even though his Mentor had told him it wasn't important, he still found it intriguing.

The increasing light brought nearby features into view. From this vantage point he could see much more of them than he could from the edge of the teaching hollow. The tall plants undulating in the current near the hollow looked lacy and truncated. And the large mounds and stacked flats downstream appeared small and insignificant. When he looked across The Flow, he could just make out the jutting rock under which the Boktow Grouping was starting to stir. He watched the Others with great interest. Last night his mentor told him he would meet the Others when it was *right*, but he'd refused to elaborate on this, no matter how many questions Droplet had asked.

A sudden movement in the teaching hollow drew his attention. His mentor had awoken and was whirling around looking for him. Droplet backed away from the edge of the ledge and stilled himself. As The Flow continued to lighten, he wondered how long it would take his mentor to find him.

Finally, the thrill of hiding began to pale and he peeked over the edge to find the teaching hollow empty. He looked all around, but didn't see his mentor anywhere.

Just as he was becoming concerned, his mentor startled him by dropping onto his perch from above.

"Ha! Just as I thought. Trying out your new skills, weren't you?"

"I . . . ummm . . ."

"It's quite all right, Droplet. But please don't wander off like that without letting me know. If I didn't know you as well as I do, I might have worried more. And as you'll discover, many groupings have *customs* regarding coming and going, so you should get used to letting someone know your intentions, all right?"

"Yes, all right. But I've been wondering . . ."

They chatted as they returned to the teaching hollow and then travelled upstream a ways so that he could practice using attractor/repulsion charges on objects that were further apart. He enjoyed mastering this difficult skill and reveled in the freedom he was starting to attain.

Droplet's focus and patience started to fray by early afternoon, so his mentor suggested they take a break. While resting, Droplet looked around and noticed a waterlogged mass of roots near the bottom of the bank. He got permission to investigate it, which was good because he felt like being alone. He used an attractor-charge to pull himself into the gloomy slickness of roots and then relaxed all of his senses. In his mind he imagined that this root-ball was his home, but he could also travel in it. He let his thoughts wander into all manner of unlikely encounters—with strange creatures, foreign landscapes, and unusual Others. In all of his imagined wanderings he was always alone.

Quite unexpectedly a wave of longing swept through him, bringing him back to the present.

Longing for what? he wondered, as he set himself spinning softly by using brief micro-pulses of repulsion. He explored the feeling until his mentor approached to suggest they do some more work together before heading back, but he never understood why the feeling came or what it meant.

On the way back to the teaching hollow, Droplet appeared distracted. Mentor Sootan found the recent changes in his pupil's behavior concerning. After spending the morning on self-locomotion, he had deliberately focused the rest of the day's teaching on things Droplet had an interest in. But instead of asking the expected questions about Others of their kind and how and why they form groupings, his pupil had wanted to learn more about light, currents, creatures and things *beyond* The Flow.

What had started out as a normal progression of interests had veered into the unusual and worrisome. He had also noticed that Droplet was having trouble focusing on one thing at a time; his questions often bounced around and lacked any order or pattern that he could discern.

As he pondered these things, he also had to admit to himself that Droplet was well into the optimal time period for *cresting*, yet he showed no signs of it. He reminded himself that each foundling matured a little differently, and Droplet hadn't displayed any of the mood instability that would indicate he was moving into a *cresting flux* rather than a true *cresting*. So, there was probably still time.

That evening, just before retiring, Droplet asked his mentor a question he'd been wondering about for a while.

"Mentor Sootan, what is sleep?"

"What do you mean, Droplet?"

"I mean, why do we get tired and lose awareness? And why do we have strange imaginings when we sleep?"

"I'm very tired right now. Can you ask me again tomorrow?"

For some reason this answer annoyed him. He felt stifled and suddenly frustrated with *everything*. Working so hard to learn things he wasn't really interested in, and not able to find out about what he really wanted to know—*Ugh!* It was like constantly trying to stay on the tiny point of a slippery shard. Nothing he tried worked for long, and he wondered why he kept trying.

He stewed quietly in frustration until he finally edged into sleep.

Right next to him, a now very alert Sootan felt his pupil's emotional storm and took it as a bad sign. He waited until Droplet had entered deep sleep, and then he slipped away from the teaching hollow and made his way across The Flow to the Boktow Grouping. He needed to confer with an elder.

He approached the grouping and waited politely until they finished their evening convergence. Then he moved toward one of the elders, waiting quietly until he was addressed.

"Ah, Mentor Sootan, welcome. Your young pupil is resting, I take it?"

"Yes, Elder Bonn, but I have some concerns about his progress."

"What kind of concerns, Sootan?"

Mentor Sootan took some time to formulate his thoughts.

Then he sent, "Well, he is very bright, but he is also quite unusual. I would even say some of his interests are bizarre, and he seems to be developing in tangents. Frankly, I'm worried about him."

Elder Bonn knew Sootan to be an experienced, if not a particularly inspired, mentor.

"Perhaps he just needs more contact with Others," he sent carefully.

"But he hasn't *crested* yet!" Sootan replied in true distress.

"He hasn't? But I thought . . . Now I understand your concern." Elder Bonn knew that until the complex integration of thought, emotion, and experience called *cresting* had occurred, a foundling could not mature enough to form abiding relationships, become part of established Groupings, or access the realms of higher thought.

Mentor Sootan and Elder Bonn spent the better part of the night discussing the foundling's situation and what could be done about it. They both knew that the optimal opening for cresting was fairly brief, and if missed, a foundling would remain mentally and developmentally stunted. Because of this foundling's exceptional qualities, neither was willing to accept this outcome.

By the time they'd concluded their exploration of options, they both agreed that Elder Bonn would try to contact Wise Elder. Their hope was that because of Wise Elder's brief, but significant, early connection with the foundling, he might be able to help him before it was too late.

Early the next morning, Wise Elder, who had been well up-flow of the Boktow Grouping when he received Elder Bonn's distance-sending, caught the current and arrived as requested. After a brief talk with Elder Bonn, he made his way across The Flow to the teaching hollow. There he found Mentor Sootan on the edge of the hollow pensively watching his pupil, who appeared to be exploring the far side of a stand of plants.

"Ah, Wise Elder. I'm very glad you could come! I believe the foundling you helped revive a few twelve-days ago is slipping into a *cresting flux*. He's fixating on odd things and has recently become unstable emotionally. I'm not sure why he hasn't already crested and I'm very worried about him."

"So I understand from Elder Bonn. Would you like me to take over here, Mentor Sootan? I'm familiar with this foundling's mind and think I can help him."

"Yes, that would be much appreciated. I believe I've taken him as far as I can."

"And done a fine job of it, too, I have no doubt. Would you like to introduce me and let him know you're leaving?"

"Yes."

After rolling around aimlessly all morning, Droplet had finally settled down to watch a small *creeper* making its spiraling way up a plant stalk. He wondered how it would feel to be a creature like this; then he imagined being the plant. Letting his awareness move from object to object suddenly became almost unbearably boring. His next feelings were listlessness and impatience. His mentor had seemed uncharacteristically distant this morning, and when he'd asked if Droplet was still interested in talking about sleep, Droplet didn't answer. *Sleep*, he wondered, *why did I want to talk about sleep?*

He sensed his mentor's approach, but didn't turn.

"Droplet, I have someone I'd like you to meet."

That got his attention. He turned to find his mentor with an Other next to him. As he studied the newcomer, he realized there was something familiar about him. Then his vision shifted somehow, and he noticed a brilliant light deep inside of the Other, to which he felt instantly attracted.

"Droplet, I'd like to introduce you to Wise Elder."

Droplet forgot everything he'd learned about the social courtesies and just stared.

"Hello, Little One," came the newcomer's strangely familiar sending.

"*You!* Umm, who *are* you?" Droplet felt an uncomfortable mixture of affinity and confusion.

"Droplet! I just told you." There was no mistaking the annoyance in his mentor's sending. "This is *Wise Elder.*"

"Oh, hello," said Droplet, briefly remembering his manners. "But . . . do I know you?" He couldn't shake the feeling that he did.

"You may remember me. I'm a friend who was present when you were first found."

"Droplet, Wise Elder has agreed to work with you on the next phase of your training."

Droplet didn't respond. He felt strange—very quiet and still—as if he was watching himself from a great distance. Then with little transition he switched back to being fully present to what was transpiring.

"He's going to work with us now?"

"No, Droplet. He's agreed to take over your training, and I will be going."

"Oh." Then it hit him. "You're leaving?"

"Yes. I have enjoyed our time together, but I think the change will do you good." His mentor paused briefly, and then sent him the formal phrase he'd learned: "Farewell, until The Flow brings us together again, Droplet."

This was an *ending* then. He thought for a minute, trying to remember his training, and then sent, "Thank you Mentor Sootan for teaching me. I wish you fair travels."

"Thank you, Droplet. Wise Elder, again, I appreciate your coming."

And with that Mentor Sootan turned and left.

Droplet watched him make his way across The Flow toward the Boktow Grouping. Then, feeling shy, he glanced at his new companion.

"Why don't we travel up-flow together a ways, Droplet. There's no reason I can think of to stay here. What do you say?"

"Oh." He had trouble understanding what had just happened. Then, in a flash of insight, he realized he was going to get a whole new experience, and eagerness started to bloom.

"Yes, I would like that."

Five

Droplet and Wise Elder traveled upstream for most of the day and were now resting together on a sandy bank in a shallow portion of The Flow. The late afternoon sun had just sunk beneath the wide stretch of clouds high above them, illuminating their surroundings with scintillating light.

The hard traveling, and all of the day's changes, left Droplet feeling tired but also exhilarated. He didn't know if he wanted to explore the new area, learn more about his companion, or just nod off.

He could sense the Other next to him. *Wise Elder*, he reminded himself, observing him. This awareness brought subtle new feelings with it. Just as he was trying to sort through them, he received a feeling-tone-only sending of calm and what he could only describe as rightness. He instantly relaxed.

"So, Little One," his companion sent a little while later, "you have had a day full of changes. How are you doing with all of them? Do you have any questions?"

He thought about this and then sent, "I know I've been different lately. Is that why Mentor Sootan left?"

"Those two things are related, Droplet, but not in the way you might think." Wise Elder's sending was composed and clear. "Mentor Sootan has mentored many foundlings, but he has rarely met one like you."

"What do you mean?"

"It's the way your mind works, Droplet. You yearn to understand things far beyond the usual interests of our kind." Wise Elder paused to regard him. "You are inquisitive yet decisive; capable of great clarity and leaps of intuition one moment, and then completely unfocused the next."

"Yes, that's true. Especially lately," he admitted.

"But there is nothing wrong with this. In fact, your mind works a lot like mine."

With this sending, Droplet felt a distinctly positive sense of connection between them. This awareness brought him a deep sense of relief, and another inner relaxing.

"It does?"

"Yes. Let's explore some of the many questions I know you must have, Droplet. Tell me about what you perceive and think about."

"All right," sent an excited Droplet. *Finally, I get to learn about all the things I'm really interested in!*

Droplet and Wise Elder spent the next two days exploring the area—with all of its new creatures and vegetation—and discussing all manner of things. They talked about everything in The Flow he wondered about, including Others of their kind and why they formed groupings.

"We are social Beings, Droplet, which means we generally enjoy one another's company. Groupings are usually formed by Others with interests, beliefs, or just their location in common. Groupings can be remarkably different from each other, as you will likely discover."

He watched six small, identical flashers swerve away from the bank and swim downstream. Then he sent, "In the grouping across from the teaching hollow all the Others spent the night-cycle next to each other. Why do they do that?"

"Different groupings have different preferences regarding close personal contact, and most have standards of membership. I promise I will introduce you to the Boktow Grouping as soon as you are ready, so you can experience it for yourself, Okay?"

"Hmmm." He found he was much more willing to just listen to Wise Elder than he had usually been with Mentor Sootan. There was something about how his new companion thought and communicated that made learning truly enjoyable. His interactions with Wise Elder were always laced with shared curiosity and mutual respect, and a deep trust was developing between them. Although his emotions were still unpredictable, he felt happy much more of the time now.

Wise Elder also felt pleased with the easy trust building between them. He found Droplet's enthusiasm, his thoughtful questions, and his insightful observations quite refreshing.

While it was true that Droplet still hadn't crested yet, Wise Elder was confident it would happen soon.

Their third day together was coming to a close and the gentle light of evening softened everything around them. Wise Elder, sensitive to Droplet's mood, suggested they spend the night at a place he knew of.

Droplet, always eager to explore new things, followed his companion farther upstream than they'd gone so far. Along the way he practiced the refinements to attractor- and repulsion-charges Wise Elder had taught him. They both agreed he'd become increasingly skilled in self-propulsion.

They traveled into a deeper section of The Flow and stopped when they reached several very large rocks near the hither bank. The light ebbed into twilight around them while the bottom was already in inky shadow.

"*Boulders*," Wise Elder sent, as he made his way to the top of the second tallest, settled into a protected dip on its upper face, and waited for Droplet to join him. This placed them quite near the surface of The Flow, and as Droplet had never been allowed this close to the surface before, he was excited.

"Calm down, Little One. Being this close to the surface requires some special care. It's best to be cautious and respectful around it."

"Why is that, Wise Elder?" Droplet settled himself and leaned in toward his companion.

"Well, the surface is where The Flow ends and *Big Blue* begins. These two powerful aspects of existence are mutually exclusive. This means that under most circumstances they don't mix well with one another, and a strong boundary naturally forms between them."

"Oh," sent Droplet as he looked up toward the surface of The Flow. This was the first time he'd had an opportunity to observe it closely. Suddenly, the low-angled sun illuminated a riffle on the surface so that it glowed with a life of its own. *Beautiful*, he thought, as he watched the light intensify briefly and then slowly fade away. Just then, a flyer glided high above the surface catching the very last of the light. Droplet concentrated on its motion until it disappeared into the shadows.

"There are so many things beyond The Flow," sent Droplet, calm, but alert. "But Mentor Sootan taught me The Flow was everything."

"To many of our kind, it *is* everything, Droplet," Wise Elder responded serenely. "To other kinds of Beings, The Flow might be either the beginning, or the end of what they know and experience. There are many, many kinds of Beings and creatures who exist—in and beyond—The Flow."

As Droplet let this sending sink in, he felt a subtle shift in his thinking. This shifting sensation had been happening more lately, and he had grown accustomed to it. Usually the thought shifts brought him an increase in clarity, but not always. Sometimes they just confused him.

Watching the huge, indistinct shapes beyond The Flow, Droplet got his first hint of how big everything really was.

:The world, came an inner transmission from Wise Elder, who was lightly touching him and aware of his thoughts.

:The world, responded Droplet quietly as he relaxed his consciousness. His mind instantly filled with the image of a round *sphere* which quickly expanded into a form so big he lost it. Then Wise Elder showed him how to work with the image. He helped him envision the sphere in ever-increasing sizes, while gently stretching his ability to fathom the true massiveness of what the image represented. *:It is this which supports and gives form to The Flow. Without the world, The Flow as we know it would not exist.*

After another moment of shared experience, he felt Wise Elder recede from his thoughts, but stay near.

Then something extraordinary occurred.

As Droplet pondered the notion of what supported The Flow, he noticed a pressure building inside of him. When he explored this inner sensation, as Wise Elder had taught him to do, he perceived several different streams of information or awareness starting to converge in his consciousness.

Then, without warning, the separate streams became a *unified force* which swept into and through him, building in vigor until, like a mighty wave, it *crested* throughout his being.

His individual awareness expanded and he became an integral part of this powerful force, which hurled up and over itself into vastness. There, he and the magnificent force hovered *as one,* for a brief eternity.

This experience, both profound and purposeful, contained more potency than anything he could have imagined.

As the intensity of the force gradually dissipated, he felt alert and completely calm: he experienced himself as a boundless, shining pool of liquid awareness which contained everything he had ever known or felt, and much, much more.

Then, again with no transition, he became aware of the infinite number of Others of his kind. For the first time he perceived them as a collective, and he could feel their *essence* in himself, almost *as* himself. He sensed their thoughts, affections, worries, activities—both individually and as a large, singular group.

As he focused on this, he realized that he and Wise Elder were once again sharing thoughts in a way that far surpassed sending. They were thinking and experiencing together, through their linked essences.

:Yes, Little One, came the intimate and infinitely tender awareness. *:This is the direct experience of our kind. Through our conscious essence, our esse, we are part of the Sacred Flow, the great circle of awareness that ALL conscious Beings on this world share. Through the Sacred Flow we are united in ways that far surpass our individual experiences.*

Droplet perceived a bright corona of conscious light shimmering around the world-sphere he had seen before. An unknown, but very strong, emotion welled-up in him.

:This feeling, one of unconditional acceptance and deep appreciation, is called Love. Welcome home, Droplet.

And he felt it. For the first time in his short existence, he felt truly received and *welcomed*. To himself, to The Flow, to his kind, and to this wonderful, wise Other.

Together, Droplet and Wise Elder reveled in their shared experience of the *Sacred Flow*, while the physical Flow around them darkened into night.

As his awareness slowly shifted back to their perch near the surface, Droplet noticed that the shining points of light in the nightsky above them looked very close. For the first time, he thought he could detect patterns in the sparkling lights.

The last gift Droplet's wonderful companion shared with him before he drifted into a profoundly deep sleep was the word *star*.

Wise Elder felt Droplet's awareness fade into sleep, and was well-pleased.

In all of the crestings he'd witnessed, rarely had he seen one as powerful and synchronous as the one he'd experienced tonight with Droplet; a foundling no longer.

Yes, he was very pleased, and deeply moved as well.

The next day dawned resplendent with discovery. What Droplet thought he had understood about his immediate environment held no comparison to what he now experienced.

The moment he awoke, The Flow looked different to him. It appeared richer, with vastly greater clarity and texture. The currents above and around him were now clearly delineated, and much more abundant than he had realized. And even in the subdued light of early morning, he could see particles and creatures everywhere—all shapes and sizes, many very tiny indeed—spinning and soaring in and between the dancing currents. What had happened to his perception?

He noticed that what he used to recognize as the 'edges' of the strong central current, were actually areas of ruffled dissipation which often devolved into brief, but lovely, spiraling eddies. And within the central current itself, there were long, powerful pulses, sudden and surprising heaves and changes, and gentle susurrations all in constant flux.

Before he would have been overwhelmed by this amazing amount of detail; now he felt comfortably at ease with what he experienced as the richly beautiful, ever-changing, implicit *order* of The Flow.

After giving Droplet some time alone to appreciate his new gifts of awareness, Wise Elder, who had been partway up the hither bank, but within view, leisurely made his way back to his exuberant young friend.

"I had no idea there was so much beauty around me! Why couldn't I perceive all of this before, Wise Elder?"

Wise Elder took a moment to settle himself next to Droplet, and then sent, "Because you hadn't crested yet, Little One. Now that you can access *collective* or shared levels of awareness, the amount of information you can handle is far greater than what you could have comfortably managed before."

They were silent for a moment, as Droplet let this statement settle in. *So that's what happened.*

"Your increased ability to perceive is not the only thing that has changed. Tell me, have you noticed a difference in your thinking? Think back to your cresting experience."

Droplet immediately turned his focus inward the way Wise Elder had taught him. At first nothing seemed different. Then, he recalled the shining pool of awareness he'd been part of during his cresting.

All at once, he was drawn back into the immediacy of the experience, but now he was aware of the pool stretching into a tall object. As he watched, this inner form shifted into the shape of—a *tree*. But it was unlike any tree he'd ever seen.

This tree was massive, completely clear, and filled with brilliant light. It had a vast root system and a long, thick trunk which supported an expansive array of branches.

Droplet immediately understood that this tree represented levels of awareness. The roots of the tree were deeply grounded in experience, while the branches held many different types and categories of information. Before he could even formulate a question about what he was viewing, he became aware that through this vast but somehow intimate *Tree of Light*, he had unprecedented access to *knowledge*.

As this realization cascaded through him in a miniature version of last night's cresting, he began receiving information about The Flow, greater rhythms and cycles, Others of his kind, and a vast array of things which surpassed his understanding.

Very quickly, with Wise Elder's competent assistance, he learned how to shift his awareness between the roots, trunk, and branches, which were *symbols* but also *containers* for experience, presence, and knowledge. This allowed him to manage what might have been an overwhelming amount of information with ease. With a start he realized that thinking, learning, and understanding his experience had become effortless.

Moreover, he could now comprehend complex concepts and the purpose and value of symbols in thinking about them.

Sophisticated patterns and subtle connections he had struggled to understand were now stunningly clear. He reveled in the intellectual awakening that cresting, and accessing this powerful process/symbol of a Tree of Light, afforded him.

It was far more appealing and rewarding than anything he'd ever known, and as Wise Elder later explained, this experience completed and signaled the full integration of his cresting.

The day sailed by as he delighted, again and again, in his ability to perceive the complex simplicity within and around him.

The next morning, Wise Elder took Droplet downstream to a place where the exposed roots of a gnarled tree protruded from the aft bank. *It looks a little like the Tree of Light—only less beautiful and far simpler,* he mused.

Wise Elder guided them to a wide flattish root toward the center of the woody mantle. They perched there, near a couple of low bumps, while Droplet looked around.

He liked the play of bright light, dimness, and deep shadow here. There were several slight, shiny-bright flashers darting in and around the stringy plants flapping rhythmically in the current nearby. He sensed a presence below him, and finally detected two burly, motionless flashers hiding in the darkness of the lower roots. Droplet also noticed several different kinds of crawlers making their way along the undersides of the roots above them.

"As you have discovered, Droplet, the Tree of Light is a very powerful symbol and access point to deeper levels of mind. It aptly represents several levels of awareness and being, which you can now access at will."

Wise Elder paused as the flashers below them made their leisurely way into the current, then he continued. "This physical tree here cycles through several dramatic phases with the turning of the seasons. I enjoy the symbolism of trees, as well as this tree's changeability, which is why I like to rest and think among its roots."

Wise Elder was in a philosophical mood. He watched Droplet absorb this and then sent, "There are some things I'd like to discuss, but first, do you have any questions about what you've experienced?"

Droplet gathered his thoughts. He felt very calm and centered in his new capabilities. Finally he sent, "The cresting I experienced—is it like that for everyone?"

"No. For many it is both less intense and less comprehensive; and very few experience the Tree of Light the way you did. You have an unusually bright esse, and a strong, facile mind, Droplet, and these allowed the full magnitude of what you experienced."

"But you helped, right?"

"Only during the integration phase; the rest, other than a bit of aid helping you stabilize, was all you."

"Oh." Droplet was quiet for a while taking that in. He watched one of the 'bumps' on a lower root start to move slowly; a *knobbed creeper* he realized. He easily accessed both the name and the fact they required a firm surface on which to live.

Then he sent, "What did you want to talk about, Wise Elder?"

"There are a few more things you need to know before you are ready to interact with Others of our kind. The first is, that you will likely have far greater comprehension of the 'how and why of things' than most Others you meet, so you shouldn't be alarmed or dismayed by their lack of understanding. Everyone has their own set of priorities, interests and gifts. Practice accepting Others the way they are, and you'll usually be accepted in turn.

"The second thing is obvious: even though you have had a powerful cresting, you are still very new to The Flow. There is a great deal for you to experience, and a large variety of experienced Others who will help you in their own ways. You have a strong attraction to knowledge and learning, and this should serve you well."

Droplet silently agreed, remembering his obsession with learning how to move. This reminded him he still had more to learn about getting around in The Flow.

Wise Elder waited until he had Droplet's undivided attention, and then he continued. "The third, and most important thing, is that very few Others have *esse-sight* like you do. Most of us perceive our kind as opaque, faintly glowing spheres. A few of us can sense esse in a vague fashion, but for the vast majority of our kind, nonphysical awareness, which we call esse-sight or primary-sight, is quite rare."

Upon receiving this sending, Droplet made the subtle shift in his awareness which showed him his companion's esse, blazing strong and radiant. "Why is that, Wise Elder? How can such an easy shift be rare?"

"It is only easy to those who have the capability, Droplet. Most have neither the ability nor the inclination to expand their perceptual skills."

"But don't they miss the added information esse awareness can give them?"

"Did you miss the experiences cresting brought you before you'd crested?"

"No, I didn't have even the faintest . . . Ah, I see what you mean." After a pause he sent, "But esse is so bright; where does it come from?"

"That is a discussion for another time, Droplet. For now, just remember that few Others have esse-sight, and some are very uncomfortable around those who do. Until you know someone well, it is a good idea to keep this capability to yourself, all right?"

Droplet, quietly thoughtful, indicated his agreement.

Then Wise Elder sent, "It's just about time for me to be on my way, Droplet. So, let's make our way back down-flow. Then I will take you to meet the Others of the Boktow grouping."

It was hard for Droplet to hide the eager brightening of his esse as he realized he was finally going to meet the Others he had watched and wondered about.

Observing him affectionately, Wise Elder sent, "You don't have to try to hide your own esse, Droplet; those of us who can see it will rejoice in its clarity and strength. You need only conceal your *esse-sensing* ability from Others you don't know, and who don't know you. Unless you were to tell them, very few Others would guess you had the capability, so it's not something to be concerned about, only cautious with. All right?"

"All right," sent a relieved and still eager Droplet.

With that they began the easy journey down-flow.

Six

When they got back into territory Droplet recognized, they crossed to the hither bank. As they approached the ledge Droplet had observed from the rock above the teaching hollow, he was excited to see a cluster of Others beneath it. *Finally*, he thought.

Wise Elder took him right up to a couple of Others just under the edge of the ledge.

"Elder Bonn, I would like to introduce you to Droplet, previously Mentor Sootan's foundling pupil." Wise Elder's formal sending alerted Droplet, and he found himself being studied by the Elder.

"Ah yes. Droplet, is it? I have discussed your progress with Mentor Sootan." Once again he was scrutinized. "Crested now, have you? Do you intend to join our grouping?"

Droplet couldn't read Elder Bonn's emotions, but he could detect his shining esse, and what he thought was a certain interest.

"I'm not sure, Elder Bonn. But I would like to stay with the Boktow grouping for a while if I may. Is Mentor Sootan here?"

Elder Bonn paused and then sent, "Yes, I think that would be fine. And, no, Mentor Sootan is not here. He was called away to mentor a new foundling, but he asked that I welcome you should you arrive. This is Boffel, a long-time member of Boktow," he sent, indicating his companion. "Why don't you let him show you around and introduce you to whomever is about. Then tonight we will welcome you in *convergence*."

Before he could respond, Boffel moved forward and sent, "Welcome, Droplet. Please call me Boff. I'd be happy to show you around. "

After a brief, polite sending to both Wise Elder and Elder Bonn, Droplet indicated his agreement and followed Boff to a nearby cluster of Others.

That day, Droplet casually met almost three twelves of the Boktow Others, and learned about some of their interests. Just as he was starting to feel completely overwhelmed, Boff took him to a open stretch of bank where he explained some things about the Boktow grouping and how it functioned.

"We're pretty open to newcomers, Droplet, which isn't true of all groupings. And there are actually over four-twelves of us, but eleven individuals are off visiting other groupings right now."

They were resting near a peculiar, clear object Boff called a *crystal khoot,* which was stuck into the bank a short distance upstream of the grouping's protected recess. Droplet had investigated the fascinating object thoroughly, discovering he could go inside of it and watch The Flow through the hard, crystalline material. He liked the way it caused things in The Flow to look wavy. Boff, quite familiar with the *khoot,* had waited patiently.

"Visiting other groupings . . . ?" That sounded interesting.

"Oh yes. There are several Boktow members who spend most of their time traveling The Flow. You know, having new experiences and sharing what they know."

"Have you been to many other groupings, Boff?"

"A few times, yes, but I didn't really like traveling that much. I found all the uncertainty and newness kind of uncomfortable, to tell the truth. I tend to prefer the company of Others I know."

Boff's attitude about travel surprised Droplet.

Sensing his reaction, Boff added, "You might want to talk to Fernlin sometime about his travels. He's had some interesting adventures. But right now we should start heading back, so we're sure to be in time for convergence."

"Convergence—is that where you all clump together during the night? Sometimes I would see you from across The Flow."

"Yeah." Boff seemed distracted. "Let's head back now."

Droplet looked around and saw that the shadows were indeed lengthening. They made their way back down-flow.

"So, tell me more about this convergence," sent Droplet when they paused briefly to watch the last rays of sunlight sparkle on a nearby hill.

"Well, as you already know, we 'clump together' at night," Boff responded with a certain humor as they continued on.

"But why?" Droplet had a couple of hunches, but he wanted an idea of what to expect.

"Well, we do it for companionship, mostly." Boff seemed to be thinking about how to explain it. "It's how thoughts and experiences get shared with everyone at once. You know, so we don't have to endlessly repeat information to each individual."

"So, is it like working with a mentor all night long?"

"Not at all, Droplet, what an odd notion! It's a lot more interesting than that. Comforting, actually. You'll see. Come on, it will be starting soon."

They arrived at the deep alcove where many Others of the Boktow grouping were already squeezing into position. Droplet, as a newcomer, was placed near the outside; he felt oddly nervous. Fortunately, he was situated between Boff and Fernlin, whom he had just met, and they were both calm and expectant. Several Elders, including Wise Elder and Elder Bonn, were toward the center of the clustered grouping.

It began when Elder Bonn sent a welcoming through the grouping in such a way that everyone received it and passed it on to his neighbor. Then each Other present sent his name through the grouping until everyone knew who was in attendance. When it was Droplet's turn, he shyly introduced himself, and had the uncomfortable experience of being the sole focus of the grouping's attention for a moment.

After the introductions, there was a long sharing of information regarding things Droplet knew nothing about: expected visitors, updates on known travelers, phases of The Flow . . .

The last thing he remembered was Wise Elder sharing something about a grouping far from there. By the time the stories finally started, Droplet had fallen fast asleep.

He awoke at some point in the night surprised to be touching and touched by so many Others. He had gotten used to sleeping with only Mentor Sootan or Wise Elder near. After a moment's reflection, Droplet decided that it *was* comforting to have Others so close. With this thought, he drifted off to sleep again.

Early the next morning Wise Elder came to tell him he was leaving. The two of them moved away from the alcove so they could communicate privately. Droplet had already learned that the Boktow grouping placed little value on privacy.

When they had settled on the far side of a large rock, Wise Elder watched him for a moment, and then sent, "I'm needed elsewhere Droplet, but I think you'll do fine here."

Although he had been expecting this, he suddenly felt self-conscious and overwhelmed by all they'd shared over the last few days. He knew himself to be profoundly changed, deeply enriched.

"I'm not sure how to thank you," was all he managed to send.

"Ah, Little One, there is no need to thank me, we are friends, *allies* in the truest sense. We will come together again, probably sooner than you think. In the meantime, I know you will fare well."

Droplet received this thoughtfully, and then contemplated what he wanted to send as goodbye. When he was ready he leaned into Wise Elder, whom he considered his *true* mentor, and showing off his new capabilities, sent a heartfelt composition of gratitude, respect, affection, and expectancy for their next time together.

Wise Elder received the layered sending appreciatively, and then mirrored it back to Droplet, after adding the unmistakable qualities of fondness and pride.

A moment later, Droplet felt filled to the brim as he watched Wise Elder dart into the center of The Flow, and speed away.

Droplet lingered for a while in a reflective mood, and then headed back to his new home. On the way he found Boff, who had been waiting for him near the alcove.

As soon as he caught sight of Droplet he sent, "*Swirly,* Droplet! Fernlin and a couple of Others are going to travel to the far up-flow. They're expecting to be gone most of a twelve-day. Fern said you and I could join them if you'd like . . ."

Droplet didn't even hesitate. He immediately replied in the affirmative, and followed Boff, who took him to where Fern and two Others were waiting. He was briefly introduced to Tilsen and Lozani, and then they were off, with Fern in the lead.

He was woefully unprepared for the pace they set, however. *Why do we have to travel so quickly?* he wondered for the fifth time as he struggled to keep up. *I can't even look around.*

Finally, he got better at fine-aiming his attractor-charges which allowed him to expend less effort. He also discovered that by traveling immediately behind any one of them, moving at their pace was easier. Still, he was ready for the rest break when it came.

They had been following a big curve in The Flow, and had arrived at a wide pebbly spot where the current was placid. Boff, Til and Lozani had gone to explore a rotting log poking out of the bank nearby. Fern stayed with Droplet, both lost in their own thoughts for a while. Droplet intended to show his respect—one of his mentor's early lessons—so he waited for the other to send first.

"So, what did you think of your first convergence, Droplet?" Fern asked comfortably.

"I was pretty tired, but I, ah, liked it." Droplet responded a bit cautiously.

"Yeah, I noticed when you drifted off. You actually missed the best part, you know. Sometimes the sharings and stories are amazing."

Droplet, who'd already decided he'd have to try to stay awake longer next time, asked about what he was really interested in.

"Boff mentioned that you have done some traveling. I'd enjoy hearing about that."

This appeared to be all of the encouragement Fern needed, for he eagerly launched into a detailed narrative of his most recent journey near where they were going this time. Fern, his esse sparkling, vividly described the things he'd seen. He went on at length about *paddle-flappers*—large, winged creatures paddling and feeding *tail-up*—all over the wide, marshy shallows in vast numbers. Droplet listened with rapt attention, visualizing everything Fern sent, until Boff, Til and Lozani returned and suggested they continue on.

They had been traveling through a long stretch of huge boulders and verticals, called The Narrows, when the sun moved behind a high bluff, plunging The Flow around them into shadow. Droplet, who was fully ready for another break, paused with the rest of them.

"There goes sol, time to find a good place for the night," sent Fern, the group's undisputed leader.

In short order, Til found them a suitable spot at the base of two monolithic sol-verts. They'd passed many similar rocks that afternoon; enormous stones with high, broad planes rising shiny and smooth above the surface. While in The Narrows, the Flow's dominant current had been plunging and tempestuous, but at the base of these massive stones crowded with *cuddle moss* and clumps of delicate, round-leafed plants, the current moved in calmer rills.

They clustered together in a type of convergence, sharing observations and insights of the day's journey and then stories long into the evening, until one-by-one they drifted into sleep.

It was no surprise to anyone that their exhausted newcomer was the first to go.

During the next day's journey, they passed a *divide* that had separated the creek they'd been traveling from a larger creek. The newly combined Flow became wide and gentle as it meandered through a series of low hills. Droplet enjoyed the reduced intensity of The Flow, which seemed to be reflected in his companions, who were now traveling at a more relaxed pace.

They had stopped for the day, while the sun was still high, at a strange land configuration. Fern told Droplet this bit of land, surrounded on all sides by The Flow, was called an *island*, and often contained interesting features and creatures. They took off in twos to explore, Droplet paired with Lozani.

"So, have you been here before?" Droplet asked as they rounded a bulge in the irregular edge of the island.

"Naw, but I've seen other islands splitting The Flow—some a whole lot bigger than this."

Just then they came to a deep indentation in the island's bank, choked with the roots of many wide, low bushes.

"Let's go in there," Lozani angled sharply into the root system; Droplet followed. "Ah, look at that."

Partially hidden among the first roots they came to were a couple of lumpy *crawlers*, scuttling in the dark mud. They watched silently as the crawlers suddenly raced toward something, stirring up little clouds of fine silt which lingered in The Flow.

The two observers angled closer to see an ungainly, shard-shaped creature nosing around the base of a root. Without warning, the crawlers pounced on the creature, and began to shred and devour it—sending up little bits of flesh—which then attracted a sleek, big-spotted flasher hiding deeper in the shadowy roots. In short order, the blocky creature was no more, and the crawlers had scuttled away leaving the flasher to finish consuming what remained.

Droplet was stunned. *What just happened here*, he wondered, trying to figure out how to phrase a question to Lozani, who hadn't seemed at all surprised.

"Well, that was quick," sent Lozani casually.

"Um . . . yes. Does that sort of thing happen often?" Droplet sensed it was a strange question, but he really wanted to know.

"Sure." Lozani glanced at Droplet, and what he saw made him add, "You know every creature has to eat, right?"

"Yes," he responded slowly. "But I haven't actually seen them eat much, and that seemed, well, pretty horrible."

"Oh, it can be," admitted Lozani. "I remember the first time I saw two big-clawed *quarns* go at it. It was a fight for certain, right up to the end when the smaller got the larger in a claw-lock and then pinched off its head. After that, the smaller had itself a good meal until the scavengers arrived. Then it had to dash, or be eaten too."

Droplet took this in as he looked around. After glancing at Lozani, he moved away from the shadowed roots and into the center of the little bay until he came to a pocked ledge. Lozani followed him. Droplet sat pensively on the ledge and regarded the sun-drenched bay with its dark-rooted fringe. The current was very still.

Lozani waited thoughtfully, and then sent, "I'm sorry, Droplet, I didn't fully realize how inexperienced you are. It *is* a weird thing—this rule of creatures—which is to eat the other or get eaten yourself. Doesn't seem like much of an existence, does it?"

Droplet immediately opened up. "No, it really doesn't. Why does it have to be so—I don't even know the word!"

"Aggressive, violent, brutal?"

"Yes, all of those!"

"I don't know, Droplet. And I don't know anyone who does. I just think we are blessed not to have to struggle that way, don't you?"

Droplet was very quiet as he thought it through.

Finally, he came to the realization that there was no way he could truly understand something so completely foreign to his own existence. After that he relaxed, and they talked about other things until Lozani suggested they continue on around the island, and then head back to the others.

That night, the orb was a bright half-circle. Soft light bounced and shimmered around the five of them as they huddled together sharing stories of their adventures. Droplet was grateful to Lozani for not bringing up his earlier discomfort, and he listened carefully to several tales of near-mishap involving a variety of creatures who, even at the best of times, behaved unpredictably. Finally, his companions quieted and slid into sleep.

Droplet stayed awake for a while, watching a couple of orb-illumined flyers soaring above the surface. He thought again about the strange actions of creatures, and understood in a different way that even though cresting gave him the ability to reason, he was still, as both Wise Elder and Lozani had said, quite inexperienced. *I'm sure that will change,* he thought sleepily.

Comforted by the memory of Wise Elder, he finally relaxed into sleep.

The next day, they finished exploring the perimeter island and continued traveling upstream. They passed out of the low hills that Droplet thought resembled mounds of stone in The Flow, and the terrain gradually flattened around them. The Flow widened and slowed even more. In fact, it seemed to Droplet that the current had all but ceased.

Late in the day, Fern called a halt to decide where to go next.

"There's a divide up ahead that will take us back into the hills or we can continue on into Marsh Lake. Any preferences?"

"I'd like to explore Marsh Lake," sent Til, the quietest among them.

"Okay, any other opinions?" Fern looked at each of them in turn. Boff and Lozani indicated no preference, and Droplet didn't know enough about a *lake* to chose. *Oh.*

"Umm, I'd like to see the lake," Droplet sent, hesitantly.

"Me too. The lake it is, then," agreed Fern.

They continued on the way they'd been going. The next day when they passed the divide Fern had mentioned, Droplet wondered how such a little trickle could have taken them all the way into the hills.

Then they entered Marsh Lake.

To Droplet, it might have been another world. Very quickly the current petered out, The Flow itself was dark and murky, and trees and banks and other familiar features were totally absent. If there were stones in the wide expanse of shallows he couldn't see them because the bottom of The Flow was mucky with rotting plants. And there were plants everywhere *in* The Flow; tall stalks called *reeds*, wide-leafed plants floating on the surface in large groupings, and thick clumps of bushes rooted into each other rather than a bank.

The expansive lake was also a treasure trove of flashers—many more kinds than he had ever seen. And almost all of them were huge. The whiskered flashers that like the bottoms were the size of small logs. He didn't even notice them until they moved. The limited visibility meant that if he hadn't been right next to his companions or able to see their esses, he would have been completely lost.

After exploring part of the lake's rim together, they traveled to the tallest bushes they'd seen and prepared to spend the night nestled among their twiggy roots. Convergence was a sleepy affair, and Droplet felt distracted by the strangeness of his surroundings. He glanced up and saw a few stars through the roots. Excusing himself to the others, he left and moved away from the sheltering bushes. Til followed him.

When Droplet got clear of the bushes, he noticed Til, who sent him a shy greeting and joined him on a delicate frond near the surface. The Flow around them was dark and almost completely still; only the occasional passing of an invisible creature could be felt.

Then he looked up and nearly lost his attractor-charge. The vastness of the night sky was astounding. He watched as more and more stars appeared glistening into different shapes and forms. Many more than he'd ever seen before. Perched so near the surface and without banks or trees to restrict the view, Droplet and Til shared a sense of spacious wonder. The rising of the bright, star-dimming orb signaled to both of them that it was time to return to the others.

"See that over there, Droplet?" sent Boff, indicating several rounded shapes floating on the surface in the morning mist. "Those are the *paddle-flappers* Fern told us about."

Droplet watched the nearly motionless shapes. *They don't look like any creatures I've seen.* "Why are they called paddle-flappers?"

"Well, just keep watching and you'll figure it out," Boff sent cryptically.

Droplet, who had been joined by Til, watched patiently until more shapes emerged from the reeds. A few of the shapes lowered thin *necks* to tear plants and wrigglers from the bottom, but most of them glided into the open using wide, leaf-shaped *paddlers* to push themselves along. All of a sudden, for no reason Droplet could determine, the nearest of the creatures erupted into activity. Paddling fiercely, they unfurled large wings and starting lifting away from the churning surface. In a very short time, the whole grouping was flapping high above them, circling the lake. *Astounding!*

"Paddle-flappers," Boff offered casually, "come in different sizes. Come on, I'll show you some really big ones."

Boff, Til and Droplet spent the entire day together exploring the lake and tracking down paddle-flappers. Boff took them to hidden *nests*, some complete with downy younglings straining to be fed by careful adults. He showed them the smallest paddle-flappers who dive down to the murky bottom to snag tiny flashers and other creatures and then bob back to the surface to eat them. And finally, after a very thorough search, they found a few of the huge paddle-flappers Boff had described, paddling along, pulling-up thin roots and cluster mosses with their long, pointed *beaks*. Droplet thought they looked far too large to fly, but Boff assured him they could. They watched these tranquil, long-necked creatures and myriad other lake creatures until sol dropped toward the horizon.

On the way back, they took the long way round the lake so they could practice stories of their adventures for the evening convergence.

A few days later Droplet and Lozani were traveling along the far shore of the lake, beyond the marshy areas, when they came across a ringed flasher swimming erratically.

"I think he might be sick or dying, Droplet."

Droplet agreed. The tattered flasher had just gone into a stand of curly-stalk when Droplet thought he saw a flicker of light further on.

"Did you see that, Lozani?"

"The wrinkled *gibbler* hiding under that log?"

"No, I think there's something behind that mound. Let's go look."

Droplet led Lozani between a few exposed mounds along the sandy lake bank. The daily mist had mostly lifted, revealing the first tall trees Droplet had seen since entering Marsh Lake, but sol's light had yet to reach full brightness.

There. Under a flat stone wedged into the bank Droplet could just make out three or four faintly glowing esses. He went right to them, but Lozani stopped him before he could enter the dim recess.

"Don't go in there, Droplet," Lozani sent after getting a quick look at the ragged-looking Others. "We need Fern here before we make contact."

"But why? They look like they need some help."

"I know, but trust me on this, Droplet. We need Fern's greater experience before we do anything more."

Lozani glanced under the flat again; the Others had retreated deeper into the recess. "I'll go get Fern, if you agree to wait over there and not try to communicate with them in any way. Will you do that, Droplet?"

"Yes, alright," he sent, retreating to the speckled mound Lozani indicated. "But I don't understand why."

"I know, Droplet, but it's important. I'll be back as quickly as I can." Droplet sensed him start distance-sending as soon as he shot away from the bank. *Fast*, he thought, as he settled in to wait.

Curls of mist edged away from the bank above him and then slowly ascended in long, vanishing tendrils. As directed, Droplet didn't approach the Others hiding under the flat rock, but he did watch them.

Near the center of the lake Fernlin observed the largest of the paddle-flappers intently. He had secreted himself in the reeds to the side of the low hump of their nest where one of the adults rested. When the adult got up to stretch, he could just make out five—no six—fuzzy-headed hatchlings. He had spent many, many twelves of seasons studying the habits of creatures, and these huge flyers were one of his favorite species. He recognized the parent on the nest, by its size and markings, as one who had nurtured other successful broods, and he hoped to have his most pressing question answered today.

Fernlin knew that most small creatures—crawlers, flashers, creepers, leapers and the like—came into existence knowing exactly how to be whatever creature they were. He also knew that large creatures, especially land dwellers, were raised and taught what they needed to know by their parents, just as his kind were taught and trained by mentors.

What he, and Others who studied these things wanted to determine, was whether very large flyers taught their young like land creatures; or, like smaller flyers, did the young emerge already knowing how to eat, swim, and fly?

The debate among his peers revolved around whether training young, or not needing to train them, is a function of a creature's species, it's size, or perhaps something else? Because it is hard for his kind to closely observe the newly born young of any species living beyond The Flow, his fervent hope was that the low nest before him would offer him the required vantage.

The nesting paddle-flapper stretched again, spread it's impressive white wings and stepped away from the nest. Immediately, six little heads popped up, mouths open. Fernlin turned to watch the second parent approach and climb onto the nest while the first parent paddled away. The second parent offered food to the younglings from it's beak. Clearly, the young ones knew how to get food from the parent, but . . .

Just then, he received a faint, but urgent questing sending. He quickly distance-sent his location and returned his attention to the nest. One of the young had hopped up on the edge of the nest while the others were still feeding. Would he jump into The Flow on his own, or would he wait for the other adult paddling nearby, to guide him?

Before he could learn the answer, Lozani raced up to him and told him about the strange, contact-avoidant Others Droplet had found hiding near the far shore. Masking his annoyance and cognizant of his responsibility as leader of his group, Fernlin gave a last look at the youngling teetering on the nest's edge. *Ah well, there'll always be more hatchlings.*

Then he turned away and followed Lozani out of the reeds.

The mist had cleared to hazy mid-day by the time Lozani returned with Fern. Droplet had edged a bit closer to the hidden Others, but he'd kept his word and hadn't tried to communicate with them. Still, he was relieved when Fern arrived and took charge, going directly to the edge of the recess to peer in.

He and Lozani moved closer to watch.

Fern's delicate questing sending resulted in the Others moving even farther under the flat. Fern stopped sending and looked back at him and Lozani.

"Did either of you do anything to upset them?"

"No," Lozani replied, "Droplet saw them under there and when I looked at them I knew we shouldn't do anything, so I went to get you right away."

"Droplet, did you do anything?"

"No. I just stayed over there and watched them."

"All right. I need to go in to find out who they are and if they need our help. You two stay back and be quiet. They seem quite fragile and we don't want to upset them any more than they already are."

Then Fern went into the recess. Droplet watched his bright esse approach three or four dim ones, then the occasional flicker of esses and subdued sendings. Finally, after what seemed like a long time, Fern emerged with one of the Others.

As Fern and the Other came toward them, Droplet could see that Fern helped the Other move with a subtle attractor-charge.

"Lozani, Droplet, I would like you to meet Birsted. He and the three Others are from the Symbonica Grouping up-flow of Marsh Lake."

Birsted just looked at them. Up close he appeared to be in even worse shape than Droplet had thought. His form was concave on top with splotchy areas around his middle and his esse fulgurated erratically.

"Were from," he sent flatly. After another long pause he added, "Symbonica is no more."

The finality and utter despair in the feeling tone of this sending rocked him. He looked to Fern for an explanation, but Fern was busy trying to get the Other settled comfortably. Lozani looked as shocked as he felt.

Fern looked up to gauge the time of day. "Lozani, I'd like you to find Boff and Til and have them join us here by dusk. Tell them we'll be spending the night here and then heading back to Boktow with these four survivors."

As Lozani sped away, Fern looked at him. "Droplet, I'd like you to come with me." Then he turned and went back into the recess.

Droplet glanced at Birsted, who seemed calm but oblivious, and then followed.

The recess was dark and tight. Wedged into the farthest gap were the other three *survivors*. He wasn't sure what this term meant, but it didn't seem like a good thing to be.

Fern approached the three and sent to Droplet on tight-beam, "I want you to stay near while I talk to them. Try to radiate calm."

Radiate calm? "Umm, okay."

Trying to be as still as possible, he watched Fern attempt to engage the three in sending. After quite a few attempts, two of the Others, who's esses looked strikingly similar, started giving brief responses while their esse's brightened perceptibly. But the third remained distant and dim.

With contact finally established, Fern asked him to join him. "Droplet, this is Bintner and Binny, formerly from Symbonica." Then he indicated the Other making little jerking motions in the crevice. "And that is Gern. He is a non-sender."

Fern paused as if gathering his thoughts, "I'm going to stay in here with them, and I'd like you to go out and ask Birsted to join us. Please stay nearby, Droplet, and when the others arrive, let them know I'll be spending the night in here, and that I'd like us all to leave for Boktow at first light."

Lozani, Boff and Til arrived just as dusk was setting in. They had tales of the day's adventures and lots of questions for Droplet.

"But what happened to their grouping, Droplet? I've never heard of Symbonica, have you Boff?" Til, usually quite self-contained, was all over the place.

"All I know is that they're in pretty bad shape," Droplet replied. "Fern called them *survivors*, and one of them is a non-sender. I'm not even sure what these terms mean."

Til looked at Boff.

"Well, I guess I'm the only one here with any experience," Boff began reluctantly. "Droplet, being a survivor means you've been through a catastrophic event. And no, Til, I haven't heard of Symbonica, but I have heard of catastrophes before—usually they have to do with severe storms, banks giving way, or rockslides. But they can disburse an entire grouping, and being violently torn away from those you live with and forced to leave a familiar location can be extremely difficult for some. Sudden destruction on any scale is hard to deal with; on a large scale it can be devastating."

They were all silent as they tried to imagine what this would be like. The rest of Droplet's questions evaporated like mist in the subdued mood. After what seemed like an unusually fast transition into the dark of night, the four of them huddled together for comfort, each holding a delicate attractor-charge as they slept.

An intensely bright flash of light startled Droplet awake. In the dim light of predawn he felt a sudden but brief vibration in the mound they'd slept next to. He looked beyond The Flow as another bright flash revealed huge dark clouds filling the far horizon. *Like banks along The Flow,* he thought groggily, as he tried to make sense of what was happening. Then came the vibration again; this time more sustained, and Droplet could tell that the whole lake shook briefly.

"Yeah, there's a *storm* coming, Droplet," sent Lozani as he and Til nudged Boff, who had somehow slept through this.

Droplet, who vaguely remembered learning something about storms, sent, "That's when everything gets disrupted, right?"

"Ha! That's one way to put it." Just then there was another intense flash of light which caused everything around them to look vivid and flat. "That, my friend, was a *sharp-flash* and it generally signals a *deluge* is coming. Let's get to Fern and the Others."

They hurried to the recess where they found Fern coaxing three of the Others out into the open.

"We need to leave immediately," Fern sent in a rush. "I want to get the survivors back to Boktow so that Fintan can help them, and this is no place to wait out a storm." He went back in to get the last survivor. But he returned almost immediately.

"Lozani, Til, link with these three and wait here. Droplet and Boff come with me."

They went back into the recess to get the non-sender Birsted had called Gern. Just as they reached him another sharp-flash showed him flattened into the crevice in a way that looked unnatural to Droplet.

"This won't do," sent Fern. "We've got to get him out and he can't understand our sendings. Droplet, you and Boff grasp him on either side with a firm attractor-charge while I pull him from the front. When I give the word, we'll all aim a unified repulsion-charge toward the rock behind him. As soon as he's free we'll sweep him out to the Others. Just don't let go of him, okay? Here we go: *now!*" They carefully combined their attractor- and repulsion-charges as directed.

Gern didn't budge.

They tried again. Gern remained absolutely fixed.

"I can't believe this! How can he be stronger than our combined charges?" Fern looked completely flummoxed.

They had been so focused on Gern, they hadn't noticed that Birsted had joined them. "Perhaps I can be of some assistance," he sent softly. "He knows me, and he is capable of some understanding if approached correctly."

"Okay, but . . . ?"

65

"Just give me a moment with him." Birsted exchanged places with them, and began sending an undulating murmur. To Droplet, nearby and paying close attention, it felt mostly like a calming feeling-tone, but with curious changes in rhythm.

When done, Birsted returned to where they were waiting at the edge of the recess. "I believe he is willing to come now, but it would be best if he could attach to a couple of you for the journey. His one great ability is attachment, you see, and the only way he'll feel safe once that," he sent, indicating the rampaging wind and lowering clouds, "affects The Flow, is between two of your strongest senders."

"Okay, bring him out," agreed Fern. "Droplet will you attach to him with me? Boff, you go link with one of the other survivors and wait for us to join you."

Droplet and Fern watched in amazement as Birsted slowly peeled Gern out of the tight crevice. Once he was completely free, Birsted continued to murmur to him until he regained more of a roundish shape. Droplet noticed his esse, while still quite pale, looked more stable now. Gern did look very unusual, though; the term *oddball* came to him unbidden.

Birsted brought him out slowly, and then helped transfer Gern's attractor-charge to them. Droplet immediately responded to the unwavering intensity of Gern's charge—no wonder Birsted called it *attachment*. He briefly struggled with the uncomfortable feeling of being powerfully clutched, until Fern's presence, which he could sense *through* Gern, calmed him.

Fern, Gern and Droplet turned as one to the Others, who were watching with great interest.

"Alright, pair-up and let's get going," Fern sent to everyone in a commanding tone. "We have a long journey ahead and The Flow is going to be challenging in places, so let's form a line and stay out of the strong currents as much as possible. Lozani, you and Binny take the lead; then Boff and Birstead; Til you join Bintner; and Droplet, Gern and I will bring up the rear. Use a linking attractor-charge to stay with your partner and to link with everyone else. If anyone breaks loose, we'll all stop to help. This isn't going to be an easy trip, and we're going to need regular rest stops to keep up our strength and focus. Lozani, you watch for safe patches and signal when its okay to take breaks. Any questions?"

There weren't any, so they linked-up and traveled along the edge of the lake back to where they'd entered it.

They took their first break before leaving Marsh Lake and just as the storm broke. "Here it comes," sent Boff, vanishing momentarily in the vivid light of another sharp-flash. Above them there was an intense commotion. Droplet looked up, astonished to see vast numbers of clear chunks of something plunging into the surface and then disappearing.

"Okay, break's over," sent Fern. "We need to get to the island before The Flow gets too turbulent."

"But what's happening?" Droplet asked Lozani, as Fern moved among them testing everyone's linking charges.

"It's the deluge, Droplet. It comes from the clouds and runs off everything it touches—except The Flow of course—which it unites with."

Unites with? "Something that comes from *beyond* The Flow can unite with it?"

"Ah—you should probably ask Fern about it when we've got more time. Right now, we've got to link. You're going to see a whole new Flow, Droplet. It's going to get much wilder and leaping-fast."

They left the lake and moved into the river in a line, hugging the hither bank. Above them the deluge pelted the surface and caused little rivulets to pour over the bank disrupting their progress. Except for the time a strong rivulet suddenly broke through the bank and cascaded right into them, they did a good job of maintaining their links. It was tiring though, and as Fern had predicted, they needed frequent breaks through-out the day.

It was nearly dark when they reached the island—now little more than a rocky hillock in the middle of the swollen river. Fern brought them to the relative calm at the farthest down-flow point of the island. There, exhausted but secure in large mixed stone and well below the swirling confluence of current, they slept.

The Flow transformed in the night.

In the faint light of morning Droplet awoke next to his sleeping companions, but that was where any sense of familiarity ended. At the surface the deluge had let up some, but The Flow itself had become congested with suspended particles. Something about the look and feel of the restricted visibility—the murky dimness—tugged at his memory, but he couldn't place it.

Directly above him two turgid currents whooshed around the island, merged their catch of leaves, stems, branches, rocks and other debris, and then hurled downstream in a wide swath. Along both banks new rock formations and tangled roots were exposed. The powerful current tore a small tree from the aft bank as he watched; it quickly rolled and spun away.

At his back, the diminished island lurched and shivered as objects crashed into it and then sailed past. Droplet found these changes astonishing and even unnerving. And he wasn't the only one.

The others near him began to stir and waken. While his Boktow friends reacted to the situation stoically, several of the newcomers revealed the diminished esses Droplet now associated with the emotion of fear. And the instant Gern took in the clouded current, he severed contact with Droplet and Fern and scuttled into the nearest tight crevice. Fern startled awake at the abrupt charge interruption.

"Well, that's not very helpful," sent a tired looking Fern. He shook himself a bit and then looked at Droplet and sent, "At least he's safe there, I guess. Let's see how everyone's doing and wait until we're ready to leave before we try to pry him out."

"Agreed."

They discussed their situation together in the chaotic and slowly brightening gloom. Fern explained that they weren't far from The Narrows, the substantial stretch of river choked with huge vertical boulders and sol-verts, and that Boktow was an easy half-day journey beyond.

"Some of us aren't at our best and need help, and the current through The Narrows will be fast and rough. The big question," he sent to the very attentive group, "is should we try to get through the narrows now, or should we wait to see if The Flow settles down a bit before we make the attempt?" Fern paused for a moment and then added, "And I think it should be a group decision."

Lots of concerns and points of view were shared, especially by Boff, Birsted and Lozani. Droplet, who had little experience and therefore nothing of substance to contribute, followed the discussion carefully. In the end, it was the intensifying storm above them that decided them; they would attempt The Narrows now.

This time Fern suggested they go through The Narrows in pairs rather than trying to stay together in a line. "If we're in pairs we have a better chance of avoiding a mishap that might fling one or more of us into the turbulent surface currents."

They all agreed to reunite, if possible, beyond The Narrows at the base of a short, distinctive cliff on the aft bank that the Boktow members all knew. "We'll spend the night there and then return to Boktow the next day. If anyone hasn't arrived by morning, we'll assume they got taken by the current and will hopefully be waiting for us at Boktow."

Droplet felt a quiver of unease as he studied his friends and companions. He hadn't considered that he might not see all of them at the gathering place beyond The Narrows. Not everyone looked confident, he thought, but everyone except Gern, who was still flattened into the crevice, showed varying degrees of determination.

"Remember, the current should be mildest around the base of the boulders," sent Fern, as he and Droplet turned to retrieve Gern. "Go slowly and use attractor-charges to keep yourselves as near the bottom as possible. Now link with your partner and we'll see each other again at the cliff."

The rest of their group paired-up and departed to sendings of "Safe journey!"

Droplet and Fern took their time bringing Gern from his place of safety in an effort to build trust. Neither of them thought this worked very well; Gern just strained to return to the rocks and hardly seemed to notice them. They had to use their strongest attractor-charges just to hold him.

"Why won't he attach to us? We can't travel fighting him the whole way—at least not safely..."

Droplet, who had watched Birsted's interaction with Gern sent, "Let me try something."

He moved away from Gern while Fern held him firmly and approached him from the side without touching him. Then he started a very gentle sending of nonsensical murmurs the way Birsted had. It took a little while, but Gern gradually relaxed and stopped resisting Fern's attractor-charge. When Droplet moved to his position at Gern's side, he instantly attached to both Droplet and Fern.

"Well, that was—impressive—Droplet," Fern sent as they snugged Gern between them and left the island behind. "What exactly did you do?"

"I noticed Birsted used very gentle sendings that didn't contain meaning to calm him down before," Droplet sent, as they rounded a large conical. "I thought it was worth a try."

"Yes, and it certainly worked. Having a better way to deal with him will make our task much easier." Fern stopped sending as they moved through some rooted crack-dwellers and Gern balked.

They stopped and Droplet murmured to him again until he calmed and they moved on.

They carefully rounded a long curve Droplet vaguely remembered. In the distance he could see the huge verticals that signaled the beginning of The Narrows.

"Um, why is he the way he is?" Droplet wanted to see if they could have an actual conversation *through* Gern without disturbing him. They hadn't tried it before.

"It's a good question, and I don't know the answer," responded Fern softly. "It seems some of us are just different. It isn't common to find a non-sender with Others, though, and I don't know how he ended up with the survivors of Symbonica. Usually non-senders are loners, but it's possible he's only been a non-sender since the catastrophe, which means with the right kind of help he could recover."

Droplet thought about this and then sent, "Did you have a chance to learn what happened to them, to their home I mean?"

"Not yet, but we'll have plenty of time to get to know them back at Boktow. Right now, let's concentrate on getting through that," he sent, indicating The Narrows up ahead.

They stopped for a moment to focus on the heaving Flow as it sped through the giant boulders. The movement of debris revealed erratic flurries in and around the massive obstacles, while crosscurrents kicked-up sand and silt from the bottom. This, and the fact that the main thrust of the current appeared well below the surface, meant there wasn't going to be an easy way through.

"Swirling flumett, Droplet! This is worse than I thought it would be!"

Droplet could discern that the worry in Fern's sending was for the Others who'd gone on ahead, as well as for them. This, combined with what he now saw, boggled him. As he struggled to form a question, Gern twitched next to him and then nearly severed their link; they had to fight to maintain it. Finally, Gern stopped trying to break away, but he quivered and sparked like a nervous flasher.

Fern's next sending was calmer and more determined. "Okay, here's what we're going to do. Instead of trying to use charges to slow and control our progress, we're going to ride the lowest portion of the main current all the way through. This means it will be a fast trip, and we'll be able to maintain a firm grip on our friend here. We may need to use an occasional repulsion charge to keep from colliding with something, but I'll take care of that if you'll keep a hold on Gern. Agreed?"

Droplet looked from Fern to The Narrows just ahead. He thought he could see the part of the current Fern meant, but it still looked pretty turbulent to him. "Umm."

"Don't worry, Droplet. If we'd been alone and not trying to help survivors, I wouldn't have hesitated riding through the narrows—even on a current as fast as this. I've done it before, many times. And I'm sure that's what Lozani and the others have done."

When Droplet hesitated again, Gern struggled. Fern strengthened his grip on their reluctant burden and added, "Trust me, Droplet. It'll be more challenging as a threesome, but we can do this."

Droplet noticed something as he felt the sincerity in Fern's sending: Gern's resistance affected him by heightening his own doubt. *I wonder if my doubt also increases Gern's agitation?*

He took a moment to calm himself until he felt an inner release. Then he looked ahead and tightened his hold on Gern. "Okay, I'm ready," he sent, with rising excitement. "Lead the way."

Fern didn't hesitate. He used a repulsion-charge to angle

them away from the bottom and into the rushing current. When the current grabbed them, all Droplet could do was hold tight to Gern and watch in amazement. Just as when he'd been caught in the current before Mentor Sootan had rescued him, he had the undeniably strange sensation of seeming stationary while both banks rushed by him at a dizzying rate.

Then they were into The Narrows, plunging over and around submerged boulders, getting caught in momentary eddies, and then swirling back into the main current. A couple of times Fern had to repel them away from large flotsam captured in the current with them, but overall it was a fast, exhilarating trip.

Short though, thought Droplet, both excited and relieved as Fern took them to an irregular conical jutting out of the aft bank, just beyond The Narrows. He could see that Fern was shaking a bit from exertion and needed to rest.

"That was great!" sent Droplet, as he relaxed his grip on Gern, who edged toward the stone behind them and attached to it.

"Yes, and it's even more fun when you only have to worry about yourself," Fern offered, glancing after Gern.

Fernlin felt tired and disconcerted. He wanted to keep his worries to himself, and Droplet was a bit too perceptive at times, so he settled near Gern while Droplet relaxed and watched the storm. He used their short break to review his decisions and thought he'd made a few mistakes. He probably should have taken a good look at the conditions in The Narrows before suggesting they split-up and attempt it. He strongly doubted his entire group would be at the meeting place when they got there. He knew his Boktow friends would manage fine, but he worried for the survivors who were weakened and fragile with shock. They needed help and they needed it as soon as possible.

And then there was Gern. The enigma. The smart thing would have been to find out if he'd been an actual member of Symbonica, or was just a loner they'd come across after the catastrophe. If he'd been a loner, he could manage fine on his own again. But without knowing for sure, Fernlin couldn't just leave him, even though he was sorely tempted to at times. *And I don't even know why I find him so frustrating,* he admitted to himself.

These thoughts and worries perturbed him and kept him from getting the rest break he needed. He finally relaxed when he thought back to the paddle-flapper nest he had watched—was it only two days ago? He'd been so close to getting the answers he sought, too! So much had happened in such a short time—no wonder his thoughts were swirling.

He had to admit, times like these made him glad he wasn't considered an *Elder*, even though he was certainly old enough for the job. He preferred the uncomplicated ways of the natural world far too much to dedicate himself fully to Others the way Elders did. He looked forward to returning to Marsh Lake in the near future to see if he could observe some late hatchling. But first he had to get Gern and whoever was waiting at the meeting place the rest of the way home.

Droplet noticed Fern stir and went over to where he rested near Gern.

"Okay, time to detach him and get to the meeting place. Why don't you try your special trick again, Droplet."

Droplet complied and went to murmur gently to Gern. This time though, no matter what he did, Gern wouldn't budge.

Finally, Fern had a suggestion. "If you will stay here with him for a bit, I'll scout ahead to see who made it to the meeting place. If Birsted's there, I'm tempted to bring him back to help us with Gern. I'll come back to let you know either way. Okay, Droplet?"

"Yah, okay," he replied, after he made another unsuccessful attempt to move Gern on his own. "We'll be here."

Fern left with an astonishing burst of speed. *Kind of like he couldn't wait to get away,* Droplet thought, with a certain longing.

He turned back to Gern, who surprised him by hovering a little way from the rock he'd been stuck to since they'd stopped. He immediately linked to Gern and for the first time detected an emotion in him; something like eagerness. *That's strange.*

Detecting a disturbance above them, Droplet looked up just in time to see a tree branch sweep around the large conical they were next to and plunge downstream. Then, with no warning whatsoever, Gern attached strongly to Droplet and aimed a mighty repulsion-charge—*a repulsion-charge?*—at the conical, which catapulted them away from it and straight into the fastest part of the racing current.

Droplet had an instant to consider his two choices; he could attempt to break Gern's attachment and try to get out of the current, something he knew from experience wasn't easy, or he could stay with Gern as he'd been told.

But before he could decide, the tree branch just ahead of them slammed into a boulder and slewed around in a wide arc, sweeping them both into its shuddering leaves. Gern, with preternatural strength attached to the branch, with Droplet in tow.

The more Droplet, already tired, struggled to free himself, the firmer Gern's attachment to him became. *Not a very good feeling,* he acknowledged, his strength ebbing.

Finally, stuck fast to the branch speeding and lurching in the tumid river, he surrendered to exhaustion. The last thing he remembered was the dubious image of both banks quickly receding *from* him—strange!—and a faint emotion coming from Gern. It felt like *contentment.*

And so they traveled downstream together, hidden in the leafy-end of a small branch captured by the racing current. Past the meeting place. Past the teaching hollow. Past the Boktow grouping. And then past several of the storm-swollen river's merges and divides, quite thoroughly into the unknown.

Seven

D roplet's awareness returned to him slowly. He felt groggy and confused, trying to understand his unfamiliar surroundings. He was lodged next to a flat with a rough texture and dark blotches that looked like mud but weren't. The Flow above him appeared thick and opaque and he couldn't see either bank. Then, with a little flutter, his mind cleared and he remembered what had happened—the storm, Gern, the tree branch, all of it. But where was he now and, more importantly, where was Gern?

He pushed away from the flat and whirled around, but didn't see him anywhere. So he went exploring.

He found the branch, minus most of its leaves, a little ways upstream. He examined both ends and every nook in its bumpy bark, but found no Gern. Knowing Gern's predilections, he carefully searched the nearby mounds and flats, especially those with crevices, to no avail. He even tried a broadcast sending until he remembered Gern didn't respond to sendings.

Marking his location in his mind, he traveled perpendicular to the current until he reached the hither bank. It was sandy with very few rocks, so he turned around and eventually returned to the aft bank of this broader river—was it even the same creek he'd been in with the Others? *It feels very different*, he admitted. The aft bank had a rocky area just downstream, so he went there and searched every likely spot he could find.

He finally stopped when the light started to fade. He watched some flyers in the trees above him through the clearing current as night came on and thought about his predicament. He didn't have any idea how far they'd traveled, or how long he'd been unaware, for that matter, but he just wasn't willing to give up on the responsibility Fern had given him. A wave of loneliness washed through him as he thought of Fern and his Boktow friends. After a short rest, he decided he would use *esse-sight* to locate Gern in the dark.

Then he would bring him back.

He searched the whole night. He rested the next morning, and then he resumed his search. The Flow continued to clear and settle back into its banks. A few times he believed he'd found Gern, but it was only a strange kind of lichen that emitted light. For lack of a better term, Droplet dubbed it *false-hope* lichen.

After two nights and nearly a full day of fruitless searching, he realized he needed to let it go. The truth was if Gern didn't wish to be found, he wouldn't be. *And can I really blame him?* he wondered, as he watched hazy clouds streak across the nightsky. *He certainly had no reason to trust me, given that I was constantly making him do things he didn't want to do. He's such a strange character, I'm sure he does just fine on his own—probably even prefers it. While I—miss my friends.*

Decision made, Droplet left that very night.

Traveling back upstream at a leisurely pace and staying alert for a hidden esse, he began what he now suspected would be a long trek. He thought about his Boktow friends, sure that at least Fern would be worried, and maybe even searching for him. Him *and* Gern, he reminded himself.

He played everything that happened over again in his mind, but he couldn't imagine how anything he could have done would have changed the outcome. He wished he'd been able to spend more time with his Boktow friends, but he also knew from Wise Elder that when unexpected things happen, it's best to try to accept them. *Trust in The Flow*, was his common response whenever Droplet wanted to understand too much too soon, *It will always bring you what you need.*

So . . . Time to learn what The Flow has brought me, he thought, as he arrived at a merge where two separate Flows came together. He would have to pick one if he wanted to continue going upstream. But before he did he needed to rest, so he found a little overhang in the aft bank and nestled into it. *Strange to be so all alone...*

Gern had stayed with the branch until it snagged on something and came to a stop. After getting a read on his new location, he took the *sleeping one* to the bank away from the current, and left him. Then he moved to the center of the little river and let the current roll him downstream. Every few river-widths he would stop and sense the ambient vibrations. He sought a specific substance, and experience suggested he would find it nearby.

He found what he was looking for after allowing himself to be rolled into a shallow side-creek: piled mounds in an agreeably rapid current. No moss or other plants impeded these mounds, and they rested on hard-pack rather than dulling sand or cloying mud. Perfect!

After touching and sensing several of the smooth-sided stones, he happily flattened himself against a large, resonant angular. Now, through his attachment, he could revel in the intricate vibrations the endless current delivered.

What need had he of pesky Others who constantly tried to distract him from this joy? Oscillating, fluctuating pulsations spoke to him best through rock; comforted him, delighted him, sang to him. He loved the delicate trembles, the stutters, the throbs, and the riotous beat of The Flow in all its moods. And now, once again, he could be with them undisturbed.

Yes, here he would stay for a long time.

Droplet studied the two streams in the early light. After spending some time trying to sense the best way, he moved into the stream along the hither bank. He traveled most of the morning but nothing looked or felt familiar, and doubts started to nip at him the way a *skulker* harries little flashers.

Was this the right way? What if he'd chosen the wrong stream? How would he even know? After thinking it through, he decided he would just continue the way he was going, and if he'd made a mistake he'd go back and take the other stream.

Along the steeply sloped bank, pitted stones of all sizes rested against one another offering easy targets for his attractor-charges. On the under-edges of several, he noticed feathery plants growing—some with shiny globes clinging to them. For an instant, he thought these might be Others of his kind, but when he shifted to esse-sight he saw no esse in them, so they clearly weren't.

He approached the nearest rock for a closer look. A crawler scuttled out of one of the pits near the spheres. It approached the globes and, looking around, it carefully attached a couple of globes to the short spines on each if its thin legs. Then, as Droplet watched in amazement, it floated up to the surface where it laid in wait near the bank for a meal. After it had captured and devoured three hapless skimmers, the crawler twisted its legs until it dislodged the globes; then it sank back to its pitted home.

Droplet's estimation of all crawlers rose as he observed the inspired methodology of this crawler's actions. *How could it have learned to do that?*

Over the next couple of days, Droplet became more confident that he was following the right stream. Even though he still didn't recognize any of the features around him, it just felt right to him. And he continued to enjoy the creatures he came across.

There were a variety of different *quarn*, waving their jointed antennae and tussling one another with their snapping claws. He never saw them actually hurt one another, so even though they looked fearsome, he thought of them as playful and benign. Speckled *moss vens* made solitary sojourns from rock to stone in the shallows, while little groupings of spiral-shaped *knobbed creepers* made their slow way up and down the banks. They seemed purposeful and determined, but he could not discern their objective. He also discovered several odd looking flashers which resembled long, mottled leaves—with fins and faces. One of these darted out from under a log after a shiny fleck of something and almost bowled him over.

Late one day after an easy journey through narrow banks lined with tall, arching trees, he came upon a strange sight. It resembled a land creature, but it had a bloated body and was lolling, partially submerged near the aft bank. He approached it gingerly—in his experience creatures could be unpredictable. As he got closer, he saw that its upper side was teeming with a type of crawler he didn't recognize, some of them winged.

The creature is dead, he gleaned, *but not by another*

creature's attack or it would have already been eaten. Something wafted off the creature, making the Flow immediately surrounding it hazy. He moved upstream a ways and watched while unfamiliar scavengers helped the crawlers dismantle it—no, *consume* it. The life-cycle appeared to continue until no form remained.

He left the area just as some spotted flashers arrived, heading toward the dead creature. He didn't know if they were going to eat the creature, the crawlers, or the other scavengers, but he'd seen enough.

A short time later he felt done for the day and found a nice place along the quiet hither bank. Sol, still bright, was sinking toward the horizon. The Flow's surface and the leaves on the trees high above him shimmered in the slanting light. Even though it was beautiful here, Droplet's mood had shifted back to uncertainty. He tried to explore the feeling, but no new insights came. That night he dreamed.

The dream started like any other. He was back in the familiar environs of Marsh Lake, exploring with his friends and enjoying their company. Then it shifted and his friends were replaced by a single shining light. No, a large *esse*. An esse surrounded by the faint, luminous figures of paddle-flappers and myriad other creatures.

In the center, emerging from the brilliant esse, the image of Fernlin appeared and Droplet received, :*Ah, Droplet. I have finally found you. I want you to know that you did well, and that Gern is fine.* (Droplet caught the briefest vision of Gern flattened against stone.) :*You are relieved of the responsibility I laid on you, and you are free to go wherever the Flow takes you. Know that I appreciate your help, and your presence, Droplet . . .* (the image started to waver) *And should you choose to return, you will always be welcome in the Boktow grouping.* The final message was very faint. :*Fare you well, Droplet, until The Flow brings . . .* As the rest faded out, Droplet awoke.

He had full recollection of what had just happened and knew it was more than a dream. It was a true sending. Relief flooded through him along with a welcome sense of freedom. :*Thank you, thank you:* he tried to reply. :*Are you still there?* He felt the barest whisper of acknowledgement in return, and then nothing.

That was incredible—I had no idea a sending could come through a dream! Fully awake, Droplet contemplated the unique sending, the emotional warmth he'd sensed in the message—far more than he'd received from Fernlin before—and finally, the actual message. It was the freeing nature of the message itself, along with its somewhat daunting implications, that he kept turning over in his mind as he dozed the rest of the night away.

The next morning brought dark clouds and a small storm. Happy to spend a day relaxing, Droplet watched it all from the safety of his resting place on the hither bank. This time he could enjoy the energy of the storm as he studied its effects, especially how the trees and bushes responded.

When the surface pelting began, he moved up the bank near the surface to get a closer view. He still couldn't figure out exactly what was happening, but he found it intriguing that after disrupting the surface, there was no sign that anything had fallen. Not at all like the leaves and stems which also fell and glided downstream.

After the last of the storm moved beyond The Flow, Droplet gave more thought to his situation. Now that he could go anywhere, where should he go? No, where did he *want* to go? He quickly realized he knew far too little of the world to decide, and this took him back to Boktow.

Yes, he thought, *I will continue the way I'm going with the hope of returning to the Boktow grouping.* Even as he decided this, he understood he might not be able to find his way back. But a spirit of adventure took hold, and when he left his place of rest, it was with an open mind and a much lighter disposition.

In the early morning, a few days later, Droplet was awakened by a disturbance in The Flow. He quickly identified the cause as the commotion created by some large land creatures slowly moving into the shallows along the muddy bank. The creatures had round, cloudlike bodies and dark legs, and although they weren't nearly as large as the mighty *bigheads* he'd seen with Lozani at Marsh Lake, they were still bigger than any creature he'd seen since leaving there. Droplet counted several twelves of them as they approached The Flow in threes and fours to lower their heads to the surface. He moved a bit closer, intrigued by their unlikely shape, and then stopped when he saw that they were sucking some of The Flow into themselves. Engrossed by what he was seeing, Droplet was startled to receive a close-range sending from just behind him.

"Watch out for the *fur-faces*."

Droplet whirled around to find an unusual looking Other quite close to him. The Other had an elongated shape with several shallow depressions in it. He was also intently focused on the creatures just beyond them.

Droplet quickly switched to esse-sight which showed him the Other's glowing, but slightly ragged-looking, esse.

The Other gave him a quick glance and then sent, "I mean it, young'un, we should probably pull back."

Just as Droplet was going to ask what he meant by *pull back*, the Other sent, "Uh-oh, here come the *lungers*. We'd better just hunker down." With that, he squeezed between a couple of low mounds and sent a quick, "Come on!"

Droplet read the urgency in that sending clearly enough, and squeezed in between the stones next to him. As soon as he had, he turned around to see several new creatures—obviously the *lungers*—with longer legs and leaner bodies move to the edge of The Flow around the cloud-shaped creatures. Droplet got a glimpse of dark, shiny eyes as each of them lowered their whiskery visages to the surface and sent out a long, flat appendage—

"*Lapper-dappers;* all the lungers have them, and a lot of other fur-faces too. You'll want to stay plenty clear of the likes of them," came the quiet sending from the Other watching next to him.

As each pale fur-face finished sucking at the surface, another waded in to take its place. This happened again and again until the entire area got so murky they could hardly see the fur-faces at all. Then the lungers started jumping and lunging in the shallows until the cloud-shaped creatures retreated up the bank. Beside him, the Other sent, "Now, here come the flashers."

Around them, The Flow was suddenly churning with

glittering flashers. Many more than Droplet had ever seen at one time.

"They like what gets stirred up by the fur-faces," came the explanation from next to him. "Best we stay put for a while."

Droplet could only agree as he watched all the action. In a short time though, the fur-faces had all climbed the bank and disappeared, the flashers had flashed away, and the current had carried off the murk and muck.

Droplet turned to the stranger next to him. He couldn't sense more than a few surface thoughts, so he sent, "Thank you for warning me, umm . . ."

The Other, who had appeared distracted, sent, "Oh, I'm Dag, short for Dagrenoche, originally out of Dagram, but not for a long time now. What's yor call?"

"Ah, I'm Droplet," he sent, answering what he assumed was a request for his name. He wasn't sure how to say where he was from, originally or otherwise, so instead he sent, "I was wondering if you know the way to Bok—"

"*Swervey!* You're pretty new to all this, ain't cha?"

Droplet was startled when his sending got cut off, and he wasn't exactly sure what *swervey* meant. He decided to be a bit cautious with his response.

"Well, I've never seen those fur-faces before, but I've been here for a while."

"Shor. Yes, yes, of course," sent Dag as he looked around them. "So is this place your home?"

"No, I umm, got caught-up in the deluge a twelve-day or so ago, and I'm traveling back to the Boktow grouping. Do you know how to get there from here?"

"Nah, I haven't heard of Boktow." Dag paused and looked at Droplet. "Sorry. Feel like you need to get back right away, do you?" he asked sympathetically. When Droplet didn't answer immediately Dag added, "Cause if you're up for it, I can show ya something near here that's pretty *biffle*. You interested?"

Droplet, of course, had no idea what Dag was referring to. But everything he sensed from the Other seemed open and forthright, and he did feel up for a shared adventure. So, he decided to give his curiosity the lead and responded in the affirmative.

Dag led them further up-flow, and then they cut over to the aft bank. Here the current seemed strong and disorganized. When they came around a narrow stand of verticals, Droplet could see why. Just in front of them a wide turbulent Flow joined The Flow they were traveling.

"It's the Fair River merge," Dag sent from behind him. "And the Fair River, there, is a favorite of mine." Dag indicated the larger Flow descending sharply as it plunged into the merge.

Droplet watched the two Flows meet in chaos, and started to send, "How are we going to—"

Dag moved sharply in front of him and sent back a quick, "We'll link, but don't disengage until we're all the way though and into the Fair. It'll be worth it, for shor. Ready?"

Why not? Droplet linked with him and Dag immediately headed for the new river bottom, darting in and out of the strong, choppy current. Dag deftly avoided the little flutter currents that tugged at Droplet as they passed.

When they were beyond the fiercest part of the confluence, Dag used complex attractor-charges to move them into the wider river with its spirited current. As they paused for a rest, Droplet had to admit that he wouldn't have tried that on his own. *This Dag has some skills.*

When Droplet tried to express how impressed he was, Dag just sent back one word, "Experience," as they continued on.

Dag showed Droplet how to find the *still-run,* the quiet area beneath and to either side of the main current. Traveling in the still-run made moving against the current *much* easier and they journeyed that way for the rest of that day.

As the shadows started to lengthen, they finally stopped near a cluster of wide flats stacked in large rambling formations.

"Wow," sent Droplet after they'd found a place to pass the night, "that was great! I sure learned a lot today. But I don't know why my other friends didn't show me the still-run."

"Well, like as not, you were with a grouping, right? And groupings don't travel near as much as a *solo,* as a rule, and generally aren't as smart as they like to believe, neither."

Droplet was intrigued by the attitude in this sending, but he had already noticed that his new companion wasn't receptive to a lot of questions. "Yes, I was kind of part of a grouping," he replied, a bit loosely. "But mostly I was either with my mentor, or a few Others until the day before I, ah, left." Droplet paused. "Actually, I got side-swiped by a rogue tree branch and dragged for quite a ways," he added shyly, leaving out the part about Gern.

"Oh yeah, and that's a nasty business, to be shor! It's happened to some I've known, but never to me. Puts a real tuck in your day, I imagine."

"It did," Droplet agreed, becoming more comfortable with Other's sending style.

"If that ever happens to ya again, wait for a calmer stretch and push-off for all you're worth, okay?"

"Okay," sent a bemused Droplet. He wished he could have done just that. "So, what is the *biffle* thing you wanted me to see?"

"Further up this river is Soaring Cliff—a cliff so high it blocks most of the nightsky. And when you peer at it from the other bank it gives you an amazing sight—as long as the orb is gaining, which it is . . . "

They settled companionably into a gap at the base of the flat stones as dusk ebbed into true night. Droplet finally got up his nerve to ask Dag about what he really wanted to know: his travels.

"There's kind of too much of that to tell, young'un. Can you be a little more specific?"

Droplet sensed that Dag was willing to share, so he sent, "What's the strangest place you've ever been?"

Dag seemed to think for a minute and then sent, "That's not actually that easy of a question. I've been in some *swirly* circumstances, to be shor." Then he paused and sent, "But one of the oddest would have to be the *drowned forest*."

"The *drowned forest*?"

"Yeah, you know twelves and twelves and twelves of trees, all big-bottomed and wrinkly, living together in vast clumps. And they were in The Flow—all the time—drowned-like. And it was a strange, murky-still Flow, at that. There was all kinds of mung and scum everywhere, and some of the strangest creatures you ever did see."

Dag went on to describe his experiences, and all the creatures of that strange place, big and small. Most of his tales of the drowned forest were pretty grim. The creatures were unpredictable and aggressive, the light was always low, and the Others who lived there were "spin-witted and erratic." *Oddsters*, he called them. Droplet enjoyed learning all the new vocabulary, even if the images were unsettling.

"Even for me, well-traveled as I am, it was an uncomfortable place, and I was glad to be quit of it, I kin tell ya that!"

"But if it was as big as you say, and there was hardly any current, how did you get out?" asked Droplet, completely engrossed in the story.

"That, my little friend, is a tale for another evening," his companion sent, with what Droplet hoped wasn't the unwelcome finish it sounded like. Then, "Fair dreams, Droplet."

Ah.

"Fair Dreams, Dag."

That night, though, Droplet's dreams were far from fair. They moved and curled in dark and foreign currents. He dreamed of the drowned forest and the huge *sneaky-logs* Dag had described, with their long rows of *flinty-sharp teeth* ravaging anything that moved. He was both fascinated and repulsed by these creatures and their strange, gloomy environment.

In the peaceful light of early dawn, Droplet awoke with a start, unexpectedly alone.

A quick search of the area confirmed it. Dag was gone, and somehow Droplet didn't expect him to turn up again. *He was interesting, but called himself a 'solo,' which probably means he prefers to be alone. He taught me some good stuff though, and he 'shor' told a good story*, thought Droplet appreciatively.

Faced with the choice of continuing to travel toward Soaring Cliff, or returning the way they'd come, Droplet chose the former. He had to admit he enjoyed finding out what was around each new bend in The Flow.

Sol brightened as he continued to travel along the still-run beneath the fast-moving current. Around mid-day, Droplet came to the beginnings of a massive rock formation. Huge sol-verts gradually formed a solid foundation which rose along the hither bank until it reached a truly staggering height. Towering over The Flow, this magnificent cliff continued to rise until it dwarfed everything around it. *Soaring Cliff,* he thought. *'Biffle,' indeed.*

Droplet left the still-run and approached the bottom of the cliff. Gazing up, he could almost sense its sheer massiveness pulling at him. *Wow,* he thought, truly amazed.

Moving up the side of the cliff toward the surface, he noticed distinct eddies swirling twigs, leaves and debris in large ovals. Looking beyond the surface to the heights, he could see that the cliff had many cracks and ledges.

After watching for a while, he counted several twelves of small, bright flyers soaring to and from the ledges. Occasionally one of these would drop something into The Flow, where it would end up in a surface eddy, as often as not.

The magnificence of Soaring Cliff and the antics of the lively flyers captivated Droplet's attention for most of what became a lovely, lazy afternoon.

Not long after resuming his journey upstream along the mighty cliff, he was surprised to discern a faint, but constant sending coming from downstream and getting stronger.

He determined that the unusual sending was moving toward him so he stopped to wait. Soon he could see an Other, advancing slowly along the cliff face, investigating every nook and crack. Esse-sight showed him the Other's esse flickering in a way that made him feel uneasy.

"Horval? Hooorvaaal? You swirly gurgler, where are you?"

Droplet remained in the Other's path and waited politely until he was noticed.

"Hey, have you seen my spin-witted other half—Horval?" The Other, barely glancing at Droplet, quick-sent this as he continued his search.

Droplet, who could now clearly sense the Other's distress, moved closer and sent, "No, I haven't seen him, but um, perhaps I could help you search?"

The Other stopped searching for a moment and peered at him distractedly. "Do I know you?"

"No, you don't," he sent gently, "I'm Droplet."

"Well, Droplet, is it? Yes, you can help me. I'm Griff, and

I'm scummed if I can't find Horval!"

Droplet responded intuitively, even though he didn't know this Other, and had no idea why he seemed so frantic.

"All right. What should I be looking for, Griff?"

"Oh, he's a big, ugly lout, and sneaky too. I don't know why he always does this to me. The scraggly clot!"

With this unhelpful but anxious sending to guide him, Droplet entered into the search. Together they systematically covered the every bump and fissure of Soaring Cliff. And with both of them working it, they did it faster.

At one point, Droplet thought he had found the elusive Horval. He was using questing sendings in a deep crevasse, when he flushed out an Other who had obviously been sleeping.

"Wha, wha?" sent the barely conscious, and thoroughly annoyed, Other. "Are you frickey around the bobble? This is my hang; what are you doing here?"

Droplet backed out of the fissure quickly. *Frickey around the bobble?*

Griff came over to intercede. "Stobbs! Is that you? We're looking for Horval—have you seen him?"

"Of course I haven't seen him, Griff. I was sound asleep until this knob woke me with his probing."

Knob? "Sorry," sent Droplet quietly.

"Yeah, well. Just leave me alone, will ya?" With that, Stobbs returned to his *hang.*

Over the past two days I've learned more interesting terms than since my early time with Mentor Sootan, he thought, appreciatively. He continued the search, but stopped enjoying himself when night came on, and Griff became truly desperate.

"I just don't know where else to look," Griff lamented as they came to a large break in the cliff wall. "I hate it when he does this to me. It seems cruel, doesn't it?"

"It does kind of," responded Droplet, thoughtfully. "Does this kind of thing happen often?"

"Not really. We had an argument, as *doublets* do, and then he just disappeared."

"Doublets?"

"Yes, doublets. You know, *twinned* pairs?"

"Umm, I haven't actually heard of that." Droplet was

curious and thought a distraction might be helpful, so he sent, "Have you, ahh, always been *twinned*?"

Griff seemed to calm himself for a moment, and then sent, "Of course. That's what it means—esse-bonded from the first moment of awareness, and all that. Twinned, which is why it's painful to be apart. But of course, I seem to feel the pain a lot more than he does. Ohhh, where can he be?"

"Well, have you checked your home lately?"

"No, of course not, I've been searching all day." Then it hit him. "Oh. Let's go!"

With that, Griff took off in a truly impressive burst of speed which left Droplet struggling to keep up with him. Staying close to the cliff they traveled upstream until they came to a section riddled with shallow holes and pockmarks. Droplet could see that quite a few of these had Others in them; often a pair of Others, he noted.

Finally Griff came to a shuddering halt in front of a narrow, but deep hole. Even though it was quite dark inside, Droplet could see the faint esse-glow of an Other, who appeared to be sleeping in the far recess.

"Horval?" sent Droplet quietly.

"Horval!" Griff confirmed exuberantly and with obvious relief, as he quickly slipped into the hole. He seemed to be so relieved, in fact, that he forgot all about Droplet.

Droplet watched their reunion for a moment. Griff, no longer agitated, seemed to swell and soften slightly as he nestled next to his twin. They were gently lit with near identical esses, and he barely detected their quiet sendings.

Droplet rather abruptly realized he was quite tired. He looked around and found a little crevice not too far from Griff and Horval, where he settled in for the night.

What a strange day, he thought to himself as he drifted off to sleep.

In deepest night, something woke Droplet from a dreamless slumber. He was still tucked into the crevice near the bottom of the cliff which served to protect him from the current, the feeling of Others near, and movement of any kind. Senses on alert, Droplet realized it was the complete lack of any of these things that had awakened him. The cliff didn't allow any of the frequent, gentle disturbances in the night he'd grown accustomed to.

After a couple of unsuccessful attempts to return to sleep, Droplet remembered something Dag had mentioned about Soaring Cliff at night. He moved out of his crevice and noticed that The Flow around the cliff was brightly lit. Soon he was surrounded by orb-light. He moved further away from the cliff and into the shimmering current until something made him turn around.

Behind him, the cliff *glowed*. It was too tall to see completely, so he moved to the aft bank for a better view. Now he could see that the entire cliff shone! He discovered that there were distinct sections of intense luminosity surrounded by less radiant expanses of rock.

But what causes it to shine like this?

He moved back toward one of the brightest parts of the cliff. There he discovered big chunks of clear rock which vividly caught the radiant orb-light from above. Droplet looked up and saw that these clear chunks went all the way up Soaring Cliff in thick, branching trails. *How beautiful*, he thought, and wondered if the Others here knew of this stunning night-time phenomenon. He watched for a long time, but no one joined him.

Eventually, the orb traveled behind the top of the cliff, and the illumined chunks were just pale rocks again. He realized he was still tired, and returned to his crevice to sleep.

Droplet awoke unusually late the next morning. When he left the cleft he'd spent the night in, the sun's rays were already dancing in The Flow around him. He turned toward the towering cliff and was surprised to find that that the cliff-face, so splendid in the silvery light of the orb, looked like ordinary rock by day.

For a time he watched busy flyers swooping to and from the high ledges. *What an impressive cliff.*

Finally Droplet lowered his gaze to the base of the cliff, to see if there were any Others about. He was looking forward to actually meeting Horval, and learning more about doublets in general. But when he went to where he'd left Griff and Horval the night before, their hollow was empty. After a quick, and then a more thorough search of the area, he realized something.

All of the holes, fissures and nooks which had been occupied last night, were empty. There wasn't an Other to be seen or sensed anywhere.

This is so strange, he mused, as he widened the parameters of his search. *There had been several twelves of Others here last night—where could they all have gone?*

His extended search failed to reveal any Others anywhere. So, once again, he had a choice to make; he could wait to see if they returned, or he could go looking for them.

After waiting a little longer, he decided to go looking. Now the question was: upstream or downstream? He already knew what was downstream, and he wasn't particularly eager to face the merge again. Also, he had to admit that he was really enjoying all the new sights and experiences—now that he felt free to do so. *Upstream it is, then.*

Droplet traveled until Soaring Cliff gradually diminished and he came to an area of large, shiny-smooth sol-verts along the aft side of The Flow. Just ahead he could see some commotion near the bank.

As he approached, he discovered several fur-faced creatures, not much bigger than a large flasher, frolicking among the sol-verts. Droplet realized that three of the energetic creatures were smaller than the others—*probably young ones,* he thought, as he watched them slide down the rocks and splash into The Flow. These sleek, agile creatures were also good swimmers, he noted. Something about their playful antics caused his mood to brighten.

Eventually, the whole little grouping of fur-faces dove into The Flow using their legs and tails to propel themselves along the bottom. When they found something to their liking, they would bob up to the surface and float while eating it.

Droplet watched them swim away as a group, their little legs pushing them smoothly along.

Remarkable, he thought, as he resumed his journey. *Clearly these little creatures are comfortable both in The Flow, and beyond it.* In Droplet's experience, limited as it was, this seemed to be rare.

As he continued up the wide, rocky Flow, Droplet imagined all sorts of things the Others might be doing. He felt sure he would find them around each bend. But he didn't. And it would be dark soon.

Now he had to decide if he should continue on, stay where he was, or head back to Soaring Cliff. Just as he was about to decide to turn back, he thought he sensed an Other nearby.

He looked all around, but didn't see anyone. The feeling vanished. *That's odd,* he reflected, as he continued to look around. Then he caught a glimpse of what looked like an Other in the distance. Droplet headed upstream to investigate.

I knew I'd find them, he thought excitedly, but when he got to the spot, there was no-one there. *I'm sure this is where I saw someone!* Droplet carefully explored the whole area, but didn't find any Others, even though he again had the inner sense that he wasn't alone.

Now this is interesting. I seem to be alone, but I don't feel alone. Intrigued, Droplet explored this inner sense more fully, and discovered a subtle feeling of connection that he hadn't noticed before. *I can sense something—or someone—just on the other side of this rock.*

Droplet went very still, and stealthily let the current carry him around the large boulder. As he came to the far side of it, he felt a familiar energy. It almost felt like . . .

He quickly turned, just as the deep sending came: "There you are, Droplet. How have you fared?"

Surprised, and then overjoyed, Droplet responded with, "Wise Elder! I thought someone was here. I couldn't see you, but I could sense something and then I felt our connection."

"Yes, and you've grown in other ways too, Little One."

"I have, but I have so many questions," exclaimed Droplet. "Like, where did all the Others go?"

"I assume you're referring to the Others of Soaring Cliff?"

"Yes. I helped one of them last night. But when I woke up this morning all of them had gone."

"Ah. The Soaring Cliff Others often travel as a group to the merge. They enjoy riding the intense currents there, but doing this causes them to become widely scattered down-flow. If you had waited a few days, most of them would likely have returned."

"Huh, I wouldn't have guessed that," admitted Droplet. "That merge seemed pretty overwhelming to me. But I did learn how to get through it, and all about the *still-run*. From a guy named Dag."

"Good, good. So do you want to go back to the cliff to wait for them, Droplet, or shall we spend the night here?"

Droplet was deeply pleased to see his wonderful friend again. Somehow, spending time with Wise Elder always seemed much more important than anything else he could be doing.

"Let's stay here," he sent eagerly.

Wise Elder agreed. "There's a nice spot I know just upstream from here . . ."

Droplet and Wise Elder were settled in a shadowy depression not far from the steep bank, watching the orb— which was partially obscured by haze but still lovely—rise through the tops of a nearby cluster of trees.

They were talking about Dag, a solo, and the nature of doublets.

"So, you've started to experience some of the variety of our kind. Most of us enjoy the comfort and familiarity of being part of a stable grouping. Some move from one grouping to another; often known as *drifters*, they are always searching for—but never quite finding—a place they truly feel at home. Others of our kind go through phases where they travel a great deal, settle down for a time, and then travel some more. There are also quite a few who repeatedly travel a fixed route between several groupings, always looking forward to spending time with the same friends in each grouping. You'll also come across twinned or bonded pairings—doublets, *triplets,* and even *quads*—who are always together and seem to suffer when they are apart. There are a few groupings comprised almost exclusively of pair-bonded, like the one at Soaring Cliff.

"The two I met briefly there seemed to have matching esses. Is that why they bond?"

"It can be. Sometimes Others come into awareness together which creates a deep resonance between their esses, but they can also develop emotional and/or *esse-bonds* after meeting one another, and these can be just as strong. And then there are solos, like Dag, who generally avoid contact and prefer to wander The Flow alone."

"Is that why he talked so oddly?"

"Yes, solos often develop unusual ways of thinking and acting, and their communication style can be filled with jargon."

Droplet could easily guess what the term *jargon* meant.

"Solos often have a specific view of themselves that makes them hard to connect with." Wise Elder seemed thoughtful, like he was remembering something. "They can sometimes be-"

"-Real *gurglers*?"

"Hah! Indeed, Droplet, indeed."

The shining orb disappeared for a while. It had just emerged from behind a cloud when Droplet had another thought.

"You're not a solo, are you, Wise Elder?"

"No, I'm not. Remember what you learned about my work the night you crested?"

Droplet, who rarely forgot anything, sent "Uh-huh. You go when and where you're needed."

"Yes. And that takes me all over The Flow. I am part of an actual grouping, though I rarely spend much time there these days. I also have times when I am free to follow my own interests. Like now."

This gave Droplet a warm feeling. "But how did you find me?"

"You and I share a strong connection, Little One. That's what you felt earlier. Through this connection I can sense you—where you are, how you're doing, that sort of thing. I've returned because there is some more learning you need."

All of this made sense to Droplet, and brought him a sense of rightness and comfort. He knew he was starting to feel drowsy, but had one more question he wanted to ask. "What is your true name, Wise Elder?"

"Well Droplet, that's an interesting question. My true name can't actually be spoken. As you know, Wise Elder is my title, but it is also my use name—at least in these parts. Shall we get some sleep now?"

"Yes, as long as you promise to be here when I wake up." Droplet had had quite enough morning surprises lately.

"I can't promise that, Droplet, because of the nature of my work. But I can say that it is my intention to be here. Why don't I promise to wake you if I need to leave in the night—

agreed?"

"Agreed," sent Droplet gratefully. Droplet didn't know if it was because of their connection, or if it was just that Wise Elder was such an exceptional Being, but he always felt accepted, trusted, and trusting with him.

"Rest well, Little One."

Droplet and Wise Elder spent several wonderful days together. During this time they discussed many of his questions about creatures, Others, and the world around them. He found out Gern was an unusual type of Other called a *partial*.

"Partials are Others who, for one reason or another, haven't developed along normal lines. Gern is probably what's referred to as a *sensory partial*, in that most of his awareness is centered around a particular sensation. He preferred to be flattened against things right?"

"Yes! Usually rocks or stones—it took two of us to pry him loose."

"So he was probably focused on the vibrations he could feel through the dense stone. For sensory partials, a single sensation becomes the center of their existence."

Huh! Droplet had felt different vibrations in The Flow, of course, but he couldn't imagine creating an entire existence around them. "But why couldn't he send?"

"Partials often lack the capacity to form or send images and thoughts. While some can receive sendings in a limited fashion, they usually have very little interest in communicating with Others. They exist, in many ways, in a world of their own."

Droplet took all of this in. It certainly explained a few things. And more importantly, it absolved him of the remaining tendril of self-reproach he felt over giving up his search for Gern. That brought him to the dream sending he'd received from Fernlin.

"Dream-sending is an advanced sending skill, Droplet. I know Fernlin to be a mature, experienced elder. He is one of a large, wide-spread grouping who are fascinated by the habits and behaviors of creatures, especially land creatures and flyers. They have worked hard to develop the skill of dream-sending to stay in contact with one another. But you'll learn more about advanced sending and the scholarly groupings in your own time, Little One . . . "

Droplet continued to learn new things at what Wise Elder called an *extraordinary rate*.

He learned that drops of *rain* were actually the same substance as The Flow, which is why they could unite with it, and he liked that his name also related to The Flow. But no matter how hard he tried, he still couldn't figure out how the drops had separated from The Flow, or why they fell from Big Blue.

"Everything is a mystery until we understand it, Droplet," his friend responded cryptically. "Be patient and any knowledge you seek will come to you."

They proceeded upstream. They stopped briefly near a low, open stretch of bank lined with delicate *seedlings* bobbing in the sunlight. Droplet decided he and Wise Elder rambled through topics the same way the short-winged flyers fluttered among bushes further up the hillside. Delightfully.

At times their meanderings grew spacious and speculative. *What is time, anyway? Well, it's mostly a mystery, Droplet... Our current understanding is that time is the passage of change in the physical world, but it's also an inner flow of experience. And the perception of time is extremely individual—not only among different creatures, but among ourselves as well...*

Most importantly, though, Droplet learned about himself.

It was early morning during his third day with Wise Elder, and they were resting on the slick clay bottom of the hither verge of The Flow.

As Droplet was practicing his perception skills, Wise Elder asked him to focus on a particular leaf among several leaves rocking in the languid current. Droplet couldn't do it to Wise Elder's satisfaction.

Finally he sent, "I don't see any difference between those leaves; what do you mean?"

"Ah," sent Wise Elder as he realized the problem. "There is an aspect of seeing that you don't yet have. Here, let me show you." And with that Wise Elder gently adjusted something inside of Droplet.

"That was the strangest feeling," sent Droplet as he focused inside of himself trying to see what Wise Elder had done.

"What did you—Oh, *wow*!"

Suddenly, everywhere he looked—his entire world—quivered with intensity. Where before he only saw degrees of light and dark, now everything he saw dazzled brilliantly. He was overwhelmed for a moment.

"Steady there, Little One," sent the calming presence of his friend. "What you're seeing is *color*. Take a few minutes to get used to it."

"But I . . ." Astonished at what he could now perceive, Droplet couldn't stop looking. The Flow and everything beyond it contained a whole new dimension! *Color* was everywhere; deep, rich, faint, bright, clear, sparkly, luminous. Droplet could not only perceive the colors, he could almost feel them, and he soon learned what each color, tone, and hue was called.

From the instant of this discovery, his perception gained a depth and complexity he couldn't have imagined before. *And such beauty! I had no idea there was so much more to see. This is life-altering!*

"Thank you Wise Elder, for doing whatever you did to me."

"We'll talk more about it later, Droplet. For now, just get used to your new skill and the additional information it gives you."

Droplet spent the whole rest of the day exploring his new ability.

Now, when sunlight rippled through The Flow at certain angles, Droplet saw myriad reflected hues playing at the surface. Sometimes he even thought he detected a mysterious color to The Flow itself, invisible up close, but hinted at in the distance.

He discovered that many creatures, and most flashers, had an iridescent sheen, even the huge, whiskered flasher in the thick brown roots of the nearby tree with green and gold leaves. For the first time, he could see the nearly invisible red and blue floaters which were eaten by the tiny, orange-and-silver-striped flashers flicking around the rocks.

Looking up through The Flow, he saw bold swathes of multi-hued green, and the pinks, yellows and whites of *flowers*—what a wonder! Then the majestic expanse of vibrant blue above and beyond; very beautiful.

Oh, Big *Blue*! His sudden understandings were joyous.

Even Wise Elder looked different. His esse was a soft golden-blue color that swirled into bright flashes of silver when he concentrated or communicated.

Toward evening, after Droplet had immersed himself in all of the colors he could find, he approached Wise Elder to ask more about his amazing new skill.

"Perception is like a stream, Droplet. When you're in a certain stream that's all you experience, but when you leave it, your experience changes—sometimes dramatically. And there are many streams and rivers of perception. All I did was alter your perceptual stream a little, and you were able to see color. Think of it as a kind of fine tuning. There are a lot of different rivers of perception you can tune into, as you will learn."

"Do you mean there is even more that I can perceive?"

"Why, yes Droplet, your ability to perceive is essentially limitless. But we don't want to do too much all at once. Why don't you learn everything you can about color, for now. Take some more time with it. Then I have something else to show you."

Droplet spent the next day and a half exploring color in every way he could—studying it from different distances and angles, noticing the subtleties of tone and texture. He even tried merging with color, but couldn't tell if it worked.

He had been surprised at first, when all of the colors faded away at the end of the day, and equally amazed when they returned again with the increasing light. And he learned that the intensity of light directly affected the colors he could perceive. *Some colors make me feel a certain way,* he observed. *Bright green feels enticing and silver-blue feels calming.* He also learned that colors could signal warning—like the flare of yellow-red on the belly of a suddenly agitated crawler.

Late in the day, Droplet found Wise Elder near the center of The Flow in a state of deep concentration. For a while, Droplet hovered just out of contact, appreciating the silvery arcs and flashes inside this wonderful Being who enriched his existence so much.

Just as he was thinking of moving away without interrupting him, Wise Elder *esse-sent, :Hello, Little One, are you ready for something new?*

"Yes, and how do you *do* that? It's like your thought is inside me."

"Esse-sending is something you will learn how to do one day, Droplet. But right now, there is something I want to show you."

With that, Wise Elder turned and traveled quickly upstream. Droplet caught up and then traveled with him, while relishing the colorful scenery. At one point, they stopped to observe a couple of pink and grey *creepers* nibble at patches of bright green algae in a tree-shaded inlet along the bank. *It's all so much more beautiful than I knew.*

They continued traveling upstream until Wise Elder veered toward the opposite bank and ducked into some tangled brown roots. Droplet followed him through the network of roots and emerged into startling brightness.

Here The Flow was unusually still, clear, and shallow. Wise Elder had settled near the sun-drenched center, next to some moss-covered flats.

"Feel free to explore this *pond* for a bit, Droplet, then come join me. There's something I want you to see. It will just be a little while . . ."

Droplet traversed the pond's near-round perimeter. He pushed through some tall, thin reeds, and discovered a tiny Flow, a *rivulet*, Wise Elder distance-sent, trickling into the pond. Clusters of bright green plants sporting delicate pink flowers nodded in the breeze.

Part of the pond was shaded by the huge tree whose roots they'd just traveled through; most of the rest was sunny and bright. *And lovely*, Droplet thought, immediately enchanted by this peaceful place.

Droplet returned to Wise Elder, and watched where he indicated. While they waited, Wise Elder quietly explained that the little rivulet flowing into the pond kept it fresh and sweet, and made it a perfect location for what was about to happen. Droplet watched carefully, but other than the swaying tree boughs and occasional ripples on the surface, nothing was happening.

It is so still here. The relaxing play of sunlight flickering through the deep green leaves caused Droplet's awareness to drift a bit.

Suddenly, something plopped into the pond's surface just above them. Droplet's first thought was that it was a seedpod from the creek's towering tree. But then the object seemed to burst, and twelve-plus tiny, pale yellow *swimmers* shot away from it and disappeared amongst the rocks.

"What was that?" asked Droplet, astonished.

"That," responded Wise Elder, "was a *sack of baby leapers*. You know the big green leapers that jump in and out of The Flow in the early evening? Those are their young."

Droplet remembered what he had learned about the life-cycles of creatures. "But where did they come from?" he asked, after looking around and not finding any adult leapers nearby.

Before Wise Elder could answer, another baby leaper sack dropped into the pond and released its cargo of little swimmers.

Wise Elder waited until all the activity subsided. "The big leapers pair off and lay eggs in sacks, which they stick to the leaves of certain trees, like these," he explained. "When they have grown some, and are ready to enter The Flow, the little ones wiggle in the sack until it becomes loose and falls. Once they have joined The Flow, they grow quickly, until they become the big green leapers that we know."

Droplet took this in as another baby leaper sack fell. He watched the young dart and squirm around the pebbles as they made for the seclusion of the reeds.

"But they don't look like leapers," he sent, observing them closely. "They look like tiny flashers."

"True," responded Wise Elder. "But they are very special creatures, these leapers. Their appearance and abilities change several times over the course of their lifecycle, and they are one of only a few creatures that thrive both in, and beyond, The Flow."

This information brought up something Droplet had been wondering about.

"The world around us is so amazing! Why was what Mentor Sootan taught me so limited?"

"Droplet, your mentor had to limit your focus to what you needed to learn from him. But, as you are now discovering, there are many other types of experiences beyond The Flow, and The Flow itself is more than it seems. In fact, not only is The Flow the part of the world we directly experience, in a very real way we *are* The Flow."

Droplet tried to wrap his mind around this as yet another sac of baby leapers dropped into the pond. One of the babies spun and swam right at them until Wise Elder sent a gentle charge toward it. Then it turned and followed the others into the reeds.

"As part of The Flow we are privy to virtually limitless ways of knowing, and you have access to more than most. In other levels, or ways of existence, there are many, many different creatures, great and small, simple and wise. Some, like trees, remain in one place, while others roam all over.

"There is one thing that is true for every type of creature though, and that is that they all require The Flow to exist. I know you have observed land creatures drinking from creeks and streams. Well, The Flow also gives life to plants in ways we don't usually see. Without The Flow, *all* of Life would cease to exist in a matter of days. The Flow is an essential partner to Life, Droplet, from the greatest tree to the tiniest leaper."

"If The Flow is a partner to Life, how could Life cease to exist?" Droplet had gotten used to the fact that creatures die, but this seemed hard to believe.

"It wouldn't happen easily, and it has never happened on this world. A living creature can certainly end, as I know you're aware, but Life itself—both in and beyond The Flow—is incredibly diverse, resourceful and resilient."

Then another thought occurred to Droplet. "But what about us, aren't we alive?"

The silvery-blue in Wise Elder's esse became more pronounced and he grew still. Just above them, a translucent blossom turned slow circles in the faint current. Then he sent: "We have vitality and awareness because our esses are part of the Sacred Flow of Consciousness, Droplet. Some refer to this as mental aliveness, or *conscious life*. To us, and to all deeper levels of consciousness, thought *is* life.

"But when we talk about The Flow being in partnership with Life, we mean physical Life with its multitudinous beginnings, cycles of development, and distinct endings.

Although we have beginnings and may certainly develop in many ways, we do not *end* the way creatures and Beings with physical bodies do."

This made a kind of sense to him, but he couldn't quite fathom it. "How do you keep all of this straight, Wise Elder? I mean, there are multiple streams of perception, different levels of existence, all types of creatures with their own lives and cycles, the essential relationship between Life and The Flow, and our own connection with the Sacred Flow of Consciousness. Not to mention more experiences than I can count."

"I know, in the beginning it can be confusing. It'll take time for all of the new ideas to settle, and for experience to trickle into the gaps in your knowledge. The most important thing to remember is that you have awareness, and as far as anyone knows, *awareness can never be destroyed*. So, you will have as long as you need to make sense out of all of this information, and much, much more. Okay?"

"All right, but I still have a lot of questions."

The light gradually dimmed as sol moved behind a hill in the distance. As Droplet watched the color of Big Blue begin to deepen, he thought back to some of the Others he'd met. "Not all Others know about these things, do they?"

"Some Others do; most do not. As I mentioned before, not all of our kind is equipped to understand the deeper truths, and it's hard for one to develop an interest in things that are inconceivable to them.

"You haven't met many Others yet, but you will. And when you do, you will learn all about what is important to them. Every kind of experience has value, Droplet, and anything can teach you if you allow it to. You have a bright mind, a curious nature, and a truly prodigious ability to soak-up learning."

As Droplet was taking all of this in, including the word *prodigious,* which he instantly understood to mean considerable or vast, Wise Elder sent, "It's nearly time for me to leave you again, Droplet."

With this sending, Droplet turned his awareness inward. He found he could also feel the subtle inner sending that called Wise Elder to go somewhere else.

Day faded into evening, and the surface of the pond became glossy in the gathering dusk. Droplet appreciated the peace and beauty around them. He thought about what he'd learned, all of his new skills, and how grateful he was to Wise Elder.

Just as he was getting ready to send his deep appreciation, Wise Elder sent, "I know, Little One, our friendship inspires me too."

Droplet received this—*inspires, yes*—and returned it, adding his deep gratitude.

"You truly have everything you need to continue learning and growing, Droplet. And know this; because of our strong inner connection, wherever you go, I'll always be able to find you."

As soon as Droplet got this sending, Wise Elder moved through the pond and away so quickly he essentially vanished. *Amazing.*

Droplet was alone again, with only the baby leapers and his own thoughts for company for quite some time.

Eight

The late afternoon sun slanted into the little pond, turning a few of the large red and gold leaves floating on its surface nearly transparent. The daytime drinkers and feeders had all wandered off, and the pond was at a natural still point in its cycle of activity. The barest hush of a breeze caused some of the luminous leaves to spin in lazy circles, and stirred the slender grasses browning along the pond's contoured edge.

Droplet, now an experienced observer of the pond's inhabitants and rhythms, calmly watched the subtler currents flow into their night cycle. From his favorite vantage point, near a brown *crystal khoot* partly buried in the deepest part of the pond, he watched the last of the light slip away.

Earlier in the day, there had been a brief pelting of drops on the pond's surface; he knew from experience this would bring more nighttime activity.

Then it began.

First, there was the splashing entrance of several large, dark-spotted leapers, who widely spaced themselves around the edge of the pond. Then some of the smaller green leapers, who had been hidden and still, emerged while the rest remained concealed. Droplet, who had watched these leapers mature from tiny swimmers, knew their favorite hiding places well. He also knew their preferences in timing, partners, and length of participation in what he'd come to think of as their evening *dance*—one of Wise Elder's terms.

The large, dark-spotted leapers always started it off. They would puff-up and send long, low vibrations throughout the pond, in an insistent 'notice me' way. They would send and respond, send and respond to each other, as if they were announcing something of import. Droplet had tried many times to decipher their sendings, but he could get no actual information from them.

After this had gone on for some time, several of the large spotted leapers would leap away, leaving one or two remaining to continue sending their low, rippling vibrations into everything around them. This was somehow a signal for *his* leapers to enter the vibrational dance. They would hop and leap in pairs, and small groups. They also emitted a vibration, but it was fainter, shorter and faster than that of the big leapers.

Over time, Droplet had become adept at identifying certain individuals by the quality of their movement and vibration. There were some he especially enjoyed watching.

This evening dance would often go on for much of the night cycle. Sometimes, when the silver orb was visible high above the pond, he could see the iridescent blue streaks and deep red spots on certain leapers. On these nights, the pond itself would glitter with splashes of silver. He would watch, entranced, until the orb passed, the vibrations subsided, and the pond finally slept for a little while before the daylight routines began.

Droplet thought his pond a most magical place, and he was truly thankful to be a witness to all of its wonders.

Eventually, the baby leapers grew into true leapers, and all leapt away. The face of Big Blue was increasingly covered with dark gray clouds. Then one day, one of its own powerful currents whipped all the leaves from the trees, including the great one at the pond's edge. For several days after that, Droplet existed in a red-orange-tinged pond that was so leaf-ridden he could barely see beyond it. As the leaves slowly settled to the bottom and browned, windy storms with their pelting drops became a common occurrence.

The day cycles were growing shorter, he noticed, and the nights longer.

Droplet felt an unfamiliar sense of urgency. There was something he needed to do, or maybe someplace he needed to go.

As was his custom, he spent time exploring this feeling, but all he could discern was an increasing imperative to move, to go.

Finally, he decided he must follow it, and in an uncertain frame of mind he retraced the path through the tangled roots and emerged back into the main Flow.

Immediately he noticed the current was stronger, faster and murkier than when he'd left it several orb-cycles ago. *Probably because of the recent storms*, he reasoned.

Then he paused. *Something else is different.*

He quickly shifted through his perceptual levels trying to identify the change. *There's still a sense of something impending. And it's not like anything I've felt before*, he realized, both intrigued and a little anxious.

After carefully observing the powerful Flow around him for a while, he decided to head up-flow where it looked a little clearer. He moved gingerly along the aft bank, trying to get used to being in an active current again. As he traveled, he quested with his inner senses but gained no new understanding. Even when he came to a divide and took the smaller tributary, the disquiet inside him did not abate.

As the long night approached, bringing yet another storm, Droplet settled near a comforting root-knot to think. He didn't even notice becoming groggy.

Then his awareness drifted away.

The next thing Droplet noticed was dim light, along with a sinking sensation and a feeling of pressure. *That's odd.* He didn't seem to be moving, but the light grew fainter around him as if he was slowly moving into shadow.

He felt heavy. And found it hard to think.

For a long time, he seemed to hover without a sense of presence. His mind slowed down, and he couldn't engage his perceptual array.

Time passed, and he had no awareness of its passing.

A swirling occurred.

Droplet regained awareness, but he felt very different. An opaque light seemed to hide everything, including The Flow. The sense of pressure had lessened a little, and yet he still felt very odd.

Was he getting heavier? He felt bulkier or thicker somehow. And although he was faintly aware of his surroundings, he couldn't actually see objects.

Thaat's in-terrr-es-ting, he thought laboriously, feeling vaguely concerned.

When he tried to move, he discovered he could neither create nor send attractor- and repulsion-charges.

The discovery that he couldn't change his orientation, direction, or location brought fuzzy, unsettling memories. But the experience persisted, and resisting it didn't help.

After a while, he felt himself rise very slowly until he touched something hard above him.

He stuck to it.

There was a distinct sensation now that he couldn't identify. He thickly tried to form a sending, but all he felt was a faint vibration.

His last coherent thought was, *Hmm, I ammm commmpletelly sstiill—innsside an' oouutt.*

Then, even his flickering awareness ceased as he finished solidifying.

Interlude

⬥⬥⬥⬦⬥⬥⬥

The winter storms raged above him, and Droplet lay unknowing, near the icy bank of the frozen stream for several months.

Small thaws and refreezes occurred near him, but the edge of the stream, where he was, remained shaded and solid.

Then, as is its way, the great waterwheel of the seasons completed its quarter-turn, and light and warmth slowly returned to the earth.

At first the delicate rays did little to alter the deeply shadowed ice, but gradually, with each incremental rise in temperature, there was a softening.

Over time, the increasingly bright light caused Life in and around the stream to gently stir.

Finally, the sun sent its warmth deep into the stream for several days in a row, and the balance shifted.

Nine

Whoa, *what was that?* Droplet startled back into full awareness after several struggling brushes with lucidity. Once again he could ascertain his internal state and his surroundings, both of which were exceedingly strange. He felt big, swollen and fixed.

What had happened to the supple, resilient form he knew? The unfamiliar sense of mass—was he really that huge?—along with the sensation of being *stuck,* sent little pulses of alarm through him.

Fortunately, although he was physically immobile, he discovered he could still access his esse and quickly used it to gain a measure of calm. By shifting through its levels of perception, he discovered he was completely surrounded by shades of thick, muted grey and brilliant white. He also intuitively understood that he was both connected to, and an integral part of, what surrounded him, which was dense and fixed like him. With a leap of insight, he understood himself to be in the midst of a state change; *the solid one, obviously.* Along with this realization came a lessening of concern and an increase in his innate curiosity.

As he relaxed into an alert inner state, he felt a physical jolt followed by a subtle pulsation, and immediately recognized it as the same sensation that had brought him back to awareness.

There it is again. What IS that?

Suddenly, there was a crunching, shuddering jerk, and Droplet had the inexplicable sensation of *breaking free.* Although he still couldn't move on his own, whatever he was stuck to began a ponderous, bobbing spin. Memories of becoming thick and still rose to the surface of his consciousness as he twirled slowly.

This gentle movement lasted for quite a while. Then, without warning, it transformed into the much more intense and vaguely familiar sensation of plunging, punctuated by erratic spinning, and wobbly bouncing. A gradual thinning in the grey-whiteness surrounding him allowed him to confirm what he suspected; whatever he was attached to was definitely moving. *Going down-flow*, he realized, relieved to still be in some kind of association, however remote, with liquidity.

Finally the bobbing motion subsided and his movement seemed to slow. Then, before he knew what was happening, he was turned topsy-turvy, and found himself looking out through a transparent barrier at a wavy blue expanse. *It's like looking straight up through a perfectly clear crystal khoot,* he marveled.

He made several small shifts in his perception, and saw that he was indeed floating at the surface, close to the bank, with a stunning view of what lay above and beyond The Flow. The immediacy, and the vast, uninterrupted *blueness* of Big Blue stunned him. And the vividness of everything else—the shining greens of vegetation set against the muted browns of the hillside, the stark trees clutching white bundles instead of the familiar green leaves—astonished him.

Seen from this perspective, things beyond The Flow are even more vivid and intense than I knew, he acknowledged, taking in the full measure of the experience. He noted the differences in clarity and tone when sol was briefly hidden by the scattered white clouds stretching across Big Blue, and delighted again in the relationship between color and light.

After watching scene after dazzling scene glide by, he began to long for the softer, gentler hues of The Flow itself. But, as he was still unable to alter his position in any way, he decided to relax and enjoy the ride—and the unprecedented view.

A short time later, the strengthening current rolled him over again and pulled him away from the bank. With the abrupt reduction of visual stimulation, he refocused on his physical form.

Faintly at first, Droplet noticed an increasingly strong sense of drag, a kind of friction building-up around him. He had never felt anything like this. Then, as he swirled around some boulders, an amazing thing happened: he experienced an irresistible quickening, and identified sol as the source of this powerful sensation.

Just after this, he noticed a gentle swishing motion and then, quite unexpectedly, he rolled free of his containment.

He immediately tried to generate an attractor-charge—and succeeded in weakly connecting to a low mound. He looked back to see what he had been attached to for so long, and saw a rock-sized, completely transparent, *something,* floating at the surface. As the current tugged it by him, it spun slowly, and then broke into pieces and drifted away.

Now that he was directly back in The Flow again, Droplet felt a powerful reorienting, along with the welcome awareness of his familiar form. And a fierce surge of joy.

He could move again! He was himself again! He was home!

Glorying in his freedom and captivated by what each bend revealed, Droplet continued traveling downstream until the light began to wane.

With the coming night, he finally acknowledged both his fatigue and his need to think about his recent experience. He settled himself near a spiky clump of moss which blocked the lively current. *I was solid,* he thought with wonder. *I don't think I ever really believed that could happen.*

He vaguely remembered learning that the solid state-change occurred primarily during the Long Night Season, but could also happen during times of intense storms, especially along the banks or in sluggish currents. *Oh. That must be why I felt I should leave the pond...* He just couldn't imagine his pond becoming solid.

As the stars emerged in their familiar little groupings, he let himself relax into a natural sleep. Given the strength of the current and the brightness of the day's sunlight, he felt fairly confident he would remain in his normal state through the night.

Ten

Early the next morning, he awoke to an unsettling sight. Everything around him was pale white. At first he was alarmed, thinking he might be going back into a state-change, an experience that, while interesting, was not one he wanted to repeat any time soon. But no, this was different. He could still move on his own, and he didn't feel thick or heavy.

As he peered around at his white environment, he remembered. Sometimes at Marsh Lake and even in his stream of origin the day would start like this: hazy and subdued with no sign of Big Blue.

Droplet moved carefully up to the surface. *Yep,* he thought, *can't see anything. The whole world is misty white.* With this realization, he returned to the bottom of The Flow, and waited calmly for the mist to recede.

He must have drifted off because he came to with a start. Something bumped him, and then he received a strong sending, "Hey there! Are you awake?'

He turned and found a couple of Others quite close. The mist had started to clear, but The Flow was still pale and flat-looking.

"Yes, I'm awake," Droplet sent. He noticed one of the Others was a little darker than the other, almost beige.

"Oh good," came the reply. "Sorry to disturb you. But we're looking for Others who had a difficult time with the *freeze.* Did you go through the change?"

"The *change*?" Droplet felt muzzy-minded, and he hadn't communicated with anyone for along time.

"Yes, the *state-change,*" the larger sent, peering at him closely with what seemed to be concern.

"You know, becoming heavy and thick—quite solid in fact," sent the beige one helpfully. "Happens quite a bit around these parts. Probably your first time, wasn't it?"

"Ah, yes, it was," he responded, more alert now. "I wasn't sure what was happening at first . . ."

"Yeah, the first time can be pretty disorienting," sent the big one with the brighter esse. "Are you headed someplace in particular, or would you like to return with us to our grouping? You're welcome, either way."

Droplet liked what he could sense of these two.

"Sure, I'd like to visit your grouping. I'm Droplet."

"Greetings, Droplet," sent the beige Other. "I'm Timlyt, and this is Tiffy. We're both originally from the Tipcott Fork Grouping, but now with the Rock Shelf Grouping—which is just down-flow a ways. We'll take you there now, if you'd like."

Droplet indicated his agreement, and they started moving leisurely downstream. As he grew accustomed to their easy sending style, Droplet discovered he was looking forward to interacting with Others again.

"So, tell me about your grouping," Droplet asked as they traversed a bare stretch between two large rock formations along the aft bank. The mist was lifting, and color was slowly seeping back into The Flow around them.

"Well, we're a good sized grouping of about five-twelves," replied Tiffy. "'Course, our numbers can swell and diminish based on the time of year. Right now, we have some extras. But you'll see soon enough; we're almost there."

As they neared the second formation, Droplet could see a series of large, unusually flat, gray rocks tightly wedged into the stony bank. Droplet slowed to study it. Timlyt and Tiffy noticed, and sent him the word *slate*; then they took him to the bottom of the stack and led him into it.

The current ceased as soon as they entered the dim space, and Droplet noticed several Others as they approached a crook in the path between the slate slabs. These Others started to come toward him, but when they caught sight of his guides they receded again. Droplet detected a quick narrow-band sending pass between them.

His guides led him around the sharp curve, and into a short, dark tunnel created by layers and layers of slate.

Ahead, Droplet could see brightness, and in the brightness were many Others.

"Welcome to the Rock Shelf Grouping," Timlyt sent, as they emerged into a large, open chamber completely hidden from the outside by the slate surrounding them.

They came to a stop, and Droplet gazed about in amazement. Other than his brief time at Soaring Cliff, he had rarely been entirely surrounded by rock before, and never by anything this charming. Misty sunlight streamed in from above, giving the chamber a soft, pinkish hue. To one side of him, great slabs of slate angled sharply into the sandy bottom, as if pushed down by a massive force.

To his other side, short, narrow shelves adorned with green and yellow mosses rose vertically in step-like fashion. Directly beyond, horizontal layers of slate created jutting ledges with deep recesses. Droplet noticed small clusters of Others spaced comfortably in and amongst the shelves and ledges, while a larger group congregated on the pale sand in the center.

He instantly felt comfortable in this bright, peaceful place.

"I'll go find Nester," sent Tiffy, who moved into the nearby cluster of Others.

"Nester is leader here," sent Timlyt as they waited. "He likes to meet new arrivals right away. I think you'll like him."

A short time later, Tiffy returned with an Other whose esse shone almost as brightly as Wise Elder's. In addition to his striking esse, Droplet was immediately put at ease by this Other's calm presence, which radiated kindness and strength.

"Greetings newcomer," the Other sent formally. "I am Nester, the current leader of the Rock Shelf grouping."

Droplet could tell he was being sized-up by this commanding, but gentle, awareness.

"Greetings Nester," he responded in kind. "I'm Droplet."

They were both silent for a moment. Droplet, feeling gently probed and assessed, flared his esse briefly.

Nester's esse flashed in response. Then he sent, "Welcome, Droplet. This is the Rock Shelf Grouping, and you are invited to stay with us for as long as you wish."

"Thank you, Nester." Droplet felt an unfamiliar tightness inside of him release, and sent a heartfelt, "I am pleased to be here."

Nester received that well, and then led him to one of the

clusters of Others and began introductions as Tiffy and Timlyt took their leave.

Before Droplet could become too overwhelmed with all the names and esses, Nester sent, "That's probably enough introductions for now. I'm going to leave you with a friend of mine. Take whatever time you need to acclimate and get comfortable here, Droplet. I'm glad you've joined us."

"Thank you Nester," sent Droplet, truly pleased. He wasn't sure what *acclimate* meant, but he could feel Nester's kind intention.

A new Other joined them. "Droplet, this is Alma. He will show you around, continue with introductions when you're ready, and make sure you feel at home here."

"Greetings Droplet. I just need to tell someone something. Why don't you wait here for me; I'll be right back." Alma seemed friendly, but not as serene as the leader.

Nester had returned to the Others he'd been with when Droplet arrived, so Droplet eased back against the slate wall and watched all of the activity around him. He felt comfortable and intrigued with what he could see of this grouping. Then, with no warning, he was surrounded by three vivacious Others he hadn't yet met.

"Hi-ho! Who are you?"

"Well *nudge*, been through the change, haven't you?"

"Been here long?"

"I . . . I . . . um . . ." This was an overwhelming amount of communication for Droplet, who had been feeling very peaceful. He had no idea how to respond—or to whom. Then he got a good look at the three, and realized they were all younglings, like himself.

"I'm Droplet. I've just arrived, and yes, I went through the change. Who are you?"

The largest of the three pushed forward. "I'm Tag, that's Disk, and this nudge here, is Bobb. We haven't been here long either."

Bobb, who had been quiet until now, sent "His real name is Tagalong. He hates it, so that's what we call him." Tag rushed Bobb, and they entered into what soon became a game of chase, in and around the lower ledges.

Disk eased closer to Droplet. "They do that quite a bit," he sent. "Gets old after a while. So how did you come through the change, Droplet? It wasn't my first, but it was the most disruptive one I've been through," he confided.

Droplet shared his own experiences, and they both agreed it was "powerful strange," as Disk referred to it. About that time, Alma returned.

As soon as Alma saw Droplet with Disk he sent, "Ah, so you've found some other newcomers, have you? I need to tend to a couple of other recent arrivals who had a difficult time with their first state-change. Why don't you spend the afternoon with these three, and I'll see you this evening?"

"Okay."

Tag, who had rejoined them along with Bobb, waited until Alma left and sent, "I guess they had a *hard* time with the state-change, get it?" Before Droplet could respond, Bobb and Disk both bumped Tag.

Then they were back into the chase, with Disk sending a quick, "Come on Droplet, let's get him."

Using rapid attractor- and repulsion-charges Droplet and the others chased Tag, then Tag chased them, up and down the ledges. When each of them had been thoroughly chased, they took a break in the main chamber. Around them, Others came together in small groups for a while and then moved on. The atmosphere was calm and friendly; Droplet liked it immensely.

After they'd shared some of their recent experiences with Droplet, Tagalong and Bobb suggested they explore the upper ledges.

"See that opening up there Droplet?" Tag sent. The four of them were resting on a wide slate flat high above the grouping's central chamber.

Droplet peered straight up until he could discern the opening. "It looks strange," he sent.

"Yeah, there's a crystal khoot up there lodged in the rocks. Let's go check it out."

They climbed to the very top of the formation, and approached the khoot from beneath. Unlike the other crystal khoots Droplet had seen, this one was large, thick and pale pink. It was partly covered with loose shale and appeared to

be firmly lodged. He could also see the rippled surface of The Flow beyond it.

Just then, the sun emerged from behind a cloud and brightly illuminated the khoot. Droplet could just make out raised markings on its side. The view through the khoot was the familiar wavy scene he'd experienced with other khoots, but this time, it was bright with pink-tinged sunlight.

Droplet turned toward Bobb, who was next to him, and got a surprise. Everything around them, including Bobb, was noticeably pink.

"Hey, Droplet," sent Tag who was clearly amused, "you're pink!" Tag and Disk were in the shade under a ledge.

"Bobb is pink, too," countered Droplet, who had figured out why.

"I am?" Bobb sounded flustered. "How can that be?"

"Are you *hatched*, youngling?" sent Tag to Bobb. "It's the light through the khoot, spin-wit! Don't you know anything?"

Bobb turned to Droplet. He seemed somewhat chagrined. "Tag can be kinda mean sometimes," he sent quietly. "He don't mean much by it."

Droplet turned back to Tag and Disk. "Let's see how pink you'll be when you come out here and join us," he sent to the two in shadow.

As it turned out, Tag was the pinkest of them all, for no reason any of them could determine. He got kidded about it all the way back down to the chamber, now entirely illuminated by golden-pink light.

That evening, Droplet attended his first *evening gathering* with Alma and his three new friends. He discovered the 'Rock Shelfers' did *not* call it a convergence, and he got the impression from Alma that this grouping viewed 'converging' as something different, even undesirable.

As the five of them waited in the dusky main chamber for everyone to arrive, Alma explained the nature of the gatherings. "For the many seasons I've been here, we've used the evening gatherings to stay informed about how everyone is doing. Under Nester's leadership, we also use these gatherings to make sure all of our connections and relationships stay fresh and vital."

That night Droplet learned this meant that after a short check-in phase, the *sharings* could become deeply personal and sometimes quite emotional. Although he found this interesting, he soon tired of trying to keep track of the intricate relationships. Alma noticed all four of them were flagging, so he directed them to the sleeping ledges and suggested they reunite in the morning.

Droplet found a suitable spot for the night on a shallow ledge near Bobb. He sensed Disk and Tag nearby. The central chamber was illuminated by the half-orb's light high above and all of the esses gathered below him. He gave an inner sigh of contentment and slept.

The next morning, Alma introduced Droplet to more of the grouping. He had just met an elder named Pim, when a low sending from behind startled him.

"Can this be the youngling we found near the Boktow Grouping, Lemsel?"

"Why yes, I do believe it is, Boklin."

Droplet turned and quickly looked from one to the other. They *did* seem familiar to him. "Um, do I know you?"

"I should say you do, youngling. We're the two finders that found ya."

He switched to esse-sight and recognized their big, bright esses instantly. "Yes! I remember now. You helped me before Mentor Sootan."

"That's right, youngling. Finders Lemsil and Boklin at your service," Lemsil sent elegantly.

"But just call us Lem and Bok like everyone else does," added Bok. "And what name did you take?"

"Droplet," he responded, a bit shyly.

"Droplet, is it? Hah. Well, I reckon that's as good a name as any," sent Lem.

"Suits ya, it does," agreed Bok.

Droplet spent part of the morning with Lem and Bok until they were 'called away' on another finding. He heard in great detail about how he very nearly wasn't found at all.

"I was all ready to give up on ya, but Lem wouldn't have it," sent Bok.

"I just knew you were there, even though your esse was barely flickering," Lem admitted. "I'm just glad we got to you in time. Without Wise Elder's help, though, you probably wouldn't have made it."

"Wise Elder was there when you found me?"

"No, Bok went to get him. We needed Wise Elder's help to keep your consciousness from dissipating the way it was tryin' to do." Lem shuddered a little at the memory. "Even then, it was a close thing."

"Wow." Droplet had no recollection of any of this.

"Hey, how'd things go with Mentor Sootan," asked Bok.

Droplet watched the two finders for a minute, and then responded with, "Pretty well, why do you ask?"

"Well, we thought you might be in for a rough time."

"We didn't think any such thing." Lem turned to Droplet and sent more gently, "We obviously didn't impress the good mentor much, and wondered how things would go between the two of you."

Droplet hadn't thought much about Mentor Sootan since his cresting and later experiences with Wise Elder.

"We got along fine, but I'm not sure he understood me very well. He taught me most of what I needed to learn, though."

Alma had quietly observed Droplet's reunion with the two finders. Now he sent, "That's not unusual, Droplet. Our first mentor is charged with introducing us to a huge amount of information, and laying a solid foundation for our later development. A truly enjoyable relationship with one's first mentor is about as common as a flasher with wings."

"Ha! That says it all, Alma," replied Bok easily. "So, is it about time for us to be on our way, Finder Lemsil?"

"It is indeed, Finder Boklin. It was good to see you, Droplet. It's always gratifying to see one of our foundlings doing so well." Lemsil flashed his esse a couple of times, and then Boklin did too.

Droplet responded in kind. Then he sent, "Farewell, and thank you both for everything."

"Good finding," sent Alma.

"Until The Flow brings us together again," both finders replied formally.

As the two left the sheltered grouping, one of the finders sent quietly, "So, he's developed esse-sight."

"Yep," responded the other. "Do you think he knows he's a finder?" Before his partner could reply, the brisk current whisked them both away.

Eleven

D roplet spent his first two days at Rock Shelf relaxing in the central chamber. After meeting and spending time with some of the long-term members, and several more new arrivals, he realized that for the first time he felt truly comfortable with a large number of Others of his kind. This grouping seemed filled with calm, accepting Beings, and it didn't take him long to see why.

They had an exceptional leader.

Although Nester kept very busy, Droplet could always spot his sol-bright esse in contact with the members and guests of his grouping. He observed that Nester always left Others in a composed state, and that the strength of his esse seemed to soothe and clarify the esses of those around him. *What an amazing skill*, he thought appreciatively.

On his third day with the Rock Shelf grouping, Alma offered to take Droplet, and newcomers Bobb, Tag and Disk, on an outing. They were all in high spirits as they headed down-flow.

When they came to a divide, Alma led them into the smaller Flow. They all discerned an immediate gentling of the current in the branch they followed.

A short time later, they rounded a bend and The Flow slowed even more and broadened. They traveled through this wide *tarn,* as Alma called it, until they came to some stacked tree trunks and limbs obstructing the current. Alma took them to the cluttered edge of the blockage and had them rest on a submerged limb.

"Let's wait here for a while and see what we discover," sent Alma, mysteriously.

Disk and Bobb played a counting game until something large and sleek slid into The Flow above them, and then dove to the base of the stacked branches and into an appropriately sized hole.

"A fur-face," Droplet sent, startled. In his experience, fur-faces rarely swam to the bottom of The Flow that way.

"A *fur-face*! What kind of term is that Droplet? What, were you raised in a *bog*?" It was hard to mistake the sneer in Tag's sending. Bobb and Disk were quiet.

Alma shot Tag a short, tight-beamed sending. Then he turned to Droplet and sent, "That's a *four-legged*, Droplet. We generally identify creatures by the number of their legs. This particular four-legged is called a 'four-legged builder'."

"Or a tree-chewer," added Disk.

"Or a tail-slapper," contributed Bobb encouragingly, making it clear that creatures could have more than one name.

"Whatever you chose to call it, this four-legged is a master builder. Does anyone know why it stacks trees and branches like this in The Flow?"

No one did, so Alma explained.

"The four-legged builder eats the soft bark of trees on Land. Then it chews through the trees and drags them into The Flow where it carefully fits them together into a *structure*, like what you see here. The creature lives, mates and raises its young inside one end of the structure. We believe it does this for safety, as there is nothing big enough to eat its kind within The Flow, but there are several creatures that hunt and eat it on Land."

Just then, the four-legged builder emerged from the hole at the base of the branches and swam to the surface. They watched how it propelled itself with its legs and big, flat tail. When it reached the The Flow's edge, it crawled out, shook itself, and then climbed the bank. A short time later it returned dragging a tree limb, which it promptly wedged in place near the top of its structure.

"Each tree or branch it adds makes the structure, and its home at the edge of it, more secure," Alma continued. "This kind of four-legged is a very determined creature. It can build its structure so high that the current is slowed, as you see, or even blocked all together. Can anyone guess why it would want to do this?"

"Is it so it can trap flashers to eat?" wondered Bobb.

"That's a reasonable assumption, Bobb. But in fact, these builders only eat tree bark and some plants. Our present understanding, determined by Others whose primary interest is observing these creatures, is that they do this to increase the surface area of The Flow. We believe they intentionally flood an area they have already cleared to bring The Flow closer to new, un-stripped trees. This allows them to eat and work within easy reach of the safety of The Flow if danger threatens them."

They were all silent as they let this remarkable information sink in.

"But what happens to everything else in The Flow if it becomes blocked? Won't that disrupt the lives of other creatures?"

"A good question, Droplet. The answer is, yes, it does disrupt things. But the law of nature is one of balance. Something always happens—in a season or two—to remove the builder's structure. Sometimes it's a flood, other times the creatures are killed by those that eat them, and their structure weakens and gets washed away. Most often, the obstacle is discovered by two-leggeds and removed. In any case, the four-legged builders will find a new place to build and the whole process will start all over."

Just then, the brown, four-legged builder returned and slid into The Flow, this time without a tree or branch. It turned its head this way and that, with short little jerks, then it slapped the surface hard a couple of times with its wide, flat tail. Two other creatures like it quickly entered The Flow, and then all three dove for the bottom together and swam into the base of the structure.

"That indicates there is danger about, and generally means they're done for a while," remarked Alma. "Why don't we go back now?"

On the way back all of them except Tag, who seemed somewhat sullen, had lots more questions for Alma. Alma discussed other creatures in and around The Flow, and pointed out some interesting plants along the bank. Then Alma told them about how the different seasons affect this part of The Flow.

"The Long Night Season, or Stormy Season here varies quite a bit. Sometimes there are Great Freezes, which cause the whole Flow to solidify, but these are rare. More often we have what occurred about seven days ago, called a Rough Freeze, which affects the surface and edges of The Flow, while the central current remains fluid. Between the freezes it can be sunny and mild like today. But for the next several twelve days, this part of The Flow can experience freezes."

They asked lots of questions and even Tag participated in this discussion, admitting the most recent Great Freeze had a strong effect on him.

The next morning, the four newcomers were told about an interesting place up-flow from Rock Shelf, and were encouraged by Alma to explore it on their own. They headed out with Tag, predictably, in the lead.

"I guess Alma got busy with something *really* important," he commented, as they traveled through alternating patches of bright sunlight and shadow.

"Why do you always have to be so spiteful?" Bobb was clearly annoyed.

"Don't be such a *swirly-lugger*, Bobb, I was just making an observation."

"*Quarn pizzel.*"

"Really, Bobb? Do you really want to take me on?" By now it was obvious that irritation had been building between these two, and Tag was pretty squeezed. They all stopped as Bobb and Tag squared off.

The tension heightened until Disk somehow flattened himself, and slid between them. "Come on you two, stop *gluggin* around," he sent. Then he just hung there between them until Tag moved off muttering something that sounded to Droplet like, *buggy flumett!*

"Just let him be," sent Disk as he regained his normal shape and nudged Bobb. Then he, Bobb and Droplet continued upstream together while Tag retired to a stretch of shiny pebbles along the bank.

A short time later, the three of them came to a wide, brown *something*, hanging above the surface of The Flow and reaching from bank to bank. Even though Droplet had passed this way earlier, he was in a solid state and it didn't look like anything he'd ever seen.

"I think that's the *span* Alma told us about," sent Disk. "Alma suggested we spend some time here and implied there would be things to see."

While they waited, they talked about what had happened with Tag. Bobb, who'd known him the longest, said Tag came from a very strong grouping many days up-flow from them, and had been lost in the Rough Freeze.

"I was the one to find him, partially thawed and sending blindly," Bobb recalled. "When I approached him we got stuck together, and stayed that way for days as The Flow around us re-solidified. He seemed both frightened and annoyed at the time—now he just seems annoyed. Anyway, when the big thaw finally came, we lost one another until we both showed-up at the Rock Self, him a couple days after me. I know the experience was hard on him," Bobb added, generously.

Droplet and Disk took this in quietly. The sandy bottom around the small angulars where they rested sparkled in the flickering sunlight. Nearby, small-and-medium-sized flashers dashed through sunlit patches and then plunged into shadow. Statuesque trees on the far bank sported white clumps Droplet learned were called *buds*, the way Big Blue above them sported clouds. Even with the scuffle with Tag, it was a lovely day.

And now there was activity on the span. They watched a couple of small, sleek, four-leggeds lope across from bank to bank, then a tall two-legged sauntered over it. It took the watchers a while to figure out that the span was used to avoid The Flow. Why would anyone want to avoid The Flow?

After a furtive, long-faced four-legged crossed, three multi-colored two-leggeds arrived and settled themselves in the middle of the span along the side nearest Droplet and his friends.

The two taller creatures carried long sticks, while the shorter one put what it had been carrying down next to them. This one somehow opened the object and took things from it. The three of them, gesturing frequently, appeared to be cooperating on a joint project of some kind. Then all three of them hung their strange, hairless legs over the span and tossed something into The Flow below them.

Early on Droplet had learned that two-leggeds were clever, but other than the ability of these three to work together, he could make no sense of their activities. Disk had an idea what they were doing, though.

"I think they're *danglers*, Droplet," Disk sent, sensing Droplet's confusion. "They dangle a *line* with tempting morsels on it to lure flashers, and then they yank them from The Flow."

Droplet couldn't believe it until it happened. He watched the astonishing struggle several times—only one flasher got away when the nearly invisible *line* caught on a sharp rock and broke. The rest, the two-leggeds pulled from The Flow with great gusto once their hapless prey had exhausted their efforts to get away.

"So then, two-leggeds are like all other creatures—they must kill to survive." Droplet mused in a sending. Wise Elder had mentioned that these creatures were highly intelligent. Wouldn't true intelligence have found a better way to exist?

Bobb stirred next to him. "It would appear they do, friend," he replied quietly.

They watched as several more flashers were yanked from The Flow, quite thoroughly dampening the mood of the day.

Then they headed back to the Rock Shelf, picking up a conciliatory Tag along the way.

That night Droplet had an unusual dream. He had become accustomed to his normal dreaming process, which had started after he'd crested, and usually involved a jumbled review of the day's events. And this dream began that way, but then it shifted into something else entirely.

In the dream, he was watching twilight deepen into full night from one of the upper ledges at Rock Shelf. With no transition, his new friend Tag was sitting next to him. But this Tag looked older and seemed to radiate unease. For the first time in any dream Droplet could remember, he shifted to esse-sight and saw Tag's esse looking wilted and tattered.

Then Tag began to send. "I hate it here, don't you, Droplet?"

"Um, no . . ." The dream orb, round and partly obscured, sent scattered shreds of light into The Flow above them, reflecting Droplet's confusion. "I don't understand. What don't you like about it, Tag?"

"*Everything!* The way The Flow always changes. How it takes things away from you—or you away from them. Even the constant, maddening pressure pushing in on me all the time. Everything about this so-called existence bothers me. It just doesn't feel right, you know?"

Although he was acutely aware of his dream surroundings and Tag's astonishing sending, Droplet had no idea how to respond. *The pressure pushing in on him? What could he be talking about?*

Tag shifted on the ledge. "Oh, don't mind me, Droplet. I'm just not happy with anything these days. Sometimes I just wish I could leave The Flow and have a real life."

A real life? "You mean as a *creature?*"

"Sure. A flyer's life looks like fun. And on four-legs I could really go places . . . even being a tree would be better than this shadowy *half-life.*"

Truly baffled, Droplet sent, "I had no idea you felt this way, Tag."

"Yeah, well don't tell anyone, squirt, or you won't like the consequences."

Before Droplet could respond to this, the dream changed and he was watching the two-legged danglers on the span. This time one of them pulled a ragged, familiar-looking esse from The Flow.

He startled awake.

Twelve

Droplet's interactions with the Rock Shelf grouping members were often interesting and educational. He enjoyed learning about their society, including their beliefs and customs. He learned they believed they were a special grouping, and although they often welcomed newcomers, they took their relationships with one another seriously and guarded against losing their togetherness. This didn't mean they spent all their time together, though. They could often be found alone or in little groupings of three or four during the day, both within and beyond Rock Shelf. Privacy, especially when one was on a sleeping ledge, was both valued and respected.

Droplet had discovered that while several of the Rock Shelfers were truly exceptional Beings, not all of them were as inquisitive or as aware as he was, and some were very old. Formally called Ancient Ones, but referred to as *Oldsters* by the young, this group generally kept to themselves.

Droplet especially enjoyed the sharing of stories and experiences during the evening gatherings, and he gradually became more comfortable with the powerful emotions the Rock Shelfers would express. Many of the highly emotional sendings drew the grouping together into shared experiences; a few, he noted, drove them apart. After these, Nester and the four other Elders in the grouping were all especially busy mending misunderstandings and strengthening frayed connections.

Although he spent a fair amount of time with Tag, Disk, and Bobb, Tag was pretty aloof, and Droplet hadn't found a good time to mention his dream. He intuitively knew it would need to be when they were alone together, which rarely occurred.

Finally, one morning a twelve-day or so after the dream, he spotted Tag alone a short way beyond the Rock Shelf entrance gazing at the surface where an early mist curled.

Droplet approached and settled in next to him in a way that brought his dream back eerily. He waited to be acknowledged.

"What is it, Droplet?" Tag seemed his usual, abrupt self.

Droplet reconsidered mentioning the dream, but his curiosity won out.

"I, ah, had a dream about you the other night, Tag."

"You had a *dream* about me? You're an odd twist, Droplet."

He hadn't known what to expect, but this reaction baffled him into sending, "Don't you dream, Tag?"

"No, Droplet. Only Finders and Seers and Elders dream, thick-wit. Whatever you think happened, it wasn't a dream. And it certainly wasn't about me."

Droplet sat quietly as he took this in. A few minutes later, Tag moved off toward the central current and distance-sent, "See you later, oddball."

And that was that.

Gradually, Droplet started spending more time with Alma. Alma knew everyone and was well respected by his grouping. Though not officially an Elder, he often worked at Nester's side, their esses shining harmoniously. Not only was he especially friendly to newcomers, Alma was also a great guide to the richly varied environment around the Rock Shelf.

"The Growing Season is finally upon us," sent Alma as he led Droplet down-flow to a divide a short way beyond the one they'd explored before. They took the branch that angled away from the main Flow along the aft bank. This branch, though smaller, had a lively current.

They traveled along its shaded bank as Alma continued.

"Sometimes I can hardly wait for the Long Night Season to release its hold on everything. What I'll be showing you soon will only get more magnificent as the Growing Season progresses into the Warming or Bearing Season, as some call it."

This was the first time Droplet had heard anyone state a preference for a particular season.

"That's not all of them, is it; the Long Night, the Growing and the Warming seasons?"

"No, there's one more, and while most folk call the first three by names resembling these—although the Long Night is also referred to as the Stormy season—the fourth is called by many different names. Around here we call it the Turning Season, but I've heard it called the Season of Reversal, the Flooding season, and in some parts, just The Passage. It's the season that undoes everything on Land and helps prepare for the deep stillness of the Long Night Season, which is what starts the whole process over again."

"Ah, here we are."

Droplet noticed the current had smoothed out and they were now at a shallow, pebbled bank which fronted a large area Alma referred to as 'cultured vegetation.' Everywhere he looked he saw different kinds of plants and trees, many of which were covered in clumps of pastel flowers. There were several kinds of large and small *winged-ones*, another new term for Droplet, flying and hopping around the bushes. The area was both ordered and busy in a way he found subtly unsettling. It was a lot to take in.

Alma indicated his favorite plants and talked about the riotous colors that would emerge as the growing season progressed. It was easy to see that Land plants were his passion.

Just as they were about to move on, a strange sight came out from behind a dark brown structure. It was a slow, bent two-legged, Droplet thought, but with round parts traveling along the ground toward them.

"And here is one of the *tenders*," sent Alma, obviously pleased.

"Isn't that a two-legged?" asked Droplet. "What's wrong with it?"

Before Alma could answer, the two-legged, came to a stop and moved away from what Droplet realized was a container holding dirt. The two-legged emptied the dirt around the base of the plants and started spreading it with a long stick.

Suddenly, a strange and completely unexpected awareness flashed into his mind. He *knew* what kind of place this was, and what the two-legged was doing—it was *gardening*— growing and tending the plants for food and beauty. *Now, how could I possibly know that?* he wondered, as he looked at Alma in shock.

"You okay there, Droplet?" Alma didn't know what had happened, but he could clearly see that something had.

The bent, two-legged tender had shuffled back toward the structure before Droplet could respond. "I think so. I just had the strangest experience. All of a sudden I knew what the two-legged was doing and why. How can that be?"

Alma studied him for a moment and then sent, "I think you should ask Nester about that, Droplet. I can arrange a meeting with him if you'd like. Let's go on now, all right?"

Alma took him back to the main Flow where they went further downstream to what Alma called his 'favorite tree.' This huge, old tree had a vast root system that licked along The Flow's edge for quite a ways. Within the roots, Alma showed Droplet several different kinds of mosses and spiny crawlers. Alma's obvious delight with the physical world had a calming effect on him, and he thoroughly enjoyed the rest of their day together.

On the way back, he and Alma came across a couple of familiar Rock Shelf members also on their way home. Timlyt and Tiffy still routinely scouted for Others who were disoriented after a state change. Droplet was surprised to learn that freezes were still occurring well up-flow of them.

The last of the day's light glinted on the surface in rosy tones as the four of them approached Rock Shelf's slate formation. Droplet noticed several small Flashers nosing around the entrance.

"What keeps the flashers from going inside?" he sent, as he watched them start to move into the passageway, and then dart away at the last minute.

"They don't like our sendings," sent Tiffy. "That's why a few of us are always stationed at the entrance. When a flasher or other creature approaches, we link together and send out a unified pulse which repels them."

Oh, similar to a repulsion-charge, he thought, reminding himself that different groupings had different terms and uses for things.

As they passed the entrance, Droplet observed the tight-focused sendings of the Others who were braced against the rock, deflecting another nosey flasher. *And a very strong repulsion-charge, at that.*

When they rounded the curve, he could see the Rock Shelf

grouping members already clustered together for the evening gathering. He thought they looked very beautiful, all softly aglow with consciousness, and sharing sweetly with one another.

It's good to be home.

Five bright and sunny days later, Droplet and Alma were once again at Alma's favorite place of cultured vegetation.

Droplet noticed that each time they visited the spot, new displays of foliage and colorful flowers delighted them. He especially liked the tiny pink and white flowers that grew near the bank because they reminded him of his pond. They often arrived early enough to watch the bent two-leggeds carefully attend to the flowers and shrubs.

Alma confided to Droplet that he appreciated the care these gentle tenders offered the plants, and that they were healthier and more beautiful because of it. This was the first time Droplet had ever heard one of his kind talk affectionately about two-leggeds. It impressed him.

"I mentioned you to Nester and he said he'd like to spend some time with you, Droplet. Of course it may be a while before that happens—he tends to be very busy."

While Droplet enjoyed the company of Alma and several Others, it hadn't taken him long to realize that Nester was a truly exceptional Being. He loved to watch him with Others and would have liked to spend some time with him, but he was always occupied. When he mentioned this to Alma, he learned that Others often arranged time with Nester in advance, and he could do that for Droplet if he'd like.

Up on the bank, a second two-legged, wrapped in flowing colors, carefully directed a 'controlled rain' onto the bushes closest to The Flow. This one was less bent than the other, but they obviously worked together well. Droplet was briefly reminded of the coordinated movements of some of the leaper pairs in his pond.

"Thank you, Alma, I'd appreciate that," answered Droplet as he watched the sparkling 'rain' arc over the foliage. If he looked through and beyond the droplets he saw bands of misty color.

Alma noticed Droplet's fascination and sent, "That's a *color mist*—an effect of rain-filtered sunlight. Not something we usually see in the natural world is it?"

Droplet thought about this as the two-legged turned to another set of bushes and the colors faded. In his experience, when it rained, sol was always hidden by clouds.

"No. I've never seen anything like that."

"Come on, I'll show you something else," Alma sent as he moved away and headed downstream. Droplet watched the two-legged tenders for an instant more and then followed.

Alma took him to an area where The Flow was brightly lit by the sun, but the tree-covered bank was in deep shadow.

"Wait here for a moment, Droplet."

Droplet watched, mystified, as Alma positioned himself as far as he could from the shadowed bank without being in sunlight. Then he moved a bit one way or another until he finally stopped.

"Ah, here we are. Take a look at this, Droplet."

Droplet joined his friend and turned to observe the aft bank as indicated. Part way up the trunks of several trees he saw a wide silver shimmer. It undulated as if it was in motion, but it stayed right there. He'd seen flashes of something similar a few times, but never this broad or vivid. He watched it for quite a while before he sent, "What *is* that Alma? How does it move like that?"

"It's called a *glory*; an effect of sunlight bouncing off the surface of The Flow and then being reflected on the tree trunks. It only happens when the angle of the sun is just right in relation to the shadowed bank. Pretty biffle, isn't it?"

"Yeah."

They watched it for some time. It gradually got shorter and narrower, then with no warning, it vanished all together.

"How did you learn about this stuff, Alma?"

"Oh, I traveled with a Solo a while back. Plink had a bright and keenly observant mind. He also told a great story when the mood struck him. He found me as I was traveling on my own between groupings, and for some reason, he offered to accompany me. I welcomed both his company and his remarkable insight into the natural world. He left me without warning shortly before I arrived at the Rock Shelf grouping."

"Yeah, I know how that goes," sent Droplet, sharing his

brief meeting with Dag, as he and Alma returned to Rock Shelf.

That night, just after the evening gathering, Alma found Droplet with Disk and Bobb.

"Hi there," he sent as he approached, "I just wanted to let you know that I will be visiting a neighboring grouping at Nester's behest, and will be gone for a few days. I also wanted to let you know, Droplet, that Nester has some time tomorrow morning to meet with you if you're interested."

"Yes, I am."

"He'll be available just after dawn on his ledge. Do you know where that is?"

"I'm not sure." Droplet had seen Nester on a couple of different deep-set ledges since he'd arrived.

"I can show him," sent Bobb.

"Great. I'll see you later then," Alma sent as he moved off toward his own ledge.

"So, you're meeting with Nester, huh?" Both Disk and Bobb seemed interested.

"Yeah, I had a couple of things I wanted to talk to him about," he answered vaguely.

"Well, you'll have to tell us how it goes. I'll show you his ledge now so we don't have to worry about it tomorrow morning, if that's all right with you, Droplet."

Bobb showed him a deep, narrow ledge near the top of the formation and then bid him a goodnight.

Excited about the opportunity to meet with Nester, Droplet didn't fall asleep easily. When he did, he had several dark, vaguely disturbing dreams.

He awoke a bit groggy the next day. The light was dim in the Rock Shelf, but Others were up and about. With some concern he realized he might have over-slept. He bolted out of his ledge and went immediately to the ledge Bobb had shown him the night before.

Deep within it he saw Nester's shining esse, along with two Others. Vexed and realizing he might have missed his chance, he waited politely at the edge of the ledge.

By the time the two Others were finished with Nester, Droplet had calmed himself.

Nester joined him quietly after his guests departed. In short order Droplet felt bathed in the calm acceptance radiating from Nester, and realized he needn't have worried.

"Alma tells me you have some questions about your experiences, Droplet. Would you like to talk about them?"

Suddenly shy, all he could think to talk about were state-changes.

"I, um, had my first state-change recently. It was pretty strange."

"Of course. Our first of either kind of state change can be unsettling."

Either kind? "You mean there is more than one kind?" Droplet asked.

"Why yes, Droplet, there are two. State-changes are when you go from your normal fluid state to a solid state or to vapor state—called by some, a non-state. Over time, you can go through any number of either kind." Nester explained.

"Oh," replied Droplet, slightly taken aback. "I've only been through the solid state-change—I got very thick and heavy and still, and then lost consciousness. I didn't find the experience very pleasant," he admitted.

"Yes, that sounds like the solid state-changes I've been through. The first time can be disconcerting, I know. How far from here were you when it happened?"

"I think I passed a couple of merges, but I'm not really sure. My memory of that whole period is hazy."

"That's pretty normal, Droplet."

"But what causes state changes?" Droplet was truly interested.

"It's an intriguing question," responded Nester. "This is how I understand it: As part of The Flow, we are subject to certain forces in nature. These include weather, seasons, and the constant attraction force which keeps The Flow in close contact with Land. The attraction force is also why The Flow always moves from higher ground to lower ground."

"Oh." Droplet had never realized this. He was fascinated.

"State-changes occur when weather and seasons combine to create special conditions which affect large areas of The Flow. The solid state-change primarily occurs during the time of long nights when the trees lose their leaves and sol stays low in the sky. Conversely, the vapor state-change happens

133

most often during the Long Light or Bearing Season, when the days are long, and sol is high and bright. We know that both of these state-changes occur more frequently in smaller Flows, and along the edges and surface of Flows in general. For reasons we don't understand, they also occur more readily in some places than in others—even within the same Flow. For instance, the solid state-change you recently experienced did not occur in this part of The Flow, and they are still occurring far upstream of us."

Droplet, who knew some of this, was silent as he thought it through.

After a respectful pause, Nester sent, "Any memories of your *emergence*, Droplet?"

He focused on Nester. "My *emergence*?"

"Yes, the circumstances of your becoming conscious."

"Oh. No, just some strange dream-like memories about my first experiences. But I do remember my Finders—in fact I met them again just after arriving here."

"That would be Finders Lemsel and Boklin?"

"Yes. They helped me before my mentor came. I—"

Just then they received a distance-sending from one of the grouping's other Elders. Droplet, who could sense distress in the sending, realized their short meeting was over. He felt disappointed, but also subtly relieved.

"We'll make some time to talk again soon, Droplet," Nester sent as he left the ledge and headed quickly toward the Elder.

Droplet found Disk, Bobb and Tagalong just outside the Rock Shelf entry, arguing about what to do with their day.

"Done so soon, Droplet? We've just about decided to head downstream to a little spot Disk found—right Tag?"

Tag, in his usual testy mood, declined to comment.

Bobb continued undeterred. "It's a place in the rocks where the current spins up to the surface."

"Yeah, it's *swirly*—for real," added Disk.

"Oh, all right, let's go," sent Tag.

This wasn't the first time Droplet observed Tag resisting something someone else suggested, even if he really wanted to do it. *He always seems so troubled*, Droplet thought, remembering his dream again as they traveled downstream together.

The four of them spent the rest of that morning and part of the afternoon darting in and out of the whirling vertical current, seeing who could ride it the longest. It was tricky because if they weren't positioned just right, the strong, steep spin would eject them well before they had to leave to avoid the surface. And trying not to be displaced by the occasional small twigs and leaves the current trapped made it even more challenging.

When they finally took a break at the base of some willowy plants waving in the current, Tag was in an uncommonly generous mood.

"Go on, Disk, show Droplet what you can do."

"Naw," replied Disk, who was the shyest of the three, "you know we're not supposed to go too close to the surface—it's one of Nester's rules."

"Rules-pools" countered Tagalong. "Those rules are only for Others who don't know what they're doing—not you Disk—you're a master."

Disk, clearly uncomfortable with the extravagant praise, retreated slightly. Then Bobb, the most level-headed of them added, "You know, Disk, you really do have an amazing skill."

By this time, Droplet was intrigued, and couldn't imagine what they were going on about.

"Oh, all right," sent Disk. He led them further down-flow until they came to a quiet place along the bank and then sent, "We need to get near the surface, but try not to get too close."

After they'd all ascended the bank, Disk urged them to wait there, while he approached the actual surface.

"There's an invisible barrier at the surface, like an edge between The Flow and the non-Flow," explained Bobb quietly. This made sense to Droplet, who had just learned that sunlight could bounce off the surface.

They watched as Disk carefully made contact with this edge, and then started to loosen his shape and flatten out. He worked at it until he was as flat and wide as he could get. Droplet was amazed; even though he had seen Disk flatten himself to get between his two arguing friends, he didn't know anyone could change his shape *that* much.

Disk was in such close contact with the edge of the surface that he bobbed up and down every time a ripple played along it. When he was done with his demonstration, Disk slowly moved away from the surface, and then regained his normal, round shape.

"Whew," he sent as he rejoined his friends, "sometimes that feels really weird, depending on how the surface is doing. Today there were some ripples, but it didn't feel dangerous. There are times when one would be a fool to try this," he added sagely.

"Wow, that was amazing! Can anyone do that?" asked Droplet.

"Well, Tag and I can," sent Bobb, "but not as good as Disk. He's the best."

"Would you show me how?" asked Droplet.

The four of them spent the rest of that day, well below the surface, practicing changing their shape: long and thin, flat and circular, round and bumpy. Droplet got pretty good at most of the shapes, but Disk was clearly the best at flattening himself out.

The next day, Droplet wanted to practice at the surface. Tagalong and Bobb were busy doing something else, but Disk was willing to go with him. They went to a quiet little bay Disk knew of and started practicing—well below the surface, at first.

After a while, Disk started to open up more. "The most important thing to remember at the surface is no sudden moves, Droplet, calm and slow is best. And it's probably not a good idea to try to look out, at first."

Droplet was concentrating on holding his shape as flat as possible. "What?"

"You know," sent the large flat Disk next to him, "the view can be pretty overwhelming when it's unfiltered by The Flow."

"Oh, sure," he sent, remembering his time bobbing at the surface as a solid. He and Disk, who had become small and round again, briefly compared their state-change experiences. Then they returned to shape-shifting.

"So am I ready to try the surface yet? I'd really like to experience the edge" admitted Droplet.

"Well, all right," sent Disk, "just be careful, okay?

"Always," sent Droplet, as he repelled up the bank toward the surface. Well before he reached it however, he slowed and waited for Disk to join him. Then he flattened himself out as he'd been taught.

"Okay, now using the gentlest repulsion charge possible, rise until you can feel the *edge of the surface* right next to you then stop. The tension at the edge will hold you," flat Disk sent to flat Droplet, as they rose delicately together.

Then Droplet felt it: the edge of the surface. He pressed against the barrier and felt it give a little. *This is fascinating*, he thought, as he slowly focused his awareness upward and looked beyond The Flow. He was watching a winged-one soaring high in Big Blue, when he felt a tiny flicker near him. He quickly adjusted his awareness, and discovered a thin-legged *surface skimmer* next to him. As he was getting ready to slowly move away, the *skimmer* jerked and sailed right across him.

Droplet was so startled that he involuntarily contracted and pulled violently away from the surface.

As he got over his shock and tried to regain his normal shape, he discovered there was something *inside* of his usual form.

Confused, he turned to Disk who observed, "Uh-oh, you've got a little bit of Big Blue in you, Droplet. Can you get it out?"

Droplet spent the rest of the afternoon trying to dislodge the bit of Big Blue inside of him. He configured himself into every shape he could think of, and some he couldn't have imagined. He tried squeezing it out. He tried shaking it loose. He even tried jerking away from it at the suggestion of a concerned but mirthful Disk.

Eventually, Droplet became philosophical about the whole experience and tried—unsuccessfully—to absorb the alien thing into himself. But no matter how hard he tried, he couldn't alter the tiny silvery globe of Big Blue, or get it out of him.

Finally, exhausted and disheartened, he and Disk quietly returned to the Rock Shelf. Droplet didn't attend the evening gathering, and he spent a difficult night in the dim recess of a remote sleeping ledge. Several times a strange sensation woke him; he was shocked to discover himself gently bumping against the rock ledge *above* him. Clearly the subtle attractor-charge he usually maintained while sleeping was being overpowered somehow by the bit of Big Blue.

After trying everything he could think of to keep himself stationary, he wedged himself firmly into a corner. His dreams were equally strange; he either had something he didn't want, or needed something he didn't have.

As night gave way to morning, Bobb and Tag found Droplet hiding in the gloom next to Disk, who was trying to cheer him up. As soon as he got a good look at Droplet, Tagalong sent, "Hey, what happened to you? Pick up a baby *creeper*, Droplet?"

Disk explained what had happened, as Droplet demonstrated his inability to get rid of the bit of Big Blue inside of him.

Bobb thought they should ask Nester for help, but Droplet was reluctant. He felt self-conscious and embarrassed. And he didn't want to have to admit to breaking one of the grouping's rules. However, he finally had to agree that the evidence was there for all to see, so they went in search of Nester.

As they moved through the grouping, Others would notice Droplet's strangeness and pull away. He could feel some of their sendings and picked up terms like 'spin-wit' and 'rule-breaker.' These sendings hurt him in a way that was completely unfamiliar to him.

"Serves him right!" One Other exclaimed, as they moved past.

"Oh, mist-off," replied Tag, as they continued their search.

When they finally found Nester, Droplet felt worse than ever. *Why did this happen to me?* he wondered. *Disk does this all the time, and nothing like this has happened to him.*

Nester took one look at Droplet and sent his friends away.

"Droplet and I have some things to discuss."

Nester took Droplet to a secluded area behind the Rock Shelf. As sunlight angled onto the sand around them, Nester asked him what happened. After Droplet told the story, and apologized for breaking one of Nester's rules, Nester asked "Do you know why we have rules, Droplet?"

Droplet thought for a minute and then answered honestly, "No, not really."

Nester explained that just because you can do something, doesn't necessarily mean you should.

"So we have rules to help keep everyone safe and together. Do you know how dangerous what you did was? You might have been lost to Big Blue, and I don't think you're ready for that."

Lost to Big Blue? "Oh," sent Droplet picking up on Nester's concern. "I didn't even know that could happen."

"Exactly. And that is partly my fault," sent Nester. "You are far too bright and curious to be left on your own, or to spend so much time with our more rambunctious newcomers. So, has anyone told you our other rules?"

"Um, no, I don't think so," admitted Droplet.

"The Rock Shelf Grouping has three basic rules, Droplet: Don't go near the surface. Don't leave without telling someone. And treat Others as you would like to be treated. Any questions about these?"

The last rule made sense to Droplet when he thought about it, and he was painfully aware of what could happen at the surface, but . . .

"Um, why do we need to tell someone if we're leaving?"

"There are hazards and unpredictable things that can, and do, happen, Droplet. That bit of Big Blue inside of you is one of the less serious outcomes. By always telling someone where you're going and when you expect to be back, we will know if you're missing and need help. You haven't been here long enough to be part of a focused search, but believe me they happen. We wouldn't want to lose you, Droplet."

"Okay, I understand, Nester. But is there any way to get rid of this thing now?" The tiny sphere of Big Blue slowly revolved inside of him.

"Most likely, yes," replied Nester. "What have you tried so far?"

Droplet went through all of the shapes, moves, and gyrations he'd already tried. When he was done, an amused Nester sent, "Well, that was more moves than I knew existed, Droplet. But have you tried accepting it and relaxing?"

"Accepting it and relaxing?" Droplet was confused.

"Well, yes. It's been my experience that it's usually helpful to accept what is inside of us—even when it seems foreign. You are of The Flow, but you have a bit of Big Blue inside of you. What do you know about these two great forces, Droplet?"

"Not very much," admitted Droplet, thinking back to conversations he'd had with Wise Elder.

"Well then, let me show you something," sent Nester, and they headed further downstream. Along the way, Nester shared more of his ideas on the natures of The Flow and Big Blue.

"Although they are forever separate, they complement one another. And when they interact they always maintain their separate natures. It might help to think of them as having a friendly rivalry . . ."

"Like Tag and Bobb?"

Nester paused for a moment and then sent, "Yes, a little like that. You know that Life requires The Flow to exist, right?"

"Yes, Wise Elder told me about that," sent Droplet as they negotiated a sudden surge in the current.

"Ah, you know Wise Elder," Nester seemed surprised; then he looked at him intently. "That is good—and it clears up a few things. He is an important friend of mine."

Droplet couldn't explain the profound sense of relief he felt, but his esse flared briefly with joy. And was answered instantly by an increase in Nestor's already radiant esse.

"So. Now I begin to understand, Droplet. We have some significant things in common, don't we?"

Droplet knew no response was necessary to what had become obvious to them both.

They traveled the rest of the way in comfortable silence.

A short time later they came to a fast-moving part of The Flow choked with large granite verticals. Nester took Droplet around the side of a rough silver-gray boulder away from the turbulent current. On the long down-sloping edge of the rock, Droplet could see layers of dark green moss.

"Take a close look at that moss, Droplet, and tell me what you see," sent Nester, as he settled into a small dip on a nearby mound.

Droplet approached the boulder's slope and moved in close to the moss, but he didn't notice anything remarkable.

"I just see moss," he sent back to Nester, pleased that he'd been improving his distance-sending skills.

"Get under it a bit more, Droplet."

Droplet maneuvered himself toward the bottom of the huge rock and looked up. As he grew accustomed to the dimmer light, he discovered that the undersides of the moss were covered with tiny silvery globules of Big Blue. "Oh!"

"Now come back over here with me, and watch for a while."

Droplet joined Nester on his rock, and settled in to watch. *Nester's esse has such a soothing quality. And even though I've broken a rule, he is understanding and kind,* Droplet thought as they waited quietly.

Presently, a group of small, blue-striped flashers came around the side of the boulder, and started nosing the moss. Almost before Droplet could register what was happening, many twelves of the little silver globules shot up toward the surface in long, arching streams. Although he'd seen something like this before, it now seemed to Droplet that the little bits of Big Blue wanted urgently to get to the rest of Big Blue, but they needed help to do it.

Does the little bit inside of me want to return to Big Blue too? As Droplet pondered this question, a new possibility occurred to him. *If it does, perhaps all I need to do is relax and allow it to leave me. That's probably what Nester meant!*

After a quick sending to Nester of, "I'm going to try something," Droplet moved to a calm place between two mounds, and tried to relax. But no matter how hard he tried, nothing happened.

Nester watched his efforts. After a few minutes, Droplet received his distance-sending.

"You're going to have to go deeper, Droplet, and don't try so hard. Relaxing is the opposite of trying."

The opposite of trying?

He went within again and then he sensed it, a still, tranquil place inside of him that reminded him of his Tree of Light experience. When he moved his awareness into this place, his thoughts quieted and he felt very calm. From this inner place of stillness, Droplet thought about how The Flow and Big Blue never merged, but always stayed separate. As Nester had said, "they stay true to their own particular natures." He considered the nature of the little bit of Big Blue inside of him, and why he hadn't been able to absorb it into himself.

Then, from within his calm center, Droplet experienced a subtle shift of perception which allowed him to accept the bit of Big Blue's different-ness. This acceptance enabled him to truly relax around it for the first time.

He moved more deeply into a stance of peaceful acceptance, like what he had experienced day-after-day in the seclusion of his little pond. As he allowed memories of the wonder and comfort he'd experienced there to wash through him, he could feel the bit of Big Blue in him start to move upward. But, as soon as he focused on it with any kind of anticipation, the movement would stop.

Droplet pondered this and then experimented a bit more.

It seemed that accepting the bit of Big Blue so that it would leave him wasn't the right kind of acceptance. Nor did feeling any kind of urgency—or even encouragement—work. Was the hope or expectation that it would change interfering with its release, he wondered?

:Less thinking, he received in a delicate inner sending from Nester, the way Wise Elder could do. So, Droplet went back to just relaxing and accepting it as fully as he could. He came into an even deeper state of calm, where he completely let go of his embarrassment and discomfort, and started focusing again on his time in the little pond. He allowed himself to merge fully with the sweet, joyful memories and not let any thoughts, urges or feelings interrupt him.

In the same way that he had accepted and released his attachment to 'his' leapers, Droplet now accepted and released his resistance to his bit of Big Blue. *Attachment and resistance,* he realized, *they seem like opposites, but they aren't.*

When it happened, when his bit of Big Blue slipped free and went sailing up to the surface, Droplet felt only a deep appreciation for it. In a state of profound peace, he watched it hover at the surface for a moment, and then vanish.

Droplet felt a remote and unexpected sense of release, and wondered if maybe some small bit of the discomfort he'd been feeling wasn't his at all, but the yearning of Big Blue for Big Blue.

He was quiet as he rejoined a beaming Nester.

"That was exceptionally well done, Droplet."

They sat in silence, as the last of the blue-striped flashers finished with the moss. Then they returned together to Rock Shelf.

Droplet felt deeply moved by his whole experience, and knew he needed time to reflect on what he had learned.

Nester, new friend and ally, agreed.

Thirteen

O ver the next few twelve-days, Droplet spent as much time with Nester as he could. Many times he marveled at Nester's remarkable patience when dealing with any problem that might arise between the Others in the grouping. Most of the problems were in the nature of misunderstandings, and Nester's keen insight made him very adept at identifying the source of the disturbance and helping resolve differences. Droplet learned a great deal about what it took to be a wise and compassionate leader by watching Nester.

Droplet wasn't too surprised when one of the problems Nester had to deal with involved Tagalong. He hadn't seen much of Tag lately, but had heard mumblings under the shelf at night about him. Apparently, Disk and Bobb had stopped spending time with him shortly after the Big Blue fiasco (as some referred to Droplet's experience), and Tagalong had "gone rogue." By this Droplet gathered that while Tag was still technically part of the Rock Shelf grouping, he spent most of his time alone, flagrantly ignored the rules, and had very little interaction—even less of it civil—with the rest of the grouping.

Clearly, something needed to change.

Droplet was with Nester when they discovered Tagalong barely concealed in a shallow, pitted creeper lair near the center of The Flow. Nester asked Droplet to wait for him as he went in to speak to Tag alone. Although Droplet tried not to listen, he found his distance sending skills refined enough to give him an awareness of the intense sendings inside the creeper lair. Without even trying, he could discern angry retorts and high emotions coming from Tag, although Nester's sendings were predictably calm and measured.

Suddenly, after a particularly heated exchange, Tag pushed roughly past Nester and shot into the center of The Flow.

Then, before Droplet could even react, the rapid current swept Tag away.

"That is one way to resolve difficulties, Droplet, but it's not generally recommended," sent a droll Nester, as he returned to Droplet's side.

"What happened?" sent Droplet, who was still reeling from Tag's sudden departure.

"The details aren't important, Droplet. What is important is that Tagalong was feeling increasingly unhappy and confined by our grouping, and rather than work on his dissatisfaction, he chose to leave—in a most dramatic way."

Yes, that would be Tag's style, he thought, *and he was able to break a couple of rules doing it!*

Droplet remembered Tagalong's cavalier, and at times callous, attitude toward the Rock Shelf Others, not to mention his frustration with their 'annoying rules and traditions'. Droplet also remembered his dream.

It seems right that he has moved on.

Before Droplet could ask any more questions, Nester sent, "I feel like visiting my favorite place. Would you like to come along, Droplet?"

"Sure," replied Droplet, who could discern a certain sadness in Nester's sending.

They traveled up-flow together for quite a ways until they came to a petite merge and entered a little side-creek, which was one of the smallest moving Flows Droplet had been in. He was intrigued, but after a few unusually terse replies to his inquiries, he kept his observations and questions to himself.

Finally, Nester stopped at a bend in the tiny creek.

"Just ahead," he sent, "is something very special to me, Droplet. When we go around this bend we should move slowly until I determine the state of 'the bed'. Sometimes, it's not right that we intrude, other times it's fine. I will let you know if we need to retreat at any time, okay?"

Droplet answered in the affirmative to this rather oblique sending, and they moved forward.

As they rounded the bend, The Flow widened, and what Nester had called 'the bed,' came into view near the aft bank. It was a wide, shallow, bowl-shaped depression, completely filled with round, iridescent globes. Some of the globes were pink, and others were golden, but all of them seemed vibrant with life.

They stopped at the outer edge of the depression, and then Nester indicated they could proceed.

As they moved into the shallow bowl, Droplet could make out faint forms in the more transparent globes, flickering with movement. Droplet was immediately reminded of the baby leapers dropping into his pond, but these were smaller and already gathered together.

Nester slowly took Droplet down into the very center of the large grouping of globes. They settled on a bit of moss between two of the faintly glowing spheres.

Very softly, Nester sent, "This place is very special to me. It is the home of many, many baby flashers. In this great nest, Life itself is born and grows, until it changes shape and flashes away. Can you hear it around us Droplet, the sound of Life?"

Droplet calmed himself, letting go of his active, inquisitive mind. He let his awareness expand to include the two shining globes nearest him. He could feel their intensity and could easily perceive the subtle movements inside of them. But he wasn't sure he 'heard' anything.

He gently sent this to Nester, who seemed preoccupied. After a while, Nester sent back "What do you perceive here, Droplet?"

Droplet shared everything he could sense and feel.

"Ah," sent Nester. After another pause, Nester sent, "There is something you're missing, Droplet. I'd like to show you, but it means I'll need to merge with your thoughts for a moment. Is that all right with you?"

Droplet, quite curious, indicated his agreement. He felt Nester's next sending from inside of him. :Go into a lower band of perception, Nester suggested. :Here, like this.

Droplet 'followed' Nester 'down' into a range of perception he hadn't known existed. As soon as he did, he started to perceive something in addition to the tiny movements in the globes around him.

Each little flicker of motion created a subtle vibration, a physical sensation he was well accustomed to, but now these vibrations somehow coalesced into the awareness of a shushing *sound*.

Working to refine this inner perception with Nester's help, he began to discern interwoven layers of sound coming from The Flow around them. Another subtle shift in awareness allowed him to focus on one particular sound by moving all the others to the back of his attention.

:This inner awareness of sound vibrations is what we call hearing, Droplet.

It wasn't the onslaught of perception that suddenly seeing color had been; it was a subtle, elegant sense that required finely-tuned focus. Over the delicate sounds of the baby flashers, Droplet began to perceive more distant sounds as well; a couple of large flashers swishing their way up-flow, the rhythmic clank of two stones jostled by the current, the susurrations of plants rubbing together; even the low pulsing of The Flow itself.

Sound is everywhere! Droplet was truly amazed. *How could I not have perceived this?*

Nester, still communicating inside of him, helped him make sense out of what he was experiencing.

:Everything in motion makes a vibration, and every physical vibration can be perceived as sound, Droplet. It took me a while to realize you were unaware of this. I know this might be a bit overwhelming, but before we leave here, there is one other thing I want to show you.

With that, Droplet felt another shift in his awareness, facilitated by Nester's consciousness.

:I want to help you put it all together, Droplet. There is a place in your awareness where you can perceive and accept vast amounts of information about everything you can, and will, experience.

Droplet, still enticed with his latest discovery, had to deliberately switch his focus so he could pay attention to what Nester was saying.

Nester, from within Droplet's mind, made an adjustment that Droplet could barely discern. There was a quick whooshing sensation. The next thing he knew, they had moved into a bright inner spaciousness together, similar to the relaxed space he went into when he released the bit of Big Blue, but different too.

Droplet instantly felt boundless and calm.

:Just here, within you, there is a 'place' of centered

147

expansiveness, Droplet. This quiet place, called the Inner Sanctum, can help you achieve peaceful detachment. Nester paused for a moment and then continued.

:There are many levels of awareness, and some of them can be quite overwhelming until you become accustomed to them.

:Here, in the Inner Sanctum, you have direct access to your esse. From this place of calm strength you can always regain your composure, and learn how to distinguish and sort through all of the sub-levels of awareness. In this way, you can choose what to perceive at any given time. If you want to perceive color and movement without sound, you can. If you want to perceive sound, sendings, and feelings, but not color, you can do that too.

:There are times when you will want only absolute peace, Droplet, and that is also possible within the Inner Sanctum. Take some time now to familiarize yourself with this inner space. It's especially important that you are able to reach this place of inner calm no matter what's happening around you—or within you.

Droplet felt a slight surge of emotion, and immediately realized he had left his Inner Sanctum. It took practice, but with Nester's help, he learned to enter and leave his Inner Sanctum at will.

Later, Nester acknowledged his progress. *:Good, Droplet. This skill will continue to deepen for you, and I believe you will find your Inner Sanctum to be a place where you can access deeper wisdom. It will also offer you an opportunity for true peace and refuge any time you need it.*

Although brief, Droplet's experience supported Nester's assertion. He had a feeling of limitless possibilities when he was peacefully ensconced in his Inner Sanctum, and his awareness seemed particularly deep and clear there.

Then Nester stirred. *:Now let us return to our outer awareness and go home. I know you have a great deal to think about and experiment with, and the baby flasher nest, with its intense Life energy, is wonderful for discovery. But experimentation is better done elsewhere.* With that, Nester receded from Droplet's inner awareness.

As Droplet eased back into his usual state of consciousness, the baby flashers around them made tiny shushes and squeaks, literally pulsing with Life.

"Wow, that was incredible, Nester. Thank you . . ."

"You're quite welcome, Droplet. I know you began this work with Wise Elder, and I'm honored that you allowed me to facilitate this new level of perception. The Inner Sanctum is a particular center of presence and knowledge that not everyone can attain. I believe it will serve you well . . . And sound awareness brings its own richness to our existence."

On the way home, Droplet was stunned several times by the intensity, tone and rhythm of the sounds now resonating through him.

Just like when I got the ability to perceive color, he marveled, *my whole experience is forever changed.*

As wave after wave of sound washed through him, Droplet felt filled with gratitude—for friends like Nester and Wise Elder, and for the endless wonders of The Flow.

A few days later Droplet had a delightful surprise. As he was exploring more of the general area, he happened upon two mature, spotted leapers, and paused to watch them. As the daylight ebbed away, they became more boisterous, sending out their signature vibrations.

All of a sudden, Droplet could *hear* the low sounds they sent through the vibrating ripples around him. *Why, they're sounding too,* he thought in amazement, *and I never knew!*

Droplet thought back to his beloved pond, and wondered what his grouping of leapers would have sounded like. *I bet they sounded better than these two,* he thought, as the rhythmic sounds around him degraded into toneless bellowing.

A wave of nostalgia swept through him, and it occurred to him that he might like to visit his pond again one day.

That night, he had a very strange dream. As the dream started, he was—*outside* of The Flow!—sitting on a branch of the tree near his pond. Suddenly, a gust whirled him up and into Big Blue. He couldn't see much, but he felt that he soared far.

The next thing he knew, his awareness twisted or wrenched somehow, then sharpened dramatically, and he experienced himself in an alien form, entirely as *other*:

I am still. Not asleep, yet not fully awake. The sun is just clearing the rocks and I am waiting for its warmth. When the first rays touch me I start to rouse, slowly at first and then more surely. I rest with eyes closed waiting for the full warmth to give my legs the strength they need. In a little while I am almost ready. I hunger and seek. Suddenly I hear/sense something and my legs raise me up off the sun-warmed rock. Yes, there is a small commotion near me, stealthy, but easily discerned by my awakened senses. I move with short bursts of speed to investigate. I rest in a shadow and observe a medium-sized leg-singer angling its antennae in my direction. Without warning it uses its powerful hind legs to leap away. I move forward on the hunt. Again I detect something—a regularly repeating clicking noise. I move toward it, my legs, with their slim claws make their own faint tapping. This time it is a hairy eight-legged adjusting the hinged opening to its deep lair. This one has a sharp warning scent, so I go a different way. As I come around a little sweetbush, I surprise two more leg-singers distracted by each other near a glistening puddle. Without hesitating I race in to grab one while the other leaps away to safety. The leg-singer struggles in my mouth which causes my jaws to lock. I move to a small hidden place and my jaws relax as I crunch the prey a few times and then swallow it whole. I scan my environment. When I determine there is neither threat nor additional prey, I approach the puddle and lower my snout to drink . . .

Droplet startled awake, disoriented. He took in his familiar sleeping ledge and calmed himself the way Nester and Wise Elder had taught him.

The strange, completely unique dream hung vividly in his mind like fruit from the limb of a tree; attached, but also quite distinct. He had no idea what to think of it. *I was a creature*, he finally acknowledged.

Some time later, the intensity of the dream slid far enough away from his immediate awareness that he was able to return to sleep. *I must ask Nester about this . . .*

Fourteen

B ut I don't understand!" Droplet's confusion was high, and building. While returning to Rock Shelf after spending a quiet morning alone, he had come upon Orry, one of Alma's older friends, acting strangely near the center of The Flow.

Orry spun in a tight little circle just below the forceful current. His esse throbbed in a way that pained Droplet, and he'd snapped at him when he'd asked if something was wrong.

"What don't you understand?" came Orry's angry reply as he circled. "Like I told you, Pilan was following me fine. Then a rogue current sucked him up and away. I didn't notice until it was too late to help him. Now he's gone. He doesn't even know he has to fight not to become one of the *Singers*." Orry's strong sending moved from anger to fear and sorrow. All at once, he stopped circling abruptly, as if something had hit him.

"I just can't believe this has happened. My little Pilan is lost for good." Orry turned away, his esse going flat and dull.

Droplet watched with increasing concern. He could understand Orry's sense of loss, but something more was going on here. After another look at Orry, now resting on the bottom in a collapsed state, he made a decision.

"I'm going to get Nester," He left without expecting or waiting for a reply.

He discovered Nester already on his way to them, and stayed out of the way as Nester calmly handled the upset Orry.

Finally, a couple of Others joined them, and Orry allowed himself to be escorted back to the Rock Shelf by his friends. Droplet watched them go thinking he looked forlorn and diminished.

Afterward, Droplet and Nester went to the top of Rock Shelf together. The day's storm clouds had moved on, and high, lacy white clouds edged in yellow slanted toward the distant hills. Open-winged flyers swooped low to the surface in gentle arcs, and there was a welcome sense of calm after the high emotions of the afternoon.

As they got situated, Droplet sent, "I understand that Orry lost someone he cared about, but I don't know why he reacted so strangely. And what did he mean by *Singers*?"

"Orry was upset because this has happened several times recently," sent Nester. "As you know, the central current near Rock Shelf is very fast. Newcomers don't always realize how strong that current is and can get swept away."

He paused as two flyers nearly collided above them and then flew off screeching. Droplet had quickly learned that a variety of sounds can come from beyond The Flow, too.

Nester continued, "Orry and Pilan had formed a strong bond, Droplet. As I'm sure you've observed, Orry has a strong, expressive esse. I don't know if you knew Pilan, but his esse was fairly undeveloped. In fact, Pilan showed signs of having had an incomplete emergence."

Nester paused and gave Droplet a chance to take this in. He surmised that an incomplete emergence into consciousness would give one a very different type of existence.

"If they were that different, I'm kind of surprised they became friends."

"Oh, sometimes our strongest bonds are with Others who are quite different from us. In fact, Orry and Pilan had become very close since the Stormy Season, and they complemented one another nicely. Pilan's weaker esse offered Orry the opportunity to guide and nurture, while Orry's stronger esse offered Pilan opportunities to grow and be supported. It is often thus in relationships, Droplet."

Droplet thought about this and realized he did understand how powerful a bond could be, for he had a similar relationship with Wise Elder, and increasingly, with Nester.

For some reason, thinking of Wise Elder brought his dream experience whooshing back. He felt the strangeness—no the complete foreignness—of it acutely. Nester, sensing the change in him, asked if he was all right.

"I, umm, just remembered a weird dream I had last night. At least I think it was a dream."

Nester observed him in the familiar way Droplet found both accepting and encouraging.

He took a moment to gather his thoughts and then sent, "I dreamed I was a creature."

"That's interesting," sent Nester calmly. "What kind of creature?"

"A land creature, I think. I've never seen or felt anything like it. I was *it* completely. I experienced its thoughts and impulses as my own. As this creature, I had a tough body, four legs with claws that clicked when I ran, and I ran short distances very fast." After a pause he added, "I, um, consumed another creature."

Nester focused his attention completely on his young friend as he sent, "Was the dream disturbing to you, Droplet?"

"Not while I was in it; then it seemed perfectly ordinary—I was just a creature doing normal creature-things. But it was so intense! After it ended I felt shocked and disoriented for quite a while."

"I have heard of extreme dream experiences like this, but I've never had one myself. It may signify a gift of some kind. What other types of dreams do you have?"

"Mostly just normal dreams about what happened the day before. My dreams often turn things that have happened into a story. A couple of times I've had dreams about Others that seemed unusual. I had one about Tag before he left where he told me how much he hated being in The Flow . . . I'm not sure I want to have dreams like these, Nester."

Nester, silent, seemed to be thinking deeply. Then he sent, "I think you probably do have a gift related to dreaming; an ability others don't share. My suggestion is that you don't resist or try to control your dream experiences in any way. There are many kinds of dreams, Droplet, and I believe some of them come to us directly from the Sacred Flow. These extreme dreams of yours may have important things to teach you. Learn to relax and roll with them, and see where they take you. One thing I know for sure, you will always return to yourself when the dream is done."

Droplet hadn't realized he had concerns about this until Nester addressed it. "That's a relief."

The light around them shifted slowly as the first hint of twilight graced The Flow. The clouds, now edged in a delicate pink-orange, looked lower and fuller behind the trees along the bank.

As he relaxed, Droplet remembered an odd thing Orry had said. "Nester, what are *Singers*? Orry said that Pilan was vulnerable to them, that he didn't know he needed to fight them. What did he mean by that?"

"Ah." Nester, lost in thought, visibly shifted next to him. "We don't know too much about the Singers, Droplet, and that tends to make some of us nervous or superstitious. What we do know is that the Singers might be similar to us in some ways, but they are also very different. They exist at the Center of The Flow where the current is fastest, and we believe they have an intense, but sadly brief, existence. They are *all-of-a-group* and don't seem to experience themselves as individuals. I'm not sure if they think thoughts at all, but their singing is very beautiful. In fact, it is an alluring sound that some find very hard to resist."

"Their *singing*?" Droplet realized Nester was referring to a *sound*, and thought of all the new sounds he could perceive. "What does it sound like?"

"Oh, you probably haven't heard it yet if you've stayed away from the central current as advised." Nester thought for a moment. "But this is something you should know about, so I'll show you—but only if you promise to stay right next to me."

Intrigued, Droplet agreed.

He and Nester left the top of Rock Shelf, and traveled along the gravelly bottom toward the Center of The Flow. There, in the dimming light, they followed a narrow clear-run until they were directly under the swift central current.

"Be careful that you don't let yourself get sucked-up into the Singers, Droplet. As I said, some find them hard to resist. Now, let me show you what they sound like; it just takes a bit of fine tuning."

With Nester's help—inside of him again—Droplet began to *hear* the Singers for the first time. It started as an inner experience of a subtle undulating sound, but gradually evolved into a lovely multi-pitched tone with a swelling intensity, which Nester called their *song*.

"Why, it's beautiful," sent Droplet, after listening quietly for a while.

Nester, right next to him, also listened to the swelling

tones.

"Yes, it is. But it's also quite seductive, so you need to limit the amount of listening you do." Nester seemed unusually intent.

"Why? What does *seductive* mean?" asked Droplet, a bit distracted by what he almost heard in the Singer's song. *There is something I can't quite sense—some lovely message or meaning I can almost detect. Maybe if I got just a little closer—*

"Droplet, attend!" The force of Nester's sending caught him completely by surprise. "You must use restraint when you listen to the Singers. Go into your Inner Sanctum. Now!"

Shaken, but alert, Droplet did as he was bid. From within his Inner Sanctum his experience of the *song* fundamentally changed. He could still hear/sense it clearly, but now he could appreciate the beauty of the tones, without the desire to get closer—no, to *merge*—with them.

In a moment, he felt Nester's comforting presence inside of him. *:This is probably the last time I will join you in your Inner Sanctum, Droplet, but you needed to be shocked out of the attraction building in you. As I said, the Singers' song can be very seductive—especially to one so new to the inner sense of hearing. Now let's return to our normal awareness and then move further away from the central current. Ready?*

As soon as Droplet returned to his usual awareness, his attraction to the song began to build again. But this time he aimed his consciousness away from the enticing tones by focusing on physically moving further from the central current.

Big Blue had deepened into indigo while they'd been *listening*. Soon it would be time for the evening gathering, but before they approached the Rock Shelf entrance Nester stopped them so they could finish their discussion.

"That was so unexpected," Droplet sent first. "I didn't even notice how attracted to their song I'd become until I went into my Inner Sanctum. Then, while I still found it beautiful, I no longer felt compelled to move toward it. I think I understand what seductive means now."

"Yes, I should say you do," sent Nester, humor intact. Then he added, "You had one of the stronger reactions I've seen, Droplet—do be careful from now on, won't you?"

"I will. But I have to admit I find the whole thing pretty intriguing. What would have happened if I had followed the attraction?"

"You might have become so enamored with the song that you would have been swept away—not just by the current, but by the song itself. I've known a few to get caught up in the Singers' song, and lose themselves to it. When this happens, they drift closer and closer to the Singers until their esse starts flickering. Then the current grabs them and they are just GONE—never to be seen or heard from again."

"Wow. Do you think that's what happened to Tag?" asked Droplet.

"No, what Tagalong did was intentional. He chose to leave the way he did. What's happened to some Others is unintentional; they just get absorbed in the song and vanish. We don't believe they remain individuals, Droplet, because after this happens there is no trace of them—anywhere. And believe me, some of us have gone to great lengths to try to find those who have been lost this way."

Now Orry's dismay made more sense.

A few solemn minutes later, Nester sent, "Let's get home now."

"Okay."

That night, Droplet's dreams were predictably troubled, causing him to wake several times. Near dawn, he dreamed he was trapped in a fast moving current. All around him were huge dark flashers using their tails to push him this way and that. He was completely at their mercy until a thin, pale yellow film insinuated itself between him and the giant flashers.

This misty, diaphanous film gradually edged him out of the overpowering current and deposited him onto a lightly pebbled bottom. Just as he was beginning to discern the presence of a faint, dispersed esse in the mist, it started to fade. Then it unraveled into the tones of *song*.

As soon as he heard the delicate sonance he jolted awake, both attracted to and alarmed by the tantalizing tones trailing through his mind.

Two days later, Droplet found Nester at his favorite place, the baby flasher bed.

Droplet noticed Nester's deep state of peace and joy as soon as he saw him. He waited quietly until Nester acknowledged him, and then joined him. They watched the tiny flashers together in silence. Droplet could easily perceive that the flickering shapes in the globes were noticeably bigger than the last time he'd seen them.

After a while, Nester indicated that they should move away a bit. They settled on the far edge of the flasher bed, basking in the golden glow of Life nearby. Following a respectful silence, Droplet asked if they could talk about something that was puzzling him.

"I still don't understand something, Nester. Why were the feelings Orry had so strong, and why does he still seem so distraught?"

Nester gave Droplet his full attention. "Well, Droplet, what do you know about feelings or emotion?"

"I'm not sure. I've received feeling-tones in sendings, and I've felt emotions before—wonder, gratitude, joy, concern, curiosity—but they seemed to be a natural part of what I was experiencing. I just don't understand the depth, or power, of Orry's feelings. Does it have to do with how strong his esse is?"

"Yes, in part. When I was about your age, my favorite teacher gave me this bit of clarification on the subject: 'From awareness can come preferences, and when preferences combine with familiarity, attachments can form.' Think back to your favorite experiences, Droplet. Can you recall favoring one aspect of your experience over another?"

Droplet thought back to his secluded pond and remembered liking some leapers better than others; the ones he'd thought of as 'his' leapers. He shared this memory with Nester.

"If something had happened to one of your favorites, how would you have felt?" asked Nester.

Suddenly, Droplet remembered that something *had* happened to one of his favorite leapers; it grew a bump and could no longer leap with the others. Droplet had watched in concern as it had slowly stopped moving all together. One day it simply sank to the bottom of the pond, pale and unmoving. Eventually mud covered it. Still adjusting to the life-cycles of creatures, Droplet remembered feeling confused and sad about it, before getting caught-up in the antics of his other leapers.

"That sorrow, Droplet, was the result of losing something you'd developed a preference for. Imagine if that brief sorrow had been much more intense, and lasted much, much longer. That is what Orry felt—and still feels—after losing his young friend."

Oh, thought Droplet quietly.

"It's not always clear why we become emotionally attached to things or Beings, and some of us have a stronger feeling sense than others—which does seem to be related to our esse. Also, many of us find that our ability to feel emotion increases over time. Orry is nearly an oldster and has a very well-developed feeling sense. He can experience a wide range of emotions with great intensity, and he identifies strongly with this capability."

Nester paused a moment, and then continued.

"Because experiencing emotion has to do with the capacity of our feeling sense, our ability to feel positive emotions—like joy, wonder, gratitude—is equal to our ability to feel the more difficult emotions—like sorrow, fear and anger. For many of us, feeling the full range of emotions brings richness to our existence, while others prefer less emotion and a more thought-oriented existence. It all depends on an individual's preferences, and their natural attributes."

"Will my ability to feel emotions get stronger, Nester?"

"Quite possibly, Droplet. Your ability to perceive the feeling sense is already increasing. A lot of it will depend on your experiences, your intent, and even your destiny."

"My *destiny?*"

"Yes, those currents of experience to which you feel strongly and innately drawn, and which help determine and reveal your character."

Droplet took all this information in as they returned to Rock Shelf.

The more he thought about it, the more intrigued he became with all of the different perceptual currents he could access, thought and memory, vision—including color, communication and attraction-repulsion sendings, sound, emotion, and the rudiments of chemical awareness that Alma called *taste*. Emotion was especially appealing to him because of its richness, breadth and depth.

Droplet secretly hoped that his ability to experience emotion would increase as he grew, and he eagerly looked for opportunities to feel things with and for the Others he lived with.

Fifteen

A s the seasons glided by, Droplet became increasingly involved with the Rock Shelf Grouping. His strong friendships not only offered him interesting ways to spend his days, but also exposed him to a variety of thoughts and opinions on everything from appropriate interaction styles, to creature cycles, and the nature of The Flow itself.

Over the course of many evening gatherings, he learned that The Flow—'Ever changing, always the same'—had existed *forever*. He learned that while the seasons always affected them, Rock Shelf was in a *moderate* part of The Flow, which somehow mitigated their effect. He learned that far upstream, The Flow sometimes stayed in a solid state for more than one season, and that when these deep, deep freezes finally thawed, it caused major disruptions in local currents, merges and divides, and in the size and intensity of The Flow itself. Fortunately, a freeze this intense hadn't happened in quite a while.

One evening, just as the gathering was breaking up, Droplet overheard something which unsettled him. He went in search of Alma, who had finally returned from yet another extended time away. Alma quickly confirmed that yes, there were barely conscious beings in The Flow who vaguely resembled Others and were commonly referred to as *Hummers*.

"But how did I not know this? Why haven't I ever seen one?" Droplet asked, vaguely reminded of Gern and unaccountably concerned.

"I'm sure I don't know, Droplet."

Droplet, a little taken aback by Alma's tone, finally sensed his friend's fatigue and sent, "I'm sorry, I can see you need sleep. Perhaps we can get together sometime soon to talk about this?"

"Of course, Droplet. I need to meet with the Elders

tomorrow morning. Let's meet at the entrance around mid-day tomorrow if you're free," Alma responded.

"Yes, let's," replied Droplet eagerly. He hadn't realized until just then how much he'd missed Alma.

Mid-day found Droplet waiting patiently at the Rock Shelf entrance. He'd given his strong reaction to learning about Hummers quite a lot of thought, and realized most of his questions would be answered if he could just see one of them.

Alma arrived—back to his usual self after a night's rest—and suggested they go downstream past the divide to the tended gardens to a place he'd seen a Hummer not long ago.

On the way there Alma answered some of his questions. "No-one knows what Hummers are. They don't seem to be individuals, and can't or won't communicate with us. Also they have very limited self-propulsion."

"But are they as common as Kipsi suggested?" Droplet shared his strange experiences with Gern, who had seemed pretty unique. "Would Gern be considered a Hummer? If not, I'm sure I've never seen one."

"No, I would say Gern was probably a Partial; someone quite different, but likely more aware and self-directed than a Hummer. And as you should know by now, Droplet, Kipsi often exaggerates; they aren't as common as he implied. Hummers tend to be found in areas of calm current, so they're hardly ever around Rock Shelf. It's also possible they were nearby and you never noticed them. They naturally blend into their surroundings and can be very hard to detect."

When they finally got to their destination, Alma's statement proved correct. After searching the entire area to no avail, they took a break along an open stretch of bank. High above them, grey and white clouds glided from one side of Big Blue to the other.

Alma had just admitted he didn't know much more about Hummers when he stopped suddenly.

"Just there, Droplet, beneath that frond. I think it's a Hummer."

Droplet quickly looked where Alma indicated, but could see nothing under the plant frond. "Can we get closer?"

"Of course. I'll go around to the other side of it."

They positioned themselves on either side of the drooping frond, but the area between them appeared to be quite empty.

"I don't see anything there," Droplet distance-sent.

Just then, as if reacting to the sending, the barest outline of a delicate form wavered into view.

Alma came around to where Droplet stared and sent, "Now do you see it?"

"But it's barely there! How can that be a Being?"

"It isn't completely. You have esse-sight don't you?"

This was something they'd never discussed, but Droplet answered simply, "Yes."

"Use it and tell me what you see."

Droplet shifted to esse-sight and saw that under the frond, there was indeed an Other-shaped outline of form which was glowing faintly. He couldn't detect an actual esse, but something similar to esse-light illuminated the form very slightly from within.

"Huh."

"Now shift through your other perceptual skills and see what else you notice." Alma's quiet suggestion came from beside him.

And then he heard it. The Being made a low, but distinct humming noise, now the easiest thing to perceive about it.

They stayed near the Hummer long enough for Droplet to determine that it wouldn't acknowledge them or respond to their communication attempts; in fact, it didn't move or change in any way. Then they returned to Rock Shelf.

Later, during the evening gathering, Droplet asked the assembly about Hummers. He learned that, despite a few wild speculations, the grouping as a whole believed Hummers were most likely "Singers who had fallen out of the center of The Flow." The going opinion was they were not very interesting, and could easily be ignored.

That night his dreams were jumbled. Then, with little transition, he was suddenly cast wholly into another astonishing experience as a creature:

> *I am in a high, safe place. Around me the night gently gives way to daylight. I hunger, but first I must call. My toned call lets others know I am alive, awake, alert. Also, that I near the time I will take a mate. I listen to the other morning calls and determine the*

mate-time is not yet. Then I stretch my feathers and hop away from my perch, letting air catch the edge of my wings. For an instant I soar and then I push the air downward and rise above the trees, briefly scanning the area for hunters. Seeing none, I descend to a span of ground protected by low branches. Here I know plump night-wrigglers will be digging into the moist soil to avoid the heat of day. When I spot one, I grab it and neatly quarter it with my beak. Its segments wiggle even as I swallow them, but not for long. It is quickly followed by another, and then another. When I am sated, I scan again for hunters, and then fly to a clear pool and lower my beak to drink . . .

Droplet returned to his sleeping ledge with a jolt. *I was a flyer!* Even though he was back in his own form, he felt stretched for a while, almost like he still had wings. *So many odd experiences—eating, hopping, flying, and concerns about mating and safety . . . how strange these dreams are.*

Just before he sank into a sweet, dreamless sleep, Droplet realized how similar flying felt to being carried by The Flow's current. *Amazing...*

The days were getting shorter as they moved out of the Turning Season and into the Long Night Season again. Storms were so frequent that Big Blue commonly became known as Big Gray. Sweeping rains pounded powerfully into The Flow's surface, while sharp-flashes and rolling crashes of thunder made it hard to think, or do much of anything else.

One day, after several long, strenuous deluges had whipped The Flow's current into a torrent, Droplet noticed an inward turning in the grouping's energy. They had all spent the last few days nestled together in Rock Shelf's central chamber, as the current everywhere was too erratic for even the strongest of them to manage easily.

When Droplet finally asked Alma about the change he was sensing, he replied simply, "Yes, we're tuning our awareness in preparation for tonight's Origins Celebration." And that's all he would say.

That night, instead of disbursing after an unusually subdued evening gathering, all of the Rock Shelf members stayed close together, so that everyone was touching on all sides. Nester and the other Elders including Elder Pim, were in the very center of the grouping.

The Elders started the celebration, which began by focusing on what each member of the grouping was grateful for. Many Others warmly shared appreciation for their grouping, the quality of their existence, and for certain individuals they were close to. Droplet wasn't surprised to find Nester mentioned frequently.

When his turn came, Droplet shared his gratitude for being so kindly received when he had first arrived—almost a full turning of the seasons ago—and for the true friends he'd found there, especially Nester and Alma.

Then the sharing moved on to what the Others would like to experience together as a grouping in the coming year. Droplet listened carefully to the first few contributions, then his attention wandered a bit.

A sudden shift in the grouping's energy brought his awareness back into focus.

From next to Nester, Elder Pim formally sent: "Now for the *Celebration of the Origin of Life*. As most of you know, some of this will be shared by sending, and some will be experienced as group memory. We ask that each of you receive what is sent, add your awareness to it, and then pass it on to those next to you. In this way, all will have the fullest experience. We appreciate your thoughtful participation."

Well, this should be interesting, thought Droplet. But before he could think another thought, a shockingly powerful sending moved into him from several of the Others with whom he was in physical contact. What came was this:

In the beginning, the three great powers—Land, Big Blue, and The Flow—decided to come together to support the unfolding of physical Life on this world.

Droplet saw the startling image of a blue and white sphere, the *World*, he remembered, against a midnight background— even more vivid than what he'd seen with Wise Elder during his cresting.

Land wanted to provide a strong, stable foundation; therefore the attributes of Land would be solidity, vastness, and long periods of stability with occasional eruptions of change.

Big Blue and The Flow were both strongly attracted to fluidity and movement, and wanted their role to contribute to the change and growth of Life.

In fact, they both wanted to provide exactly the same things and couldn't agree to compromise.

Big Blue wanted Life to start as tiny airborne forms that could move quickly and weather any storm, while The Flow wanted to be the nurturing birthplace from which Life could grow and transform into any form at all. Their lack of accord profoundly affected this world, and for eons there were major upheavals, and Life as we know it could not survive.

Again Droplet saw the blue and white sphere, but this time there were immense spiraling clouds and large patches of red and gray spewing upward. He got the sense of profound turmoil.

Finally, Land intervened by showing them that they would never support Life until they could come to an agreement, and after all, wasn't supporting Life their primary interest?

Eventually, Big Blue, who had become increasingly erratic in behavior and attitude, was able to listen to reason. It was agreed that The Flow, with its gentler nature, would be the 'cradle of life,' while Big Blue would surround the world with its protecting presence as long as it could move and change constantly. Land, of course, would provide solidity and structure, and also maintain the constant attractor-charge necessary to keep them all together.

So, The Flow nestled onto Land in vast hollows, great bowls, and the tiniest of crevasses, while Big Blue enveloped them both. And as part of the agreement between The Flow and Big Blue, they would always influence and reflect one another.

Here Droplet saw a tremendous expanse of The Flow exactly the same color as Big Blue.

Now, with all of the supportive elements in place, Life could begin, and it grew and changed into all of the common forms we know today, plus many, many more.

With the conclusion of this narration, the grouping pressed closer together as image after image swept through them.

They saw: tiny almost-swimmers growing and changing, some becoming gigantic; all different kinds of flashers and leapers, some crawling out of The Flow onto Land, and spreading feathered fins to soar into Big Blue. They saw eight-legged, six-legged, four-legged creatures scampering around on Land, thriving and then vanishing in unknowable numbers; then tiny fur-faces gradually becoming very large, and roaming in great herds over vast stretches of Land; with two-leggeds running and hunting them in groupings. They saw periods of upheaval where Land, Big Blue and The Flow would almost lose the thread of Life again and again. But always, in secreted parts of The Flow, Life would begin anew; tiny, insistent, determined.

There was a brief pause after the last of the group memories moved through, and then Droplet received this power-etched sending, which was magnified by all of the Others in the resplendent grouping:

The Flow is our sacred home;
It is part of us, as we are part of it.
Ever changing, always the same;
The Flow is now and forever.

This was repeated by everyone six times, including Droplet after the first time or two. Droplet felt his awareness loosen and shift.

Suddenly, but very briefly, he was aware of The Flow around him *in its entirety*—from its trickling start somewhere high in the foothills of great mounts of Land, to its eventual emptying into a broad, sparkling, deep-blue expanse of stillness. Droplet could feel its movement and moods as one great Being or Self; no, as *himself.*

Then the experience passed, and he was his regular self once again, feeling tired, but deeply moved.

After a few minutes of lingering resonance, the grouping broke into ones and twos, and retired for the night.

Droplet went to his favorite sleeping ledge and settled down with *"Ever changing, always the same; The Flow is now and forever"* echoing in his awareness, until he drifted off into primordial dreams.

Sixteen

D roplet didn't have much experience with these things, but even Alma agreed the Long Night Season seemed to be lingering. Although the days were finally lengthening, they were dim and often dismal. The close nights were enlivened by fellow Rock Shelfers telling increasingly elaborate stories of their travels and experiences.

After listening to many of these stories, and with encouragement from Nester, Droplet shared a few of his own adventures. With practice, he learned how to share just the right amount of description and feeling to make a good telling. He found both the sharing and receiving of stories very satisfying, and looked forward to milder days so he could have more adventures, not only to experience, but also to share in the evening gatherings.

Droplet was out on patrol with Alma and Timlyt when the weather finally turned. They had found a friendly but disoriented Other, named Notch, who had just come out of a protracted state-change, and were returning home with him. The thaw-swollen current made the return trip long and laborious; Droplet and Alma held Notch securely between them with a calming attractor-charge, while Timlyt sought the still-run—which was anything but still right now.

As they finally neared the familiar Rock Shelf formation, two Others rushed toward them with such reckless speed that Droplet became alarmed.

"What has happened?" He sent on a tight-beam to Alma as the Others raced to meet them.

"Isn't that Disk and Bobb?" Alma just had time to respond to Droplet before the two barreled up to them, sending urgently, "Notch? Notch is that you?"

Notch, muzzy-minded and largely uncommunicative until then, suddenly focused on the newcomers and sent a weak "Bobb?"

"Great Good Wave, it is you!" This from Disk who had dislodged Droplet in his urgency.

"Excuse me Disk, Bobb, but we need to get Notch back to Rock Shelf and if you're not going to help, at least move out of our way." Alma's clear sending cut through the elated reunion.

Disk and Bobb immediately moved behind them to support Notch, and together they worked their way to the Rock Shelf entrance and then into the welcome calm of home.

"You obviously know one another," Alma sent to Disk and Bobb, who were completely focused on Notch. "And after your friend has met Nester, I'd be happy to release him to your care."

"Oh, of course," sent Bobb.

"That would be great," agreed Disk.

While Alma took Notch to meet Nester, Bobb told Droplet about their friend. ". . . all from the Boreal grouping—a wonderful grouping many merges and divides up-flow from here. Disk and I have thought many times of trying to return there, but couldn't imagine how we'd ever find it again." This sending contained more fervency than Droplet had seen in Bobb for a long time. *Since before Tag left,* he realized.

"Was Tag from that grouping too?"

"No, we met him later. Notch was our closest friend before we got separated from Boreal in a sudden freeze and thaw," sent Disk. "We never thought we'd see him again. I still can't believe he's here!"

A short time later, Alma and Notch returned; Notch looking a good deal more alert. With Alma's approval, Disk and Bobb took him to one of the ledges where they would help him adjust to his new circumstances.

Droplet watched them go quietly.

"Seems like they have a strong, healthy connection with one another," mused Alma next to him.

"Yes, it does, doesn't it?"

Late the next day, Disk invited Droplet to join him and Bobb as they showed a much-improved Notch around Rock

Shelf.

"This flat area here is the main chamber where we have our Evening Gatherings. Now that you're better, you'll be able to join us."

Notch looked around carefully. "It's kind of small isn't it? How does everyone fit?"

"Oh, we fit well enough," sent an amused Bobb. "We, most of us, enjoy the close contact. And the Rock Shelf Grouping is smaller than Boreal—several twelves less in size," he added slowly, having taken a moment to calculate it.

Droplet was impressed. "I had no idea you were from such a large grouping. What's it like there?"

"Well, it's a pretty amazing place, actually," sent Disk.

"Yes, the Boreal Grouping is located right next to the Boreal *spring*—a constant up-welling of The Flow from deep in the earth," added Notch.

Droplet had a little trouble visualizing The Flow coming from inside the earth, and said so.

"Oh there are many springs where we come from," continued Notch. "The Boreal spring-fed Flow is constant and ever-fresh, and even though the Barren Season there lasts much longer than it seems to here, the spring—and The Flow issuing from it—never freezes."

Droplet thought about this. "Then how did each of you end up in a state-change?"

"That's easy, Droplet," sent Bobb. "There are a number of little tributaries off the main Flow, a few with their own small groupings containing friends of ours. They usually spend the Barren Season with us in Boreal and then return to their own groupings with the Growing Season. But for several twelve-days before and after the worst of the long Barren Season, storms can come-on very suddenly. It's not uncommon for portions of The Flow farther from the spring to go through snap-freezes well into the Growing Season. Usually these are brief and uneventful—often just overnight—and cause no difficulties.

"Are you telling me that you, and whole groupings of Others, might go through multiple state-changes during one Long Night—um, Barren—Season?"

"Not really by choice, but yes, it does happen. Like I said, though, it's considered a normal part of traveling the

170

tributaries and isn't usually a problem. But occasionally, a major portion of The Flow, well away from the spring, can freeze long after the Barren Season. When a thaw comes after a late, deep freeze like that, whole portions of the solid Flow can break apart and travel far down-flow. This is usually what we find so disorienting."

Droplet remembered his own state change and agreed.

"But the main reason we invited you to join us today, Droplet, is that we have news. Bobb, Notch and I have decided to try to return to Boreal." Disk seemed inordinately pleased.

"How? I thought it was impossibly far up-flow."

"It is, but we believe that together we can do it. Of the three of us, Notch is by far the most experienced traveler, and he believes he can get us home. Isn't that great?"

Droplet was genuinely pleased for his friends and said so. But he also had a slight sense of foreboding about their plan, which he kept to himself.

Early the next morning, Droplet, Alma, and several other Rock Shelf members gathered at the entrance to offer the threesome a fond farewell.

Droplet sent the leave-taking, "Journey well, until The Flow brings us together again," with feeling to his departing friends.

He didn't realize how much he would miss them, and that their leaving would mark a turning point for him.

A few nights later, after an especially moving evening gathering, Droplet had another of what Nester called his 'extreme dreams.'

In his third, which he'd had about a twelve-day ago, he had become a large, boisterous paddle-flapper, like those he had seen—but not yet heard—at Marsh Lake.

Surrounded by fellow paddle-flappers, he had squawked his intentions, and then murmured to his mate as they lowered orange beaks to grab tasty vegetation from the bottom of a flooded field. This extreme dream had the crisp feel of limitless Big Blue, a sense of comradeship with his fellow creatures, and the familiarity of The Flow supporting him. While the experience included the usual shocking reorientation, it had been relatively enjoyable.

Tonight's extreme dream was very different.

It began with looking at the stars high above him. But instead of seeing them through the familiar and comforting presence of The Flow, he saw them sharp, unwavering, and unusually bright. Just as he was getting used to this, he felt the strange sideways wrench that preceded the abrupt shift in his perspective. An instant later he dropped into an experience of decisive physicality:

> *I wake alone. Alone and cold and hungry. I have vague memories of a safe place with beings who care for me, keep me safe and warm. But that place is long gone, and no matter where I go or what I do, I cannot trace my way back to it; the scent is old, the trail cold. So I travel on, seeking food and finding little. Seeking companionship and finding none. Others shun my scent or they lunge with bared fangs when I approach. I know I smell of desperation, but there is no help for it. It is what I am. Finally I catch the oder of something dead nearby. As I approach it, I scent that it is long dead, and that it has been taken over by the white squirmy ones. I know this means I should leave it, but hunger overpowers my nose and I take a few tiny bites. The sharp-bitter taste finally warns me away, but before I've taken two steps I retch-up what I'd swallowed. Eyes and tail downcast, I move on. I smell the moisture long before I find it. A shallow pool with a scummy crust that doesn't smell too bad. I use my injured paw to make a clear place and lower my muzzle to drink . . .*

Ugh, he thought, after the extreme dream abruptly released him. *That was very weird!* As he worked to reclaim his normal awareness—*I'm on my sleeping ledge, there are Others sleeping near me*—he started to relax. Eventually, still wide awake, he became philosophical.

This dream had a haunting quality that troubled him, and the face that the pond had reflected back to him looked familiar. He had seen four-leggeds similar to it drinking at the edge of The Flow, but none as thin and haggard looking. He didn't like to think that a creature's existence could be so horribly bleak, but this dream, like all of his extreme dreams so far, carried a sense of certainty.

He had no idea why he'd had this dream, and he certainly wasn't sure he wanted to tell anyone about it. In the end he decided to 'roll with it' as Nester had suggested; some things were probably best kept to himself.

The increasingly mild and fair days, punctuated by the occasional squall, signaled the full arrival of the Growing Season. Droplet hoped this boded well for his friends as he watched The Flow alone from one of his favorite perches above the Rock Shelf, feeling restive. *I wonder if I should try to follow them,* he mused, idly. *Maybe it's time for me to move on too.* He had to admit he found what they had shared about the large, diverse Boreal Grouping during their last evening gathering, very appealing.

The muffled clank of a floating log colliding with a rock upstream brought his attention back to the present. A brief, but intense storm the night before had swelled and strengthened The Flow, littering it with sticks, twigs, and other debris.

Suddenly, a wide, flat, floppy brown khoot angled toward the Rock Shelf. It sailed up over the slate wall and ploughed into him, breaking his attractor-charge as it spun away.

Caught between disbelief and astonishment, Droplet tumbled out of control. With nothing to attract or repel from, the storm-strengthened current easily captured him.

The next thing he knew, the rough central current had him, powerfully plunging him away from everything he cared about.

As this realization struck him, he felt numb and then incredulous. *Not again!*

Grappling with these feelings touched on difficult memories, and he reacted by retreating into his Inner Sanctum.

Moments later when he shifted his awareness back to his physical predicament, he discovered he was in the midst of many twelves of strangely elongated Singers making their haunting tones. These tones quickly became a balm to him;

like liquid sunlight amidst the discordant sounds of the turbulent Flow.

No, wait—he needed to remember Nester's warning!

With this, he contracted himself and tried not to listen too closely. But even in his contracted state, the tones soothed and buoyed him. More importantly, he realized that he was still safely 'himself', even though he was entirely surrounded by the unique tones of the Singer's beautiful song.

Ah, I'm in my Inner Sanctum again. From here I can listen to the Singers and not get swept into them. So he allowed himself to relax, and as he did, his awareness and appreciation of the tones weaving around him deepened.

He began to discern qualities of harmony and rhythm, and was surprised to discover that each individual Singer only created one tone at a time. What these discrete tones did was amazing, though, as they flowed into and out of the tones of the other Singers. There were times when all of the Singers united in one astoundingly rich intonation, only to break into their own unique cadences and tones, again and again.

Most strangely, while focused on the Singers, he seemed to hover in a place out of time, where nothing but their joyous Song existed.

After a while, Droplet dreamily noticed that the intensity and variety of tones around him had diminished. He could still hear the Singers, but now they were only to one side of him.

All at once, in a shocking reorientation, he experienced the rest of The Flow and his own movement again. Large objects sailed by him, and both banks were quite close.

At one point, Droplet felt himself flung away from the Singers, whose tones had become high and thin.

With terrific speed, he pitched and bobbed over and around obstacles in the whirling Flow. There were new sounds around him now, loud thuds and whooshing swishes that seemed to echo, and even foretell, his changes of direction.

His sense of inner calm prevailed though, and for the first time Droplet had a sense of 'riding The Flow,' which Alma had mentioned. Remembering Alma brought a brief flash of sorrow, but it was quickly eclipsed by feeling himself an integral part of The Flow. He found the experience *exhilarating.*

Yes, I am alone again, but I am a part of something moving and brilliant and wondrous, he thought, as he hurtled headlong into his future.

Toward evening, after being halved by a significant divide, the current subsided.

The slower pace allowed him to think more about his situation, including his abrupt departure. He felt a sharp pang of sorrow as he realized that after all of the merges and divides he dimly remembered surging through, it was unlikely he would be able to find his way back to the Rock Shelf Grouping any time soon. And, of course, heading far up-flow to try to follow his friends was now totally out of the question.

As he rounded a large bend, he took a moment to go within and distance-send a message to Nester; a short summary of what had happened, and a goodbye, with his love. He had no way of knowing if Nester would receive it, but he thought he might.

Finally, in a dusky creek, he fell to the bottom of the current and used an attractor-charge to settle himself along the hither bank. Gazing at the thin orb ascending above a distant hill, and feeling in its silvery light the faintest of songs, he fell into a dreamless sleep.

Something woke him in the dark. The orb was no longer visible, and the pale brightening on the far horizon suggested the end of night was near, but he still felt exhausted. He detected a strange buzzing noise near him followed by a soft nudging. He oriented on both and fashioned a sleepy sending.

"Hello?"

After a pause and more buzzing, there was a weak answering charge: "Are you somebody?"

Droplet, struggling to awaken, attempted to focus on his surroundings. He could just make out the shadowy form of an Other. "Yes I am—aren't you?"

"Umm . . ."

The persistent buzzing coupled with this odd response roused him to full wakefulness. *Am I being contacted by Hummers,* he wondered? He instantly switched to esse-sight and saw four discrete, but muted esses hovering near him.

175

Not Hummers, then.

"Yes, yes, of course," came a different sending as one of the four pushed another aside. "We all are." After a brief pause in which the buzzing diminished, this one sent, "We are from the Inlet Grouping, which is just down-flow. Come back with us so we can have more contact with you, won't you?"

Droplet knew he hadn't gotten enough sleep, but the weird buzzing, the plaintive quality of their sendings, and the strange manner of these Others intrigued him.

"All right," he finally sent, "lead the way."

Seventeen

He followed the Others a short distance downstream and into a calm, shallow area near the gradually sloped aft bank; an 'inlet' he supposed. His guides stopped for a moment and sent among themselves.

A scattering of pink-tinged clouds high in Big Blue confirmed the coming of a fair day. Yesterday's intense storm with its unexpected consequences seemed dream-like in the pristine dawn.

As the light increased, Droplet noticed an unusually dark cast to the sand and pebbles near the shore. He turned to ask the Others about it and got a shock: each of the four Others had a shimmering glossiness to them that perfectly reflected the deepening pinks and oranges of Big Blue.

Before he recovered from his surprise, they concluded their brief conference and quickly moved toward the bottom of a wide slab-shaped rock. Then, without even looking his way, they disappeared into the gap between the rock and the black-sand bank.

Droplet, left unaccountably alone, didn't know whether to feel relieved or put-off. They certainly looked strange, and had displayed some unusual traits, but they had also invited him to join them.

As the daylight continued to strengthen, he took another look around and finally approached the big flat, noting its rough texture and noticeably orange cast. *Reflecting the dawn,* he wondered? He paused at the opening, feeling unusually leery.

Finally, his curiosity won out and he moved into the dark recess.

He immediately switched to esse-sight to help him locate the Others, and discovered an unexpectedly large grouping—all with strangely muted esses similar to the four he'd met—

clustered tightly together against the back of the gap.

He moved toward the nearest of them. As soon as he got close, several Others slid into contact with him, each with a odd, slick surface. Immediately he sensed a certain, what, *taste,* he wondered? Then they all moved toward him and he received an onslaught of questions and impressions.

"One at a time please, I can't understand you all at once." His strong sending went directly into the jumble of Others sliding around him.

It took a while, but eventually they made way for one individual, who rolled *over* the rest of them, to connect directly with Droplet.

"Back, back!" he sent to the Others crowding them. Then to Droplet, "I am the Inlet Grouping Elder. Where are you from?"

What kind of a question is that? "I am from The Flow," he finally sent. *Where else could I be from?*

"Yes, of course," came the curt reply, "but which aspect?"

Aspect? "I'm not sure what you mean," admitted Droplet.

"Well, are you from the Clearness, or from another congestion?"

Droplet was mystified, and not particularly comfortable, with the apprehension and wariness he sensed coming from the Elder, not to mention the queer slipperiness of those surrounding him.

"I'm afraid I still don't know what you mean," he answered. "I was recently with the Rock Shelf Grouping, but I got spun into the center of The Flow during a storm, and now I'm here. What is a *congest—*?"

"Oh," interrupted the Elder, "then you're probably all right. I am Elder Zoel, and we are the Inlet Grouping. You are called?"

"Um . . . Droplet."

"Yes, so. Be welcome among us, Droplet. Why don't you come into the center of our grouping so we can get to know you better."

With that, a narrow opening slowly formed in the midst of the tightly-packed grouping.

Even in the shadowed recess, the strengthening daylight beyond the entrance allowed Droplet to get a good look at them. They looked bigger than most Others he'd known, but maybe this was an effect of their uniform glossiness. They also shared a color—an unlikely grayish-green, observable even in the dimness.

Droplet hesitated for a moment, and then moved deeper into the grouping. He noticed moving among them wasn't easy; the surfaces of some of the Others were very slick, while others were sticky.

Eventually, Droplet got to the center of the grouping. With everyone touching everyone else, he was reminded of an evening gathering, but here it was day, and the shared feelings and camaraderie were missing—for him at least. Though they still struck him as quite bizarre, he could sense the affection in the Others around him for one another, and he could tell they were very curious about the newcomer in their midst. All the same, they refrained from mobbing him with their questions—for the most part.

"So," came the sending from one of his guides, who had introduced himself as Kollat. "Welcome to the Inlet Grouping, Droplet. It's always nice to have someone from the Clearness join us. Hopefully, there won't be another Occurrence anytime soon."

"I'm sorry," sent Droplet, still a little flustered with the strange Others and their unfamiliar ways, "I don't know what you're referring to."

"Oh, it's nothing really, or anyway, we're used to it now. But every so often, something enters The Flow here and kind of mucks everything up, if you know what I mean."

"No, I'm afraid I don't." This sounded a bit ominous to him; then again, they were probably just referring to a storm rill or a Great Freeze.

"Well, don't worry about it. It hasn't happened for quite a while now, and may never happen again. We don't get many visitors, won't you tell us about yourself?" This request was seconded by many soft sendings of, "Yes, oh yes!"

Droplet obliged them and tried to relax as he shared some of his past experiences with the tightly packed grouping. It was clear by their reactions that they didn't have much contact with outsiders or the rest of The Flow, and Droplet wondered about that. Even though he felt a little uncomfortable with the intensive contact, he was encouraged by the eagerness of his listeners, and their simple but bountiful questions.

Over the course of the morning, most of it spent sharing his own experiences, Droplet discovered that these Others didn't have much interest in his deeper realizations, but they loved hearing about other groupings and different parts of The Flow.

By that evening, he'd grown more accustomed to their unusual appearance and ways, and he had to admit he enjoyed being the center of their rapt attention.

Although he couldn't imagine staying for long, he thought he'd gladly spend a couple of days with them. He still had quite a few unanswered questions, but he was used to that.

The next day, he asked if someone would show him around the area. Kollat explained they didn't usually go out during the day—something about the bright light and all the colors—but he would be happy to show him around come evening.

At dusk, Kollat took Droplet out of the cleft and into the little inlet. Before the light failed completely, he showed him the larger chunks of black amidst the dark granules of sand, and how the stream's gentle current left the inlet calm.

But Droplet's favorite discovery occurred later when he noticed how lovely the nightsky looked above the dark sand, without any trees or other vegetation to obscure it. Others came out to join them as the slim orb slowly followed it's own current to the far horizon.

They watched together well into the night, as more stars than Droplet had seen since being in Marsh Lake adorned the sparkling expanse above them. *Beautiful.*

The following afternoon, after dredging up yet another story to share with the grouping ensconced in their shadowy recess, Droplet decided he felt ready to move on. Although he'd been welcomed by the Inlet Grouping, they were just too foreign for him to relate to comfortably. He considered the least disruptive way to leave, and had just decided to make a general announcement that evening—giving him one more night with the amazing star-scape—when he detected an unusual tone in the sendings coming from the far side of the tightly packed grouping.

At the same time, a low rumbling noise, which he'd heard intermittently since he'd arrived, grew in intensity. It gradually transformed into a loud booming, which made the ground under them shudder rhythmically.

"What's going on?" Droplet asked a triplet of Others he'd gotten to know.

"Well, we can't be sure," came their reply, "but it could be the beginning of another Occurrence."

"An *Occurrence*—yes, what *is* that?" sent Droplet, wondering if he'd finally be able to get some answers to his questions.

"Well, no one really knows for sure. There are just times when the shaking erupts into something weird."

"Yeah," sent the smallest of the triplets, "something really weird, and not very nice."

"Ah, okay—but what is that noise?"

"That sounds like the noise that tells us an Occurrence is coming." Droplet noticed the furthest triplet becoming agitated.

"Usually we just get the noise," added the closer third reassuringly, "but sometimes the other stuff happens too. Don't worry, you'll get used to it. We all do."

Just as he was about to ask another question, a massive sending arced through the grouping, carrying a powerful sense of fear and urgency.

Droplet, who was still getting used to the interconnectedness of the grouping, was truly astonished by the sending's intensity.

The triplet next to him went into action. "Come on! It's important to get to the inner edge if you can."

Droplet had no idea what the 'inner edge' was, but he started moving as quickly as possible through the slick and sticky Others, and away from the onslaught of fear which was coming from those closest to the opening in increasingly powerful waves. And then *everyone* tried to move away from the opening, which meant no one made progress.

This isn't right. I just need to get away, he realized, giving up his attempt to keep up with the triplets. *But which way?* He caught a glimpse of Kollat moving deeper into the cleft. He spotted an open space toward one of the sides and labored to move toward it.

This is almost like a bad dream, he thought, as wave after wave of fear moved into him through his constant contact with those he was now actively trying to escape. Although his effort did not abate, his progress slowed to nothing. In his distress, he even attempted a blind repulsion-charge, but he didn't budge.

The booming trembling around him became horribly loud and then came to a jolting halt. Thinking the worst had passed, Droplet was completely unprepared for what happened next.

The fear coming at him, magnified by the entire grouping, exploded into *panic.* Then the physical vibrations returned with a high-pitched screech.

Now everything shook and roared.

The waves of dread from those around him came on so strong Droplet could barely think, much less attempt to move.

He tried to resist, to maintain some kind of inner clarity, but his naturally strong ability to connect with Others had become a raging conduit that he couldn't break. It took all of his strength to reach his Inner Sanctum, but he couldn't stay there; the intensity surging through him catapulted him out of any state of refuge.

Ultimately, he was besieged. By terror.

It swamped him; crashed through him.

Again and again, excruciating torrents of terror lanced into him from the panicked Others struggling around him.

He was awash with their fear, adrift in a sea of formless dread. He existed only in the in-between place where dreams and reality meet. And his present experience was now the stuff of unrelenting nightmare.

Then, without warning, the sound, the vibration, the intensity all ceased. The debilitating fear-waves coming from the Others dropped abruptly to an eerie flatness.

Although he'd only rarely sensed it in Others, he immediately identified the dark emotion now spreading like a stain through the tightly packed grouping.

Despair.

As the feeling intensified, he looked up to see a thick, glistening blackness creeping toward him from the opening. He became truly desperate to get away from the grouping, and away from the dreadful blackness which seemed to be extinguishing the Others as it approached.

He was still struggling to distance himself from both the dark emotions and the wretched Others, when the blackness overtook him.

At this point something deep inside of him sundered and broke loose.

Along with the total absence of light, came a penetrating, bitter *taste*, accompanied by the slow, absolute silencing of contact with the Others around him.

Some time later, the roaring and vibration started-up again, then lessened and retreated, but Droplet hardly noticed.

He was overcome; completely depleted.

Droplet couldn't move.

He couldn't even generate a sending, much less a repulsion-charge.

He could barely think.

Unable to see or communicate, for the first time since his state-change, he was utterly at the mercy of his environment; and it was an ugly, apathetic one.

Like a *bloated-floater* sinking into the depths of a storm-ravaged lake, Droplet slid into shocked despair.

Until finally, of a mercy, he lost consciousness.

Interlude

A few days later, the human clean-up crew came to the Pebble Gulch area, near the location of Droplet and the Inlet Grouping.

The crew talked as they emptied several drums of hydrogen peroxide into the shallows to neutralize the toxic sludge that a nearby factory had "accidentally leaked" into the river.

Again.

They discussed the pending lawsuit as they assessed the damage; all agreed it was about time. This *had* to stop.

They worked hard to help the birds and wildlife affected, and lamented the loss of fish and damaged habitat. When they were done, they poured dark granules of activated carbon into the river to counteract what remained of the slick murkiness and putrid smell of the pollutants.

After a few hours of work, they left the area altered, the river's charcoal grey bed contrasting oddly with its yellow-foamed surface.

Unnatural as it looked now, the clean-up crew knew the chemical processes which would slowly cleanse the river were well underway.

Given time, they agreed, this river would run clear again.

Eighteen

⚜

A fluttering motion. Then the confusing, surreal sensation of heaviness. And dimness. *Why can't I see?*

The burgeoning memory of something frightening, unstoppable, overwhelming. A harsh, bitter *taste.*

Why can't I move? I must get away!

Struggling to move wrenched Droplet out of his semi-conscious dream state, and back into nightmare. With full consciousness, swirling memory arrived. With memory, he plummeted again into fear, where his mind spun out of control for a long time, before reeling away into emptiness.

Droplet awoke again. But unable to make sense of what had happened to him, he fell back into dismay.

There he stayed.

Mute, frustrated, helpless, his mind drifted endlessly in and out of tormented near-lucidity, until he again lost consciousness.

The next time his awareness returned, there was a little more light. This was both a boon and a curse.

He could see, yes, but things didn't look right; everything appeared wavy and distorted, as if seen through a greenish crystal khoot.

And he was still firmly stuck to the Others around him; goopy, dark-tinged, misshapen Others. *I must get away!*

Over and over again, the impulse to move caught him up short. Like a twig snared in a tight eddy, his mind kept circling through the recent horror of being trapped, while overwhelming emotional sendings surged into him, tore through him.

And then the unstoppable blackness descending and covering them all; the *Occurrence*, he eventually realized.

I must get away!

By the time he had gained some inner distance from his blasted emotions, he knew he wasn't thinking clearly—was he even thinking at all? And why couldn't he stop reliving the whole grizzly ordeal in his mind—the intense waves of terror and helplessness, along with the advancing blackness?

Finally, it occurred to him that what he'd experienced in some ways resembled an exceedingly strange state-change, and after any state-change some disorientation is normal. *Right?* This thought helped him stabilize.

He slept deeply.

Droplet's next awareness arrived with the new day. He tried to stay calm as the light gave him his first wavy look at the inlet. The surface of The Flow beyond the cleft looked very strange—foamy, orange-brown, and still.

This was more disturbing than anything he'd experienced so far. *Even The Flow is changed? How can that be? This* is *a nightmare!*

He worked to accept his strange reality; so like a dream but not a dream.

Finally he succeeded in quieting his anxious thoughts when he received a weak, unintelligible sending from one of the Others next to him. In a flash, the entire experience of the Occurrence flooded back into his mind in vivid detail.

The impulse to jerk away only made it worse. He shut-off his awareness of the Others touching him, and he gradually calmed himself yet again.

His moment-by-moment experience had become an aching contest—sometimes skillful, sometimes desperate—with the foamy, orange-tinged specter of fear.

Over the course of the next few days, Droplet worked hard to increase his tolerance and accept his situation, difficult as it was.

Panic continued to stalk him like a curious flasher; he couldn't out-swim it, but he could hide, and if he stayed very still it might pass him by.

Eventually, largely due to overload and sheer exhaustion, his panic reactions began to subside—most of the time.

Thinking about his favorite past experiences usually helped, but panic, along with its troublesome friends fear and despair, could still snag him if he wasn't very careful.

And of course, sometimes even when he was.

He found the continued unpredictability of his inner state very nearly as maddening as the constraints of his outer circumstance.

Droplet's next dilemma had to do with the weak communications now coming regularly from the Inlet Others, to whom he was still physically bound. He quickly discovered that their attempts to share what they were thinking and feeling could trigger an emotional ambush in him.

Repeated sendings like, "Oh no, the worst has happened. The very worst. What are we going to do? Oh no, the worst has happened; how can it be? . . ." really unsettled him. His susceptibility to this subsided slowly as his ability to manage his reactions improved, but he had no desire whatsoever to respond to them.

Since the Occurrence, what he felt for those he was stuck to had degraded from annoyance to disgust.

Just another of the many lovely emotions I've never felt before, he thought, adding self-pity to the list.

As the long days passed, The Flow gradually cleared. But the clearness hadn't worked its way into the cleft yet, so Droplet was still immobile.

His experience of utter stuck-ness—inside and out—led him to believe that he was lost or at least truly damaged. His former self—free, curious, expressive—existed only in memory. *An illusory glory,* he mused, *bouncing off the surface of The Flow and then vanishing.*

Increasingly, the bitterness he *tasted* around him became a part of his thoughts and moods.

As he slowly regained the ability to think more clearly, his anger and resentment blossomed. *How could these Others stay here when they knew another Occurrence might happen? Why weren't they honest about it? And more importantly, why didn't they warn me? What's wrong with them?*

Still their circular sendings continued. "Are you there, Tiggs? That was the worst one ever, don't you think? Will it ever clear? Where is Banly?"

He'd become an island of silence in their midst.

And not one of them has even tried to contact me directly, he thought with annoyance, as he worked to further insulate himself from their constant chatter.

The intensity of his reaction to the pitiful Others around him made him realize he was still far from clear-headed; he acknowledged he had more work to do.

And, of course, stuck as he was, and essentially blind, Droplet had lots of time in which to do it.

One of his greatest frustrations was his inability to go into his Inner Sanctum. He consistently found that though he could vaguely sense the place of inner calm, he couldn't actually locate it within himself, much less enter it. This penetrating loss he tried to mollify with the thought, *I'm probably too agitated to get much good out of being there anyway.*

To his increasing surprise, not to mention his acute frustration, Droplet found he *still* couldn't stop reliving all of the intense fear and panic he'd experienced before, and during, the Occurrence.

What's wrong with me? Why won't this stop?

More days passed; harsh, dim, and difficult.

Droplet continued to cycle unpredictably through his full range of overwhelming emotions.

He finally admitted to himself that the Occurrence had changed him in ways he could barely accept. His physical changes were hard enough: his reduced vision, his thick feeling, and of course, still being stuck fast to the Others around him. But his inner changes—the haunting fear and near constant state of agitation—were intolerable. And nothing seemed to help. Respite in his Inner Sanctum remained stubbornly out of reach, and even his dreams were strangely absent

With very little else to do, Droplet starting living more and more in his memories; by reliving his past he could recall the simple joys of being unconfined, calm and connected to himself in ways which were totally absent now.

While happy memories brought him a measure of peace, Droplet remained determined to leave the area as soon as he could. He remembered the longing he'd felt as a foundling: to move unfettered, and by his own will through The Flow.

To be free again eventually became his only goal.

Day-by-day, he would practice moving just a little bit more. He discovered that a simple rocking motion seemed to help loosen him, and also served to quiet the Others around him.

Rocking—moving on his own once again—gave him a measured hope as he worked tirelessly to extract himself.

Finally, during an interminable rocking trance, Droplet gently separated from the Others he had been stuck to for so long.

He rolled away, shocked and then elated—until he discovered that the sticky, bitter, opaque coating he was so eager to leave behind, left with him.

And his vision was still impaired.

How did that happen? He tried rolling around on the gravel beyond the cleft in an attempt to get the weird oiliness off him.

In rolling, he discovered something even more alarming: his mobility was affected. The coating he was unable to shed interfered with his ability to send directional attractor- or repulsion-charges. For the first time since his early days of learning to move, he felt sluggish and clumsy.

He edged laboriously away from the Inlet, attempting to reach a tendril of the current he could sense nearby. He tired long before he felt the whisper of current, so he rested and worked again to try to come to terms with his experience.

How can the Occurrence still be affecting me? Surely it can't have changed me that much!

His fatigue and state of overwhelm combined to undermine his relief at rolling free. Slowly, and against his will, he slid back into despair.

Dreamless night came as the perfect complement.

The increasing light brought him renewed determination, if not the beginnings of actual hope. By laboring all morning, he had finally reached the weak central current, and after several attempts he was able to feebly *hurl* himself into it.

Watching the grayish-orange bank slowly slide by was a mixed blessing, but by mid-day his low mood had lifted along with the freshening current.

The further away he got from the Inlet Others, the better he felt, and he noticed his vision starting to clear a little as well. *Maybe I can return to my old self yet*, he thought, more heartened than he'd been at any time since before the Occurrence.

He rode the temperamental current the rest of that day and into the next. During the afternoon of the second day, he left the current and sidled up to a long thin plant at the edge of a deep, sandy trench.

He hadn't seen any creatures in quite a while—not since before the Occurrence, he realized—but at the bottom of the trench he noticed a couple of exceptionally large, whiskered flashers slowly pulsing their fins.

The Flow here felt and *tasted* different; even this far down-flow from the Occurrence, he could still detect its subtle bitterness around him. It also looked different from anything he'd experienced before, both wider and slower, with very little vegetation, other than the occasional droopy tree overhanging the banks. In spite of being wide and open, it looked dim.

Droplet couldn't tell if there was still a yellowish-grey-green tinge to his vision, or if this part of The Flow was just that color. Then he realized that the low clouds *beyond* The Flow also looked grayish-yellow, and had his answer.

He worked his way back into the current and made his slow, lonely way through the oddly lifeless stream.

Late in the day, he spied the first Others he'd seen since leaving the Inlet. He watched the small grouping congregating near the shallows for a moment, but when he imagined making contact he shied away, unseen.

A little further on, he noticed a single Other and decided to approach.

"Hello" he sent, startling the Other a bit.

The Other seemed to peer at him for a moment and then bounded back with a sharp repulsion-charge exclaiming, "Ugh, get away! I don't want to have anything to do with your kind."

"My *kind*?" asked Droplet, reeling from the charge and unaccountably embarrassed.

"Yes, *tainted*, of course."

"*Tainted*? What is *tainted*?" he asked with a sinking feeling.

"You are! You have the dark glossiness of taint, and that weird, bitter taste. You should stay away from Others—don't you know that?" The Other abruptly terminated the sending and moved away.

Well, that didn't go well, he observed wryly, as he maneuvered himself to reenter the current. His vision and mobility had been steadily improving, and he'd allowed himself to think that his recent time in the current—lethargic as it was—had washed him clean.

But clearly it had not.

He knew he'd been changed by the Occurrence, but he hadn't realized how indelible those changes might be. Even though he had left it far behind, somehow it *still* hadn't left him. And that ugly term—*tainted*—carried a whole host of horrible feelings with it: changelessness, helplessness, remorse and shame.

As he tried to wrap his mind around this new set of restraints, it occurred to him that he might never be welcomed by Others of his kind again.

Suddenly overcome, he stopped by the bank, and let the aching sorrow of everything he'd lost—friends, groupings, beloved elders—wash through him until evening came, and he slid into sleep.

That night his returning dreams were troubled, and he woke in the middle of the night with the sad realization that even his dreams had become tainted. He realized that though his days in The Flow were totally uneventful now, the Occurrence still lurked menacingly in his nights. He could be dreaming about something quite pleasant, then be overcome by a smothering sticky darkness; or get shunned by Others who had just been friendly; or suddenly feel terror shoot through him for no apparent reason.

He stayed awake a long time thinking about how he might be able to alter or adapt to his new circumstances, but no insights came.

The next morning he woke to a brighter day, but the first thing he noticed was the bitter taste about him.

It is *me*, he realized, dismay seeping back into his awareness. The more he thought about it, the angrier he got. *I still can't believe this has happened to me!*

But, surely I won't always be this way, he finally reasoned. Then, a little while later, the unthinkable emerged, unbidden: *What if I do stay this way? What if I can't get un-tainted?*

He swirled in and out of dark thoughts until he eventually realized he wasn't getting anywhere—either in his mind or physically. So, he resolved to continue on downstream, and try to think about other things until something changed or he got more information.

After a long, uneventful day, he found a place to spend the night. But as soon as he stopped moving, he dropped back into ragged purls of troubled thought.

Why, this is almost as hard as it was during the Occurrence itself, he acknowledged with mounting frustration. *Am I forever destined to struggle with the Occurrence, when I just want to put it behind me?*

He had no answers, and he finally slid into sleep. Toward morning he came into partial wakefulness, and then felt the peculiar sideways wrench that instantly plunged him into his fifth super-vivid extreme dream of a creature utterly unlike him:

> *I stop quietly stripping bark. The sharp call of a winged one has alerted me. Quivering slightly, I strain my senses into the shadowed places in the brush around the stand of trees. There, beneath a far bush, I spot a predator approaching one careful step at a time. I must get to my home quickly, but I am slow on land and far from silent. I slowly edge toward safety, waiting to see if there is other prey for this spotted grabber. Suddenly there is a thump, and*

several furry ones flee. The spotted grabber gives chase and I am safe for the moment. But the grabber has chosen this place to hunt, and it is best to leave. I clutch the succulent strips of bark in my strong jaws and turn unerringly toward home. I move as quickly as I can, long tendrils of bark trailing behind me like the wake I make in the home pond. Finally I approach safety. With an eager leap I enter the river, blocked and widened by the work I've done with trees and branches. Before I dive to my home, I slap my flat tail on the surface to sound the warning to my mate. Then I dive into the welcome depths . . .

The dive into what was also *his* home brought Droplet into full wakefulness. He reviewed the astoundingly rich physical sensations of this extreme dream experience, and was surprised to discover he felt oddly comforted by its 'otherness'. This creature had focus, interests, purpose. He dimly recalled having those . . .

Just as he was drifting off, he remembered observing this actual creature shortly after arriving at Rock Shelf; it was a *four-legged builder*, or a *tail-slapper*, he remembered, thinking fondly of his friends Alma, Disk and Bobb. He drifted back to sleep, accompanied by pleasant memories of better times.

The next day, Droplet moved along the edge of The Flow, deep in thought. At one point, he came to a small grouping of Others who also called him tainted and moved away, unwilling to get close enough to interact with him. This was less surprising than the first time it had happened, but still disheartening.

How am I ever going to get the answers I need, if no one can tolerate being near me?

After that, Droplet's days became indistinguishable from one another. He let himself be idly borne by the sluggish current, which perfectly reflected his mood. The hazy sunlight and lack of vegetation helped him easily identify and avoid any Others he came across. Without realizing it, he had dropped into a deep, mindless despair.

He glided along listlessly until he came to a divide in The Flow. He peered ahead and almost randomly chose the smaller fork—mostly because the hither bank he'd been following veered that way.

Shortly after the divide, the aft bank of this smaller Flow started to rise into a rocky cliff and the current picked up a bit. This eased his dark mood slightly, but he remained mired in gloom.

Another change in his surroundings finally captured his attention. On the aft side, the cliff had gotten taller, while the hither bank sported a number of large, leafy trees. At the base of the trees and saplings, clumps of green-tinged flowers grew, some dipping gently over The Flow. Above him, dark-winged flyers darted between the trees or soared to the cliff; if he listened carefully he could discern their calls. High above all, Big Blue looked vast and blue-green.

The sweet loveliness of this place penetrated his loneliness, but it also hurt.

Memories of joy, and the beauty around him, sharpened the contrast between who he used to be and his current state. *Even though there is beauty here,* he realized sadly, *I can't appreciate it because there is something wrong with me. I am damaged; no, I'm tainted and lost.*

These thoughts were too painful to consider for more than a moment or two, and his consciousness retreated, allowing him the flat, simple relief of semi-awareness.

Droplet moved slowly and randomly along the tree-shaded bank and into a stretch of dense vegetation, where he discovered several groupings of tiny, startlingly-fast flashers dashing about. He stopped to watch for a while, comforted by their innocent activity. Then he traveled slowly on.

Toward evening, he came across two Hummers near some plants in a little dell. He hadn't seen any Hummers since well before the Occurrence, and he approached them slowly, sure they would avoid him as Others did now.

Through cautious experimentation, he discovered that although they always gradually moved away to avoid being too near, they didn't seem to mind his presence among them.

Over the next few days, he became accustomed to them. They never focused on anything he could see, nor did they attempt to communicate with him, but neither were they difficult or demanding in any way.

In truth, they barely seemed to register his existence, yet he intuitively felt they accepted him. *Wishful thinking perhaps,* he admitted to himself.

Nonetheless, he found their monotonous, atonal humming soothing and comforting. As the days slid by, he stopped wondering about them, tried to stop thinking so much in general, and finally began to relax.

Of course, this wasn't anything like being with his own kind, but it was a far sight better than being actively shunned and reviled.

Who knows, perhaps I can learn to 'hum' myself better, he thought, as he watched a sprinkling of stars emerge at the end of his fourth day with the Hummers. For if there was one thing he truly understood, it was that in his damaged state, he wasn't a good companion to himself or anyone else.

He gradually willed his fears and worries to leave him, and tried to release himself to the gentle humming of his companions. Very slowly he worked at just letting himself go—the way he'd released the bit of Big Blue stuck inside of him so long ago—calmly, gently, willingly.

Eventually, he found a dreamy kind of peace.

Days later, that's how they found him, a glossy, grey-green Other, hidden among plant stalks near a couple of Hummers. Humming for all he was worth.

Nineteen

⦿

D roplet struggled weakly.
"There now, friend. Rest easy. You're safe now." But he wasn't. He couldn't move and he couldn't see, which reminded him of . . .

In a sudden torrent, horrible memories of the Occurrence tore through him and he sent blindly.

"Easy, easy. Relax. You're safe now. Nothing bad can happen to you here." This sending seemed to come from within him, and it carried unmistakable calm. Even though he didn't recognize the sender, something deep inside of him responded and started to relax.

"That's right. That's right." Then, just as his consciousness started to slide away, he received his first ever melodic sending: *"You're safe, you're safe, you're in a good place. I'm here, I'm here, there's nothing to fear."*

As the words and melody repeated over and over, he grew accustomed to the simple tune, and allowed its gentle message of hope to lull him back into a blessedly dreamless sleep.

The next time he struggled to wake, he heard different words with the now familiar melody: *"I'm here, I'm here, there's nothing to fear. Relax, relax, I will stay near."*

Again he felt eased, and deeply held; he released himself to sleep.

The third time his awareness returned, he noticed the melody had changed a bit and he heard: *"You're here, I'm here, you're perfectly safe. Release, relax, let go of your fear."*

He listened in a dreamy state for a while until the gentle call to action in this sending helped rouse him. But when he came into full consciousness, he immediately discovered he still couldn't see or move.

Before he panicked, the Being next to him sent a calming charge with, "There you are, now. You're safe with me and you're on the mend. Stay calm—caaaalm yourself. Gather your thoughts now, and try to send."

"Wha . . . Where am I?"

"Good, my friend, good. You are in Steadfast; here with me, in my healing alcove."

"What's wrong with me? Why can't I see or move?"

"Because it is totally dark here, we are deep within a rock cliff. And I have you securely wedged into the narrow end of my alcove. Here, I will move so that you can."

With that, the Other next to him withdrew contact, leaving Droplet feeling strangely bereft, but also able to move again. *Clumsily*, he noted, as he aimed a weak repulsion-charge at the wall behind him. The movement, slight though it was, helped anchor his awareness to his physical form.

"There—you see?" came the quiet sending from nearby. "You are still weak, but you're mending now, and will be your old self in time."

This sending, and the bitter taste he'd become aware of as he'd moved, didn't particularly cheer him. He stayed silent as the Other moved right next to him again.

Sensing his consternation, the Other sent, "Yes, I know, it's not easy, but I will help you."

"But . . . I'm . . . tainted . . ."

"No, *not* tainted, and your strange taste doesn't bother me. Once you are whole again, you will feel much better. Rest now and we'll talk more later."

Droplet felt the soothing balm of this sending and had just started to relax when his fragile sense of self was capsized by a surge of fear.

"You won't leave me?" he sent frantically.

"No, no, of course not. I will stay with you until you are whole once again, *as I believe and know you will be*. Here, let us go back into the narrow end of my alcove where I will hold you secure."

Together they edged back into the slight indentation at the end of the alcove. Droplet felt immediately comforted by the solid rock around him again and the close contact of the Other.

"But, who *are* you?" he asked, trying to fight his sudden

exhaustion.

"Why, I am Dahzi, friend, and I am the one who will help you heal."

"Oh." Just before the need to sleep completely overcame him, he added, "Thank you. I'm Droplet."

After that, Droplet worked each day to regain his former self, always aided and comforted by the constant, yet enigmatic, presence of Dahzi.

There was something unique about Dahzi, some exotic quality that attracted Droplet and made the work he hadn't been able to do on his own seem appealing and important. He wanted to return to himself—if only to please his healer, whose total and calm acceptance of him called him to greater and greater effort.

"No, it is done this way," Dahzi sent patiently, as they worked together in the deep privacy of his alcove. "You make tones into melody, and then combine the melody *with* the words, thus. In this way you add power of intent. And through this, healing is aided."

Droplet struggled to duplicate the simple melody in Dahzi's sending. What Dahzi did was similar to, but substantially more complex and purposeful, than the singular tones he'd experienced with the Singers. And instead of pulling him away from his center, Dahzi's songs drew him into it. *How does he do that*, he wondered, for the twelfth time.

"Here, do with me. Together now: *All is well, I can tell, all is well.* With me. Relax more. Again."

He relaxed and let the worded melody sink into him. After another few repetitions, something unclenched in him, allowing the words and the melody to *merge* together into a seamless sending. *Oh!*

"Good, yes. Again." As they chanted the words with their simple notes together over and over, Droplet felt the stirring of long dormant emotions.

"Now change: *I am safe, I can know, I can feel. I can be who I am, I can heal.*"

They repeated this several times until Droplet could mimic it perfectly.

"Yes. Now *feel* the words with the melody *inside* of you, and try it on your own."

Droplet turned his awareness within—in a long practiced, but recently neglected habit—and *sang* his intent on his own for the very first time. "*I am safe, I can know, I can feel. I can be who I am, I can heal.*"

After this, Dahzi had him sing it to himself many times, as deeply as he could. At one point the power of it touched him profoundly, and he felt something within him click into place.

He stopped suddenly and sent, "Is that it? Am I healed now?"

"Why no, friend," Dahzi replied calmly. "This is just the beginning of the Journey of Return for you. But you are doing well. Truly. Now again, *I am safe . . .*"

As they practiced this and other simple-worded melodies on and off for the rest of the day, Droplet gained a much deeper understanding of what *song* truly was. *Not even close to what the Singers do,* he realized. *In fact, if this is* song, *they aren't really* Singers *at all!*

That night, as Droplet drifted off to sleep, the words and tunes of the day curled and trailed through his dreams. At one point, his dreams shifted into nightmare as they often did since the Occurrence, but Dahzi, right next to him as always, offered a song to gentle the darkness inside him.

Not entirely asleep, Droplet observed in wonder, as the simple melody turned the mounting fear within him into scattered wisps that lingered for a moment and then faded away. *I've got to learn how he does that . . .* but before he could ask, an easier sleep claimed him.

"Yes, as I said before, we are within the Steadfast Grouping. A large collection of individuals as different from one another as you could imagine. Once we both agree you are ready, you are welcome to join them. Until then, let us concentrate on your healing, shall we?"

They were still in Dahzi's alcove, and after five days of intense work, Droplet had become restless.

"But when will I be able to see for myself?"

"Why, anytime, friend. You are not restricted to this place."

Dahzi focused on him closely. "Would you like to go now?"

"Yes, I think I would." Droplet didn't feel quite so restless all of a sudden.

"Very well, I shall summon oc-Vardic to accompany you. One moment."

A short time later, Dahzi returned with only the second Other Droplet had seen since he'd awakened.

"This is oc-Vardic, and he is most happy to take you anywhere you want to go."

"Um, you won't be joining us?"

"No, my place is here, and here is where I am perfectly content to be. I will await your return, friend."

Leaving turned out to be harder than Droplet thought it would be, but he plucked up his courage and let the silent oc-Vardic lead him through a narrow tunnel and into several large chambers, all connected to one another.

The light was very dim and he didn't actually see much, but he got a sense of the scope of the place, which was very grand. He saw only a few Others, and just barely, in the far recesses. His ability to sense esses was still gone, he discovered with dismay, so he had no way of knowing if there were Others nearby that he couldn't see.

"Can you take me out? Ah, into the main Flow, please?"

Oc-Vardic grunted and led him along an upwardly sloped tunnel, until they emerged into the familiar current of The Flow. Droplet saw that it was early evening, and stars were just starting to peek through the nightsky. He thought they looked a little less green and grey than they had the last time he'd seen them, and found this encouraging.

After a few moments more, he asked oc-Vardic to return him to Dahzi's alcove.

"It seemed kind of empty," Droplet replied to Dahzi's inquiry after he'd returned.

"Yes, right now, it probably is. And you weren't gone long enough to visit more than one or two chambers, yes?"

"Yes. I, um, wanted to go out—to feel The Flow's current around me for a moment."

"Good. That is good. Now let's practice more healing tunes, shall we?"

After singing all of the earlier tunes and then learning several lovely new ones, they both agreed Droplet now had the ability to let the words and melodies touch him in what Dahzi called, "the inner place where healing resides."

Shortly after this, Dahzi determined that Droplet was ready for more advanced healing. While offering ongoing support and direction, Dahzi had him practice recalling the Occurrence using different shifts of perception.

First he had Droplet observe the Occurrence as if from a great distance, making it appear tiny and insignificant. Then he had Droplet imagine learning about it from a story told to him by someone else, while reacting with interest. Then he helped Droplet add and subtract sounds to the experience, change the taste from bitter to sweet, and create playful new visual images—like viewing the event upside-down, adding surprising new characters, or making the entire experience only last an instant or two.

Finally, he had Droplet alter the emotional current of his experience—first by viewing the emotions in an abstract way without feeling them, then by increasing their intensity like a flood, then stopping them like a freeze, and finally by bringing them down to a trickle.

At the end of this intensive exercise, Droplet felt tired, but also eased somehow, as if his fixed and difficult memories had become more natural and fluid.

Two days, and a lot more work later, Droplet hit an inner barrier. They had been discussing his past experiences, including several of the meaningful relationships he'd had—with Alma, Nester and ... and that's where he got blocked.

"What is that? Just there—what happened?"

"I'm not really sure, Dahzi. I was going to tell you about my wonderful teacher—but I can't seem to say his name."

"Ah. Then this is the next part of what must be healed. And I believe you are ready, are you not?"

Droplet thought before answering. He knew he had made good progress; he felt increasingly strong and clear, and knew that Dahzi believed he was nearly ready to complete healing what had been injured inside of him during the Occurrence. But why was it hard to talk about Wise Elder—his most important friend and teacher?

"Yes," he finally answered, "I am."

"Good. Then let us look at the fear that emerges when you think of your dearest relationship. What do you believe this teacher would think of what you have been through?"

And then it hit him. Without warning, the full devastation of the Occurrence swept through him again—the terror, the helplessness, the loss. Most especially, now, the piercing, aching loss. After Dahzi stabilized him with an intricately beautiful song, he knew how to answer.

"I believed I was being *annihilated*, Dahzi."

"Ah. And this word, *annihilated,* it means to be destroyed, yes?"

"Yes," Droplet answered, very softly.

"But has no-one ever told you that, regardless of what happens to your physical form, *you*, your esse, is indestructible?"

"Yes, I have been told that . . . by him. But why was I so afraid if I wasn't truly in danger? I am—*ashamed*—that I was so weak, so overwhelmed, so vulnerable."

"And it is this shame that holds you back now. You must accept what happened to you, *and* your reactions to it, my friend. Without acceptance, you cannot heal." Dahzi paused and looked deeply into Droplet. "Does it not occur to you that all you truly lost in the Occurrence was your innocence? Think of this. Until that point, your experience contained only the lighter emotions. Happiness, curiosity, optimism, affection, and joy were what you felt most, yes?"

"Yes . . ." he answered slowly, "along with annoyance and frustration, at times."

"Like I said, the *lighter* emotions. But they are only one side of the emotional spectra. And you are highly sensitive, are you not? Imagine then, a highly sensitive Being completely unprepared to handle either the intensity or the quality of the darker emotions surging into him from a collective of Others during a terrifying event.

"Add to this being stuck, unable to retreat or get away, with no means of handling the sheer onslaught of sendings. See that something deep inside of this unwilling participant pulls loose in a desperate attempt to shield and protect what is most precious . . . And, if this weren't already enough, my friend, add the aftereffect of being shunned as tainted by

Others of his kind, who are themselves frightened of the darker sides of their own natures. Now, tell me this. What has this one to be ashamed of?"

During Dahzi's energetic recounting of his ordeal, Droplet felt his inner self ascend to a high precipice. To one side of him, he saw the familiar fall into all the dark emotions Dahzi had just described so clearly. To the other side, he felt something so tender and so precious it took him a moment to identify it: Wise Elder's complete and uncompromising acceptance of him.

And in that moment, he knew Dahzi was right—his shame *was* unnecessary. Like choosing the wrong fork in a divide, it was simply an error, and an error can be corrected.

Finally he came to the truth: there was no shame in what had happened to him either during or after the Occurrence—it just happened, and he'd handled it as best he could.

Dahzi tracked this point of change in him and then sent, "Good, that is *much* better. But let's finish this, shall we? With your permission, I will join you as we go to that within you which is sundered, yes?"

Droplet steadied himself. Then he opened himself completely to this gentle healer he had so come to respect and trust. Together, they moved in the direction of Droplet's Inner Sanctum until they came to an empty place, a void.

:Now, this is where we will use song, my friend, for some part of you is in hiding and needs to return. And song or music is a powerful unifier. In your deepest mind, with all of the beauty of your being, sing forth with me the part of you which became lost during your overwhelming experience in the Occurrence.

In the beginning, nothing happened as they sang one of the first songs Droplet had learned from Dahzi. During the initial repetitions, he had only the awareness of blankness, or an emptiness, inside of him where none should be.

Grappling with doubt, Droplet struggled to maintain the open inner stance that he had learned healing required. *"You're safe, you're safe . . ."*

Then slowly, as they established a powerful resonance together of intent, melody and welcome, something—some delicate alignment—slipped back into Droplet's awareness.

:Yes. Now truly welcome it back; this part of you that is

bereft without you, as you are without it. Let the light of your esse shine on you and let your bond be healed, your union sealed. Now, to help, we will sing with all the loving intention we can offer, a simple song of truth:

Out of one, there came two, and separation grew.
Then from two back to one, with Love it is done.
You are now as before, your True Self once more."

As they repeated this lovely song over and over together, they entered a place of timelessness where their combined focus, along with the power of Wise Elder's unconditional acceptance, and all of the Love Droplet had ever given or received, allowed the healing to be complete.

When they finished, Droplet felt a surge of joy unlike any he had ever experienced. Speechless with wonder, he simply shone his gratitude and his love. Dahzi's beautiful, golden esse shone as well.

A short time later they were on the move.

Twenty

⊶⊷◇⊶⊷

"Now you must come to know Steadfast," Dahzi sent as he led the way into the large, dim chamber oc-Vardic had taken Droplet through earlier. But this time, with his esse-sight returned, he could see that it wasn't empty at all. There were Others everywhere, at least three twelves of them, mostly along the sides in ones and twos.

"This is Central Commons. It is our largest chamber, and where Steadfasters can come together every twelve-day or so."

"So, you have Evening Gatherings here?" Droplet asked looking around.

"I'm not sure what you mean by this term. But we do come together—those who wish it—when Sol is directly over the largest crevasse above this chamber. In this way there is sufficient light to see one another, but also enough shadow to allow comfort."

This brought up a whole host of questions, but before he could ask them, two Others left the wall and moved purposefully toward them. As they approached, Dahzi moved to Droplet's side and distance sent, "Oc-Logil and oc-Vamer, let me present our newest arrival, who calls himself Droplet."

The larger of the two reached them first and sent, "Droplet, is it? Be welcome to Steadfast. Has oc-Dahzi explained our group structure to you yet?"

Oc-Dahzi?

"No, we have just emerged from my healing alcove," Dahzi replied on his behalf.

"That's fine, oc-Dahzi. We can take it from here, if you wish."

Dahzi turned to a surprised Droplet and sent, "This is probably best, friend, for there is much to explain. When you are done, request my alcove and someone will take you there." And with that, Droplet's only friend in this place turned and left.

Oc-Vamer moved closer to Droplet and sent, "Ah, I can tell you are an Occurrence *fleer*—either Inlet, Shadow Cove, or perhaps even Bione Slope. Am I right?"

"Um, yes, I was in the Inlet Occurrence," Droplet replied, as something inside him shuddered slightly.

"You taste of it, and you are probably glossy and oily too."

Before Droplet could respond to this indelicate sending, oc-Logil sent, "Don't mind oc-Vamer, Droplet, he doesn't intend to be rude, that's just his way. You will find most of us Steadfasters to be honest and plain-spoken. Some newcomers like it, some don't, but eventually most grow to appreciate it— for it is far better than the alternative." Oc-Logil watched as Droplet grasped the meaning of this, and then he continued.

"So, you probably don't know much about us—most newcomers don't. We, of the Steadfast Grouping, are a community of *insulars*. Each of us has been reviled by Others of 'our kind' in The Flow beyond our rock barrier. Cast-out of their acceptance, we claim ourselves, with pride, to be *outcasts*.

"Belonging to Steadfast, which we signify by adding 'oc' to our name, means we don't ever have to suffer hostility and rejection, for we only choose to interact with those who are truly like us. Within these chambers we are free of the strictures and dictates of normalcy. Here, we are at liberty to accept and appreciate differences in how we look and think. Here, we can be exactly who and what we are."

Droplet, nonplussed, stared around the indistinct chamber for a moment. The two Others watched him in turn. Then, in a flash of understanding, he sent, "So, you shun Others, the way they shun you?" This ingenious way of handling something as painful as being shunned immediately appealed to him.

"Indeed we do," sent oc-Vamer, his pleasure evident in his sending. "Come, let us show you the rest of Steadfast."

That began a truly educational experience for Droplet. He learned Steadfast existed deep within the base of a cliff fronted by The Flow, and it contained six large, submerged chambers and many smaller ones, each with its own special population or function.

First, they reentered the Receiver's Chamber—complete with a network of small but deep alcoves, one of which was Dahzi's—where skilled healer/menders received newcomers. Droplet learned that most new arrivals to Steadfast were mentally disoriented, emotionally overwrought, or physically damaged, and more than a few were all three. Different healers/menders had different specialties, and several healers, such as Dahzi, were wise in the ways of inner healing and reintegration. Once a newcomer had been *revived*, they began the orientation process. Of course, they could always leave Steadfast, but very few chose to.

From there, oc-Logil and oc-Vamer took Droplet to the Event Survivors' Chambers—a series of smaller spaces containing sub-groupings of those who had been through different Occurrences and other horrible experiences. Droplet, immediately repelled by the strong, bitter tastes in these chambers, a few of which were far too familiar, asked to leave before they were approached by any of the Others there.

Next, they visited the Chambers of the Incomplete; several smallish chambers—oddly filled with the random sendings of those who had improperly emerged, partially crested, or had some form of mental deficit—plus their caregivers. Droplet was surprised to learn that these chambers also included a few Others who had not returned from a state-change completely intact.

Lastly, they visited the vast Chamber of the Misshapen. Here Droplet made out the vague forms of oddly shaped Others, most of whom stayed against the walls and were completely silent. He was offered no explanation about their afflictions, and didn't ask.

"The rest of Steadfast is made up of the Chambers of Ideology," explained oc-Logil, as they made their way back to the Central Commons.

"*Idea..?*" This was a new term for Droplet, who had grown increasingly fatigued.

"Yes, Ideology. You know, ideas, theories and beliefs—in this case, about being *outcasts*." Oc-Logil paused to let him take this in, then added after another moment, "But I can see you are growing tired, and it's best not to try to take all of this in at once. Perhaps we can continue tomorrow after the General Assembly. Would you like to return to oc-Dahzi's alcove now?"

"Yes, thank you."

Back in Dahzi's comforting presence, Droplet started feeling better as they talked about what he had learned so far.

"But how did this whole thing start, Dahzi?"

"I'm not sure this is known, for Steadfast has been here for too many full turnings of the seasons to count. I do know that the early Steadfasters, outcasts all, experienced a great deal of strife before they found this place to call their own. Now that they have a home, they are able to welcome any who need sanctuary. And many come each season—some are told of us long before they find us, while others, like you, are found and brought in. It is the way of Steadfast to help those in need."

Droplet had to admit he was impressed by what he'd learned of Steadfast so far, and decided he would like to learn more about the Chambers of Ideology. Dahzi told him the General Assembly would probably answer some of his questions, and suggested they attend it together.

That night marked the first time Droplet dreamed about the Occurrence without waking in terror.

The next day, Dahzi and Droplet went to Central Commons early to watch folk arrive for the General Assembly. The mid-day light seeping in through the fissure high above them allowed Droplet to get his first good look at his fellow outcasts. He saw the variety of sizes and shapes he expected to see, and several he hadn't imagined, as the Steadfasters filed in, mostly staying with those like them in loose sub-groupings. He paid particular attention to a large cohort of tainted—no, *Occurrence fleers*, he remembered, congregating easily to one side of the chamber.

When they were almost all there, Droplet realized they numbered well over twelve-twelves, making this by far the largest grouping he had ever seen.

Just then, a smallish, rectangular Other called the gathering to order, in what was obviously a well-known ritual:

"Who are we?" came his strong general sending.

"We are Steadfast. We are Steadfast." The assembly

answered and affirmed.

"Yes, we are. And as Steadfast, we ..."

"... Hold our differences in common," came the resounding response.

"Welcome then, to one and all."

From this fine beginning, the General Assembly quickly devolved into impassioned diatribes by the specific interests of separate Ideological sub-groupings.

With Dahzi's quiet commentary and assistance, Droplet learned about each diverse subgroup. The first to speak were the *Rousers*—these were contrarians interested in trying to force acceptance of their differences by outsiders. They wanted to rally a number of Steadfasters into going outside to agitate among the *unsullied*. Droplet quickly realized they believed they were special because they were different; yet strangely, they needed outsiders to acknowledge this.

The *Commoners*—those unidentified with an ideological subgroup—energetically opposed the Rousers on the grounds that separation served each side of the divide, and interacting with the unsullied offered nothing of value.

Then the *Oddballs* chimed in, claiming they should all rejoice in their differences, and neither need nor want anyone's acknowledgement or approval. At this point the *Malcontents*—always unhappy with everything—voiced their disgust and left the Commons.

Dahzi explained that the Malcontents uniformly blamed Others for their aggrieved list of misfortunes, and were the most reclusive of the subgroups.

Finally, the *Abiders*—those holding the general focus for Steadfast's purpose—tried to join the Commoners in an attempt to salvage the Assembly. But, as Dahzi quietly predicted, they were entirely unsuccessful.

"Well, that was interesting," commented Droplet looking around as the General Assembly broke into separate, intense discussions.

Before Dahzi could respond, oc-Vamer approached them to see if Droplet wanted to finish his tour. Glancing quickly at Dhazi, he politely declined.

"I have some things I need to talk to Dahzi about; perhaps

we could do it at a later time?"

"Of course, another time then," sent oc-Vamer. Droplet noticed he didn't look particularly disappointed as he left to join one of the animated sub-groups on the far side of the chamber.

Droplet and Dahzi retreated to the edge of Central Commons and talked privately about what they'd witnessed. Dahzi explained how the various Chambers of Ideology came into being, and how folk often moved from one to another over time.

"In fact, there is a kind of progression that is often part of the mental healing and adjustment process after becoming an outcast. I have seen that newcomers frequently go from a place of stuck-ness and overwhelm, to one of frustration and resentment where they can stay for some time. At some point, most then move into acceptance and re-orientation, and from there into the long-term commitment to staying here, building a sense of togetherness and helping others. Those in the final stage of integration most often become Abiders, but sometimes they remain non-committal as Commoners or cycle through the whole process again as a part of their healing. Our most intense Steadfasters often get swept up into one of the Ideologies where they can stay for a very long time. It's just a part of being Steadfast."

Droplet thought about all of this as they left the large chamber by mutual agreement and returned to Dahzi's blessedly quiet alcove. After getting situated in the cozy end, Droplet decided to ask a question that had been increasingly on his mind.

"Dahzi, what are *you* doing here? I mean, I know you are an excellent healer, but why here, when there are so many other—*brighter* places—you could be?"

Droplet could sense Dahzi's surprise as he replied, "But where would I go? I am an outcast, like you, friend."

Hard though he tried, Droplet couldn't perceive any kind of taint, deformity or lack that would make his healer an outcast, and he said so.

"To understand why I am outcast, we must go beyond Steadfast," Dahzi replied calmly. "Shall we do this?"

As they worked their way back through Central Commons

and the chambers beyond, Droplet noticed Dahzi becoming uncharacteristically distant, which he found worrisome.

"Are you alright with this, Dahzi?" He finally asked. They had just entered the narrow corridor which led to the outside and the light grew brighter as they ascended.

Dahzi stopped before they left the confines of the tunnel. "Yes, but going out into The Flow brings difficult memories for me, so I don't do it often. Let us continue, shall we?"

When they emerged from the tunnel and reentered the gently moving Flow, Droplet eagerly pushed away from the opening until he could feel the welcome freshness of the current. Then he looked beyond The Flow to the tree-covered bank opposite the cliff, and up to the high, thin clouds in Big Blue far above them. *Still more green in those clouds than there should be,* he admitted sadly. Yet he couldn't deny how much he had longed to be back in the light of sol.

He turned then to find Dahzi, who had hung back near the shadowy base of the cliff. He approached him slowly looking for any indication of what made him an outcast, but he found none. Dahzi looked perfectly normal, albeit a bit green, but Droplet was pretty sure that was his fault, not Dahzi's.

Dahzi, aware of Droplet's scrutiny, sent "You cannot see the flecks within me in this light, can you?"

Droplet, now right next to Dahzi, thought he could just discern something suspended within his friend's form, but before he could respond, Dahzi darted away from the cliff and into the full light of the sun, sending, "All right, what about now?"

Droplet gazed in complete astonishment at the transformation in his friend, who now appeared as a compact, brilliant ball of flashing gold. He approached Dahzi, who remained perfectly still but noticeably aloof, until he could clearly see the tiny flecks of gold twirling and shimmering inside of him. Droplet immediately realized his friend was by far the brightest thing in The Flow. He was . . . stunning.

"But, you're beautiful, Dahzi!"

Droplet's enthusiastic praise helped ease his friend's obvious discomfort. "I'm glad you perceive me thus, friend" he sent, finally. "But, as you can plainly see, I don't blend into my environment very well. Nor do most Others find me appealing, assuming I must be as strange as I appear."

211

Droplet, of course, could understand this. "But how—"

Dahzi broke contact and abruptly left the streaming sunlight. When he had returned to the shadows, he looked entirely normal again. "Although I rarely speak of it, I will share my story with you, but let us return to my alcove first. For I find I am less and less comfortable away from it."

Once they were settled back in Dahzi's small, comfy alcove he began:

"I am from a place very far from here, and very, very different. Where here we have many types of plants and creatures growing both in and beyond The Flow, I emerged in a brown and barren place where all forms of Life were sparse. Imagine a place of intense sun, blazing every day, unless blowing sands obscure it; this is where I am from. Of course, there was beauty there too—but it was usually found in the sunken caverns of the Penetrating Flow."

"The *Penetrating* Flow?"

"Yes, the Penetrating Flow. It is the name we gave the most common type of Flow in what used to be my home. Unlike Flows here which typically reside on the surface, a Penetrating Flow sinks down and burrows deep into the earth, carving out its route as it goes. Along these dark, hidden routes, The Flow moves slowly through rock and sand, but there are also lovely caverns, and in one such as this we had our home. For I am of the Iode Cavern Grouping."

"And were all of you golden?"

"Some of us were, but they were usually the eldest among us. You see, we had a favorite place to go in the evenings, a place where The Flow surfaced just beyond our cavern and seemed to merge with the nightsky. And the stars . . . the stars were impossibly bright, and as bountiful as the sands surrounding us. This place, protected by high sand-cliffs, held what we called *Star Sand.*"

Dahzi, lost in memory, stopped sending. Droplet could feel the wonder and beauty of the place through his connection with his friend.

"Star Sand was . . . astounding. Much finer than the regular sand supporting it, it was blindingly bright in sunlight. But at night it shone delicately, perfectly reflecting the light of the stars above it. To spend night after night wrapped above and below in starlight—with loved ones all around . . ." Dahzi slipped into a silence so deep no words could follow.

After a moment he reemerged, and with a pulse of fondness he sent, "Well, we shared many evenings nestled in our small pocket of Star Sand, intimately knowing ourselves to be the same stuff as the universe. This place was *sacred* to us, my friend, even though I imagine that probably sounds strange to you."

"No, I can feel the specialness of it through you. Please continue. How did you leave there?"

"One night, while in this place, I slipped into a deep, star-struck sleep. When I awoke, I was alone and the night had fled. Sol had started to peak over the sand-cliffs, and I knew if I was still there when it touched the Star Sand, it would be too bright. But just as I turned toward Iode, a two-legged *Determiner* jumped from the sand-cliffs onto the low bank next to me, and scooped me up with some Star Sand. Suddenly, I was encased with Star Sand and a little bit of The Flow, in a clear container of some kind. It is then that my nightmare began."

Dahzi lapsed again into silence. Droplet, who had received an image of the two-legged Determiner through their connection, moved closer, hoping to comfort his friend with his presence, the way Dahzi had done so many times for him.

"I don't even know how to describe what happened next," he finally continued slowly. "I was thrust into darkness and unbelievably jostled for an unknown amount of time. It was literally all I could do to hang onto my sanity, my sense of self. I believe I was dropped from a high place, while still in the enveloping darkness which surrounded me without reprieve. Then I went through a prolonged time of intense vibration, accompanied by a constant roaring, along with intermittent clanking sounds. By this time, the utter strangeness of it all overcame me, and my consciousness fled. In my very last thought, I knew myself to be utterly lost."

Droplet intimately knew this type of despair, and he was pleased that he did not feel overwhelmed by Dahzi's telling of it. He very gently sent his most comforting thoughts and encouragement to this dear friend, who was now trusting *him* with something dark and hurtful.

"Finally, finally, the jostling and the darkness both ended. My container was removed from something large and black, and placed on a flat surface. What I could perceive beyond my container completely mystified me. I had no experience, no kind of reference with which to understand what I was seeing: large blocky objects, light which wasn't sunlight, and several two-legged Determiners of different shapes and sizes. It was simply too strange. I lost awareness again, and for an unknown length of time.

"My awareness returned suddenly while I was being vigorously *shaken* and peered at by the huge, distorted *face* of a Determiner. Of course, I knew very little about Determiners at that time, but I thought it looked vaguely like the one that had removed me from my beloved home.

"Very shortly after that, my container was thrust into the *hands* of what I later learned was the youngest Determiner in their grouping. This one, too, shook me for a while and then dropped me onto hardness where my container rolled, until it was retrieved by the larger Determiner and placed on a blessedly stationary surface.

"And there I stayed for many seasons, observing my surroundings along with the growth and changes in my young, restless Determiner. It was there, in the evenings, as the little Determiner would ready himself for sleep that I first discerned the rhythmic and repetitive sounds I slowly grew to love. Night after night, the same soothing melodies bathed us both in comfort. I found myself naturally putting thoughts to them, and eventually the simple songs I made taught me a way to order—and ultimately to accept—what had happened to me. The deep and mysterious power of melody, word and intent healed me, my friend, just as it helped heal you."

Dahzi grew quiet again, and then sent, "I am now tired, friend, and would tell the rest tomorrow. Shall we sleep?"

"Yes. And thank you Dahzi, for sharing your amazing story with me. Rest well, dear one."

"And you."

"So, as I said, many seasons went by."

When they awoke the next day Dahzi resumed his narration with renewed vigor. "I know this because after a time, one of the larger Determiners placed my container near a wide aperture which allowed me to see, but not be

214

influenced by, the natural world beyond it. I call it that, although it took me a long time of careful study to realize that the vast expanse of greenness I could see was, in fact, *natural*. Where were the sands I knew? I only fully believed the rampant vegetation beyond my perch constituted a natural environment after watching it, and what you call Big Blue, day after day, and season after season."

"But how did you get back into The Flow, Dahzi?"

"That is coming, but first something very significant happened to me. One afternoon the Determiner I had come to think of as 'my' Determiner—older now and more capable in his world—picked up the strangely shaped device he would sometimes use to create vibrating melodies. These were usually simpler and more halting than the evening songs we used to listen to. Then, with no preamble, he spoke words which matched the melodies coming from his device. Although I had heard the Determiner's vocal sounds many times before, I did not realize until that moment that they could be sung. For reasons I still don't understand, this changed everything for me. I had long observed them communicating using their inexplicable voice-sounds, but I couldn't make any sense out of their strangeness; one might as well try to understand a yellow-spotted flyer clicking and trilling at dawn.

"Now, all at once, I understood that each sound they made referred to a meaningful *thought,* a thought that with enough sensitivity and determined observation, I might be able to detect. From that moment on, I studied the Determiners in earnest, searching for the thoughts behind the sounds they routinely delivered to one another. In this way I learned how they think. And this, my friend, was a revelation."

Droplet thought back to the few enigmatic two-leggeds he'd observed—the danglers on the span, several solos walking along the banks of The Flow, oh, and the stooped garden tenders. He knew there was no way he would have made the intuitive leap that Dahzi had made, and said so.

"Ah, but you might have discovered this if you had spent as much time with them as I. Remember, in all my days and nights in that strange place, I had only three ways to look—inward to my deeper self, out toward the strange green world, and into the mind of my Determiner. I worked to expand my sensing abilities until I could detect the rapid flow of his thoughts. And what I learned from his thoughts astounded me.

"First of all, I quickly discovered a mind fully as strong and agile as my own. But I also often found my Determiner filled with conflicting thoughts and emotions, or totally absorbed with some obscure thing he found fascinating. His moment-by-moment experience, and much of what he thought, made no sense to me at all. Only when he sang his thoughts while using his melodic device, did I easily understand him. And increasingly, his songs focused on his need to attract to him a mate. The enduring depth of his longing, both its magnitude and its aching intensity, was greater than any feeling I'd known save the utter devastation of being taken from my home.

"Then, one afternoon, toward the middle of the Growing Season, my Determiner reached out to give me a shake as he sometimes did when passing by, but this time he took my container out of what I knew to be his home. Suddenly, I was in the bright light of a cloudless day, held securely between his fingers as he loped along, sloshing me around. He finally stopped at the edge of a little creek near the stand of trees I'd watched change through countless seasons.

"In full sun, he gave me a shake and watched the Star Sand around and within me sparkle and spin. I could feel his joy and a sudden sense of purpose as he removed one end of my container and, without ceremony, poured me into the shallow Flow before him. To this day, I don't know what his intention was, but in a secret part of my mind—and his—I believe he somehow knew to free me. And free I was."

"Wow." Droplet had never been so completely swept up into another's story. "But what happened then? How did you come to Steadfast, Dahzi?"

"My first thought upon returning to The Flow, as you might imagine, was to try to get back to my sweet home and loved ones. But where I was had not even the slightest similarity to my home, and I had no idea how to begin to search, so I just traveled down-flow, seeking bigger Flows. Others I met along the way were friendly enough until they saw me in sunlight; at that point they grew uncomfortable and in some cases even mean, calling me names and repelling me. 'Best move on then,' was something I heard a lot until I started traveling only at night.

"Finally, I met an Other who was kind enough to tell me of a place where I might find acceptance. And by carefully following his instructions, I came to the stately cliff towering above us, and waited, glistening in the sunlight, until a Steadfaster approached me and invited me inside. When it was discovered I was good at helping newcomers heal in their minds, I was given an alcove and a purpose for which I am deeply grateful . . ."

Dahzi paused looking at Droplet, and then added, "I truly believe, my friend, that the long, lonely time I spent with my Determiner gave me the patience, the practice, and the skill to delve deeply into the minds of Others who need help. In this way, finally, I believe I have been *blessed*."

Droplet gazed at Dahzi, esse-to-esse. He let the power of their shared resonance fill him with the beautiful feeling of being blessed. As this lovely feeling grew in each of them, they effortlessly moved into a shared Inner Sanctum experience— through a connection which had developed over the course of their many days of deep healing work together.

In this profound shared space, the final healing for Droplet began; with great tenderness he brought forth the last few parts of himself that still hid from, and tried to resist, the horrors of the Occurrence, and then he opened himself more fully than he ever had.

This opening allowed Droplet and Dahzi to completely know one another, as equals, for the first time. There was an innate sense of tranquility and rightness to this sharing.

What happened next surprised and delighted them both. Each of their esses, in deep resonance, unfurled delicate tendrils of light which came together and wove into a dance of golden starlight. This gentle, spiraling dance slowly coalesced into a shining *bond* of profound connection.

As this bond deepened and stabilized, they knew themselves to be blessed beyond all limits. And through their moment-by-moment willingness to know and be known completely, a potent upwelling of love filled them both.

Together they experienced the instant when this love overflowed their esses, and became the most beautiful of melodies in an unending universe of song.

In the timelessness of their inner merging, this infinitely loving song dissolved the last of Droplet's fear, and he discovered himself to be entirely healed and whole at last.

Later that evening, they left Steadfast to spend some time together under the stars. They talked of many things, explored their most private understandings and questions, and found comfort and wonder in the astounding strength and clarity of their shared *bond*.

At one point, Dahzi, resplendent with starlight, reflected, "The Elders of my grouping would sometimes talk of a place deep within us they called the Secret Heart. I never knew this place before, but now I believe that it can only be known through being shared. Thank you for showing me this wondrous place within, Droplet."

"And thank you, Dahzi, for not only showing it to me as well, but for giving me a way to think about what has happened between us, for we *do indeed* share a Secret Heart."

It was very late when they returned to Dahzi's alcove. As they nestled into the narrow end, where Droplet's healing began, Dahzi sent quietly, "Now that esse-sight has returned to you, I believe you are also able to heal the minds of Others."

Droplet, relaxed and replete after a day filled with joyful discovery, replied sleepily, "Maybe so, but I don't think I'm ready for that. Right now, I'm just happy to be near you." As sleep finally claimed him, he asked faintly, "Do you think we will share a dream?"

He missed Dahzi's response, but not its caring feeling tone, "I think we already have, my friend."

The next morning they slept late and were awakened by oc-Vardic telling oc-Dahzi that a newcomer needed his help. Dahzi left immediately and then returned with a disoriented, and obviously deeply wounded, newcomer. After making his new charge as comfortable as possible in his alcove, Dahzi came out to apologize.

"I am sorry, dear friend, but this one needs immediate care. I will ask oc-Vardic to take you to an empty alcove until such time that you can return to mine. Please forgive me, but I cannot turn someone in his condition away."

"Of course you can't, Dahzi, I understand completely. I will use this opportunity to learn more about my new home, and we'll get together as soon as we can. Be well, my friend and give him your best care."

Dahzi, already turning back to his newest patient, sent a quick, "I will, dear one. I'll try to see you in a few days."

Twenty-One

❦

After trying out several alcoves, Droplet had finally found one he felt relatively comfortable in. It was just off a short, unused chamber, and closer to both the edge of the cliff and to the surface of The Flow, than the rest of Steadfast. Although it was considerably brighter than any chamber other than Central Commons at mid-day, it was still too dark for Droplet. And this was just one of his problems.

Since the day after he and Dahzi had *bonded* so beautifully, there had been what seemed like an endless stream of newcomers needing his friend's precious aid. Droplet had quickly discovered that Dahzi needed to give his entire attention to those requiring his healing to be truly effective.

He had also learned that their bond, easily apparent when they were near one another, became harder to sense as they moved away from one another within Steadfast. Dahzi believed this had to do with the thickness of the rock surrounding them. By conducting experiments on the few nights they had together, they confirmed that their relative distance did not affect their ability to access one another via their esse-bond when they were *both* in The Flow beyond Steadfast.

Dahzi's unavailability meant Droplet was on his own a great deal of the time, because he just couldn't seem to relate to his fellow Steadfasters.

And it wasn't for lack of trying!

Droplet had repeatedly attended gatherings and discussions with all of the subgroups except the Rousers and the Malcontents, with whom he was entirely unable to relate. Even the calmest and largest subgroups, the Commoners and the Abiders, seemed short-sighted to him and mired in negativity. He had finally come to accept that the Steadfaster's prevailing, but subtle, belief that their misfortune made them *special* felt essentially wrong to him.

Droplet discovered he deeply missed the presence of enlightened leaders and Elders who could have helped guide and unify them. When he asked about this, he was consistently told, "That isn't the Steadfast way."

Even with repeated exposure and careful reflection, he found most Steadfasters to be largely reactive and short-sighted. Many individuals he'd met seemed self-absorbed and hard to relate to. Some of them even seemed *elitist* in a manner that felt sadly compensatory to him, and in this way, deeply false.

The few times he had tried to bring up his difficulties or concerns during an open-format group discussion—very gently and obliquely—the group's members had grown hurt and defensive, which was far from what he had hoped to achieve.

When he finally shared these observations with Dahzi during one of their brief times together between healings, his friend's reaction surprised him.

"This place, imperfect as it may be, is *home* to us, Droplet, and each of us is here because we have been outcast. Have you already forgotten what that means? Do you not remember your own intense anger and frustration at what happened to you after the Occurrence? Many Steadfasters were in The Flow as outcasts for unnumbered seasons—homeless, bitter and forlorn—before finding this place of haven. Is their agitation and resentment not understandable?"

Dahzi paused, and for the first time Droplet noticed how tired he seemed. Then he continued, "Each of us deals with the losses we've experienced in different ways; often the longer the time of wounding, the longer the healing takes. Part of the healing for each one of us involves learning to accept ourselves, along with what caused us to be here. But it's also about allowing ourselves to feel what we feel, discuss difficult topics, and speak out about what we perceive as narrow-mindedness and injustice. Steadfast offers us the opportunity to do this with the support of Others who are like us."

Droplet quietly took this in. Then he admitted, "But that's

just it. Other than you, I haven't found any Others here that I feel any kind of a connection with. And I don't see how constantly bickering about opinions can be healing."

Dahzi stared at him for a moment as if something foreign had crawled into his alcove. Then he softened, and sent, "It is not opinions which are trying to heal, my friend, it is troubled individuals. After you arrived here, your healing went very fast, very sure. Usually the kind of healing you experienced takes much, much longer, and happens in stages. What you're now feeling also needs healing. You need to find a way to truly accept being here, and to open to the Others who share our home. Can you not find it in yourself to be accepting of your fellow outcasts as they struggle to express themselves and find a new way of being?"

Droplet could feel the rightness in Dahzi's sending—the wisdom in it. He knew he hadn't given it his best effort. "Yes, I can, my friend. And thank you."

A few days later, much to his surprise, he came across someone he'd known—barely—from his life before Steadfast. He had been taking a short-cut to Central Commons when he thought he recognized one of three Others having what looked like an animated conversation just outside of the Chamber of the Incomplete. He approached slowly until he was sure. Then he waited politely behind the one with the familiar esse for a break in the conversation. When it came he sent, "Pilan? Is that you?"

The Other whirled around and sent an automatic, "*Oc*-Pilan! Who are you?"

"It *is* you. I'm Droplet, Pil—um, *oc*-Pilan. We were both at Nester's grouping a while back." Droplet watched Pilan's esse dim as he pulled away and moved closer to his friends. "Do you remember?"

"Of course I remember—Rock something—right? What happened to *you*?"

Suddenly embarrassed by his appearance in a way he hadn't been since his healing with Dazhi, Droplet answered quietly, "I got caught in an Occurrence."

For an awkward moment they all just gawked at him.

Then one of the Others sent, "Is that why you're all weird

and slimy?"

The oddness of this question reminded Droplet of which chamber he was near. He also remembered what Orry and Wise Elder had said about Pilan. Obviously there were some deficiencies operating here.

He chose to ignore the question and instead sent, "Anyway, I, ah, just wanted to say 'hi.' And to let you know that Orry was very distraught—um, *sad*—when you got swept away in the current. I wish there was a way to let him know you're okay."

"Of course I'm okay," oc-Pilan sent, looking at his friends. "Why wouldn't I be? And I can't believe it would matter to Orry."

Without thinking, Droplet replied, "But of course it would matter! He was truly upset about what happened to you. He even—"

Oc-Pilan abruptly turned away from Droplet and sent to his friends, "Orry was an old unsullied. He never really cared about me." Then, intentionally excluding Droplet, he sent, "Come on. We don't want to miss the Assembly."

The three of them left without even glancing back.

And that pretty much sums up how well I get along with Steadfasters in general, Droplet thought as he turned back the way he'd come. *I don't think I'm in the mood for another Assembly after all.*

Many more days filled with earnest, but largely unsuccessful, attempts to understand and ally himself with his fellow insulars passed. And no matter how hard he tried he just couldn't get used to being called *oc*-Droplet.

Finally, he had to admit that for him, the only brightness in all of Steadfast was the time he spent with Dahzi, and while this was brilliant by comparison, Droplet didn't know if it was enough to keep him there.

In fact, lately he had become aware of an inner prompting, a vague insistence, calling him away from this place of challenge and shadow. And away from his beloved friend.

"But I don't understand. Where would you go?"

Dahzi, just released from yet another healing, had found

Droplet alone in his high alcove. Daylight from beyond Steadfast seeped into the stark space, brightening it a bit.

"That's just it, Dahzi—I have no idea. I don't know of anyplace beyond Steadfast where I won't be an outcast. And yet, I'm starting to believe I'm not meant to be an insular."

Dahzi settled next to him and thought quietly. The beauty and immediacy of their bond helped calm them both.

When he felt ready he sent, "The beloved Elders of my first grouping taught there are two ways to be in The Flow: we can use The Flow to take us to experiences, *or*, we can wait in one place and let The Flow bring to us what we need to grow. We had a saying, 'All good things come with The Flow,' which probably tells you which way of being we most often chose."

"I see . . ." Now it was Droplet's turn to think. "My way, so far, has involved a lot of journeys—and not always by my choice. The Flow has had a way of uprooting me when I least expected it. In fact, this is the way it brought me to you," he added softly.

"And for that I am truly grateful, my friend. But you're here now; you don't have to leave. What if I can teach you to heal? That would give you a sense of purpose here, and we might be able to use our bond to speed recovery. This I believe we could do."

"I know you believe I can learn to heal as you do, but I'm not sure." As Dahzi started to respond he sent, "But more importantly, I think there is something else I need to be doing; something out there, away from the safety—and the limitations —of Steadfast." With this sending, Droplet opened his whole Self to Dahzi through their beautiful bond, which had grown even stronger since forming.

After a moment, Dahzi sent, "Ah. I sense it now, this inner urging, wanting to draw you away. It is very deep within you, and more insistent than I would like." Dahzi's attempt to quell his spontaneous reaction to what he sensed was only partly successful. "And as much as I want it not to be true, I can see that it is true."

Droplet felt Dahzi reel with the intensity of this awareness, and then struggle not to withdraw in pain.

"Oh Dahzi, I would not cause you pain for the world, and yet *for* the world, I think I must cause you pain. Because the world, or something in it, is calling me, and I believe I must heed this call."

"Yes, I think you must as well, dear one. But why so soon? It seems that we have only just found one another. Must you go already?"

Droplet drew his beloved friend close in his mind. As Dahzi slowly let his distress go, their esses sang together, as they always did now—calmly, like a wide, serene river after a merge.

"Let's go beyond Steadfast this evening, and see if being in The Flow together will bring us any answers. Will you accompany me, my friend?"

"Of course, and gladly."

They spent the rest of that afternoon dozing together in Droplet's shallow alcove, taking comfort in their bond and in the closeness of one another's presence, now all the more precious because of a possible, but nearly inconceivable, future apart.

"How could our esses have become so lovingly entwined? I have never felt anything like this before," sent one of them to the other.

"Hush, beloved," came the gentle reply.

When the light filtering into Droplet's alcove finally subsided, they left the rock-solidness of Steadfast to enter the open Flow beyond. They both realized, though neither would say, that it might be their last night together under the stars.

They found a quiet spot away from the rippling current near the far bank. Starlight softly illuminated The Flow around them, while silence held them firmly in its depths.

Finally, as the merest sliver of orb rose over the treetops behind them, Dahzi turned to Droplet and sent, "So, as we both know, this is goodbye, is it not?"

Startled, Droplet sent, "No, of course this isn't goodbye, Dahzi. I could sooner leave my esse behind. If I do leave, as it seems I must, our connection goes with me—just as it stays here with you."

"But I . . ."

"Is this why you're so sad? Do you really think that our connection can be broken that easily? Look at it, Dahzi. Look at what has fashioned between, and within, us." Their brilliant esses, like twin suns, outshone the silvery stars above them—

225

outshone anything either of them had ever beheld.

"Dahzi—*you*—your essence is now a part of my Secret Heart, as my essence is part of yours. My leaving won't change that—can't possibly change that. Ever."

"I want to believe this. Truly I do. But experience has shown me how final and permanent such endings can be."

Droplet suddenly saw his friend's past in a way that went far beyond his earlier telling of it: Dahzi, abandoned and confined in swirling gold, alone in an utterly strange place, and struggling for even the tiniest glimmer of hope for a very long time. In that moment, he knew his friend's despair as his own, and welcomed it in. The welcoming became a shared song.

Dahzi immediately calmed.

"Don't you see, dearest?" Droplet sent to his beloved friend, as ripples of awareness danced through him, "We are greater than our pain, greater than any fear either of us could ever have. Because who we truly are has created this precious connection between us in a way that far surpassed any intention of ours. Who we *truly* are, Dahzi. Not just our thoughts, our feelings or our experiences, but our *esses* have bonded. I don't believe anything could ever change that."

Dahzi caught his friend's inspiration and felt the truth in it lap at the frayed edges of his doubt, easing it. He went deep into the Secret Heart of his Inner Sanctum, where Droplet immediately joined him, radiating love and truth.

Joy welled up in both of them. "Yes, I see this now. Our connection exists *beyond* time or place—and has no relation to our physical closeness, although I believe that served us in the beginning."

"Yes, and the healing you made possible for me required our nearness. I am so deeply grateful for that, and for everything else you have shared with me, Dahzi. And I promise, *I promise*, I will always welcome our inner connection in my Secret Heart."

"As will I, dear friend. Then I am at peace with you going." After a moment he added, "Do you think you will ever return?"

Droplet looked into the starry vault high above The Flow, and noticed the slivered orb had passed beyond Steadfast's rock cliff. He waited until he got an inkling of his future and then sent, "I can't say where I will go in this world, and I don't know when it will be, but yes, I will return to Steadfast. One day when our inner connection, our *esse-bond*, is so comforting and familiar that we access it without even thinking about it, I will come, Dahzi."

"Then on that day I will rejoice. Now, my shining friend, shall we spend a final night in my humble healing alcove?"

"Gladly, dear one."

Twenty-Two

E arly the next morning, Droplet made his quiet way out of Steadfast for the last time. He had left Dahzi deeply asleep and nestled in a comforting dream. They had agreed to no farewells, for if there was one thing they both finally understood, it was that their connection was as eternal as their esses, and as abiding as The Flow itself.

Before going to sleep, they had discussed how best to stay in contact on "the inner," while being apart in "the outer." They finally agreed to meet in the shared portion of their Inner Sanctum on those nights when the orb was fullest, and also when it was altogether absent—with the caveat that intensive healing might preclude Dahzi's participation, as unknown events might interfere with Droplet's.

Dahzi acknowledged that he would have to get better at keeping track of the orb's phases, and they both knew he would have to go into The Flow beyond Steadfast to facilitate contact. Even if their attempts were unsuccessful at times, they could always sense their esse-bond. But both wanted the comfort of routine contact which offered them the ability to intimately share their thoughts, experiences and feelings.

As Droplet re-entered The Flow, he felt a sense of adventure rise in him for the first time in longer than he could remember.

Increasing light drew his attention to the pink, and of course, grey-greenish clouds, high in the paleness of Big Blue. This reminded him of his biggest challenge: he would still be considered tainted by Others he met in The Flow. Nonetheless, leaving felt right . . .

He moved onto the pebbly bottom just below the central current, feeling its sweet whisper of welcome. There he paused to sense from which direction his future called: upstream or down? After checking twice to be sure, he turned upstream, and traveled until he came to the beginning of the fork he had chosen seemingly at random—the fork that had led him to acceptance, to healing, and to the enduring wonder of an esse-bond.

So, I won't be welcome among my kind, he thought, as he moved back into the larger river, blessedly clear of any sign of the Occurrence. Without pausing he immediately turned downstream, using long-dormant self-propulsion skills to steady his progress. *Surely there are Others somewhere who will accept me.*

He reminded himself he'd been on his own before, and now, of course, his esse-bond with Dahzi meant he would never truly be alone. *Even so, I am much stronger—and wiser—than I've ever been . . .*

He rounded an easy bend and came upon a couple of silver-striped flashers darting among the verticals ahead of him. On a whim he left the bottom and accelerated into the central current.

As he soared between the tall stones, an unexpected wave of joy crested through him. He was whole; he was free!

He was back in The Flow again!

Not far from the Steadfast cliffs, a third Hummer hidden in the vegetation where Droplet had been discovered many twelve-days before abruptly stopped humming.

Waiting to be certain it was unobserved by the other Hummers, or anyone else in The Flow, it turned and tracked Droplet's departure in the brightening light.

After sloughing off its Hummer-guise, the Watcher rapidly increased the brilliance of its esse, and flashed a quick inner sending to those awaiting news.

A moment later, it faded into nothingness.

End of Book One

Turn the page for a sneak peek at Book Two:
Droplet's Journey: Rivers of Being
-Available soon-

They arrived around mid-day. The creek looked like any other, save for the extensive network of exposed roots from some of the tallest trees Droplet had seen. He didn't believe he'd been here before, yet it felt vaguely familiar. He looked around for the one Wise Elder had brought him to meet, but didn't detect an esse nearby.

"Are we early?"

"No, we are exactly right."

To Droplet's surprise, Wise Elder's reply contained a measure of both pleasure and relief. He seemed different today.

"Go inward, Droplet, and I will meet you in the Inner Sanctum."

Droplet made the inward centering which took him to his Inner Sanctum. Immediately he sensed the bright esse of his companion and opened his awareness to it.

:The Being we are going to meet is very special, Droplet, and we must achieve a single point of focus to communicate. So I want you to link your esse with mine the way you've been practicing, and then be very still while I take the lead.

Quite intrigued now, Droplet did this. As soon as they linked he also got a flash of Dahzi's presence with them.

:Dahzi! It's good—

Before he could finish the greeting, he felt an immense inrushing of thought-feeling. This unusual sensation instantly reminded him of one of his extreme dreams about—

:Hello, Millie. The sending originated from Wise Elder via their linked esses and went—*where?* Droplet used a tiny part of his awareness to search for the recipient, but was wrenched back to receive:

~*AH, MY DEAR WATER SPIRIT. I'D HOPED YOU'D BE HERE, TODAY.*

This inner 'sending' was far more powerful than any Droplet had experienced before. If not for Dahzi's steadying presence in his mind, its impact might have flung him out of his link with Wise Elder.

:I am pleased to see you as well, Wise Elder replied, as Dahzi helped Droplet fine-tune his receptiveness.

In the brief quiet that followed, Droplet figured it out. On the bank opposite them sat a two-legged, or as Wise Elder referred to them, a thinker-doer. The intense sending, which was really more of a mind-link, came from this Being.

~My time here is short, I'm afraid. This old body has grown ill. And I so wanted to talk with you once more.

:Ah, Millie. I am sorry. But even though your body will pass away, I know your essence will continue in its strength and radiance.

~And that is why I've missed you, my friend! You always see more deeply, and speak truth in a way that uplifts and sooths me. I worry, though, that there is no-one of my line to communicate with you when I'm gone.

With this 'sending' Droplet saw an image of other thinker-doers doing things and communicating together with their strange sounds; there were both types, with little ones in a strange structure. (*A family, with young, in their home,* explained Dahzi through their esse-bond.)

:Do not be concerned, Millie. There are others, and we will always be in contact with those of your species who desire to communicate with us. But you, and what you've shared about your world, have been important to us. Your openness, insight, and trust are truly valued.

Droplet felt a great, hauntingly familiar, rush of gratitude and love from the thinker-doer (*woman,* provided Dahzi). Wise Elder detected his confusion and sent a quick, "This woman feels familiar to you because she played an important role in your emergence into consciousness, Droplet, and it happened in this very creek." Before Droplet could even begin to integrate this shocking revelation, they received another powerful thought-sending from the woman.

~That is good. Can I ask you about something, Water Spirit?

:Of course, Millie, anything.

~You are eternal, aren't you? Do you know what happens when we humans die?

:We have neither the physical form nor the life-death experience that you have. But I can tell you that, like ours, your Essence is eternal. It springs and flows forever from the Creator, and in this way it was never born, nor can it die.

~It's just the body that dies, then?

:The body and the belief in the individual self, yes.

~So the part of me that fears death—my ego—actually does die . . . and the part of me that welcomes it, knows it survives? . . . This makes a deep kind of sense to me . . .

In Droplet, a distant memory blossomed. He and this woman had been joined, linked by mind and unified by the unconditional Love shining from her esse. It was, in fact, his very first awareness: falling, imbued with Love and sunlight, from her finger into The Flow.

:Amazing! Dahzi, did you know this?:

Dahzi responded with warmth and a quiet promise to talk about it later. Then Dahzi gave him a soft, inner nudge, and Droplet refocused on the present: Wise Elder and the remarkable woman on the bank.

Through the immediacy of their connection with her, he felt her chest move as she inhaled a long, deep breath. He sensed her aching body and the sharp pain in her middle she believed would end her life. He perceived her strong emotional connections with her family and community, *so like our own,* he realized. He observed her remembered interactions with others of her kind and, via Dahzi's awareness, he actually understood their sounds, gestures and expressions as nuanced communication.

Through the long, winding current of her memories, he got a sense of how she experienced the passage of time, and the value she placed on the life she had lived. He felt the profound love she had for her land and the very creek he was in—that he had *emerged* in. He rejoiced with her in the sweet sounds of the birds she could hear around her *(so clearly!),* experienced the sun's warmth on her skin *(a fascinating sensation),* and caught a glimpse of her deep, but contained, sorrow at leaving this life.

Droplet felt her attention shift as she refocused on their shared inner connection.

Then she sighed, and added, *~Thank you, dear Spirit. That is more comforting than you can know . . . Do you have any questions for me?*

Dear Reader,

Thank you for reading **Droplet's Journey: Life in The Flow.** I hope you enjoyed reading it as much as I enjoyed writing it. Many times over the last few years, I have felt the ideas of this book literally flow through me, as if yearning to be known. Water is so very precious, and every living thing on our planet has a relationship with it. Although no one knows for certain whether or not water has awareness, science is far from explaining all of its mysteries. It is my own experience that consciousness can be very subtle and different from what we might expect.

If you enjoyed experiencing Droplet's world, then I have a request of you. In today's publishing industry, the success of any book lies in the reviews individual readers share. If you would like to see Droplet's Journey reach more people, I invite you to go to the **Droplet's Journey: Life in the Flow** book page on Amazon.com and write about your reaction to the book you've just read. Even a few words can have a big impact.

Book Two, **Droplet's Journey: Rivers of Being,** should be released late 2017. Visit my author page on Amazon and follow me to get updates.

Thank you for being part of the expanding readership of **Droplet's Journey.** You matter, and as you will see in Book Two, Droplet would heartily agree.

Many Blessings,
Ishara Kassirer

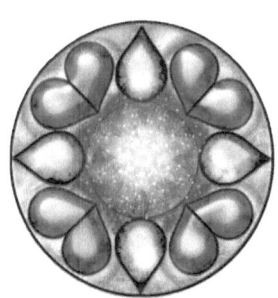

Acknowledgements

My heartfelt appreciation goes to my husband Dave for his love, support, and all of his help with the early and final versions. My gratitude also goes to Mischievous Muse Press for partnering with me in this grand adventure, particularly to Gineve Lynnara for her artistic eye, her keen insight and her persistent encouragement, and to Cat Spydell for her superb editing skills.

I also deeply appreciate the insights and suggestions of my beta readers: Ingrid Ammondson, Greg Conway, Elizabeth Greene, and Jim Rudolph. Special thanks to Chris Spurrell for his input on chemical spill cleanups, and to Dad for his abundant support and out-of-the-box thinking.

And finally, I'd like to acknowledge the collective intelligence of my fellow adventurers in consciousness, along with the Teacher in us all, whose wisdom and compassion inspires me on a daily basis.

Author's Note

After much experimentation, I chose to use the customary neutral pronouns of the English language (he, his, and him) to refer to the non-biological life-forms featured in this story. I apologize if this offends any of my readers and encourage you to remember that these are *non-gendered* Beings who naturally possess those personality traits and other attributes which we tend to ascribe to one gender or the other. If our language had a truly gender-neutral pronoun other than "it," I would have gladly used it.

Also, because Droplet and his kind communicate using thought-images and feeling-tones rather than words, I frequently had to use the best approximation in our language to convey their ideas and meanings. Accordingly, what I believe will be a helpful glossary of terms follows, with those most crucial to understanding the story listed first, under the heading, "Key Unique Terms."

Lexicon

Key Unique Terms:

The Flow – all water, still or moving. Common use: any river, stream, lake, pond.

Cresting – an early, but essential, developmental milestone; signals the complex integration of awareness-thought-feeling which gives one access to higher mental processes, as well as the ability to link with the collective consciousness of Others who have crested. Cresting signals readiness to join the society of Others.

Emergence – the original act and circumstance of becoming conscious.

Esse – spiritual *essence*. The focal point of consciousness. Common use: that which perceives or knows.

Esse-bond – a very deep, unbreakable essence-to-essence connection.

Esse-sending – communicating via the *esse*; rare and very intimate.

Esse-sight – the uncommon ability to directly use the *esse* for perception. The capability needed to perceive another's *esse*; also called *primary sight*.

Extreme dreams – the vivid dream experience, during sleep, of oneself as a completely different kind of entity or creature; very rare and unique to Droplet.

Inner Sanctum – an internal state of consciousness. Can be experienced as a 'place' of deep peace, awareness and clarity; offers direct access to *esse*, deeper wisdom and enhanced perception of many different levels of being (both physical and non-physical).

Sacred Flow – from the 'Sacred Flow of Consciousness'; the great circle of awareness that unites all conscious Beings at the deepest levels.

Sending – communicating via focused energy charge; can contain images, thoughts, feelings.

State change – the experience of transitioning to a solid state (via freezing) or to a vapor state (via evaporation).

Types and configurations of Others:

Beings – those imbued with the higher attributes of consciousness including self-awareness and reasoning. (Contrasted to *creatures,* the term referring to aquatic or land animals.)

Others – From 'Others of Our Kind.' The sentient Beings in The Flow (conscious drops of water).

Grouping – an intentional community of Others – often forms due to shared interests or beliefs; sometimes just location. Minimum number of Others needed for a functional grouping is commonly understood to be twelve.

Drifters – Others who, while social, move from group to group, never settling down.

Insulars – Others who don't seek contact with strangers, rarely open to it. True isolationists; often found in remote, exclusive groupings or more rarely, alone.

Solos – Others who strongly prefer solitude, but may be open to company on occasion.

Partial – Others who did not develop normally and lack certain abilities to think, communicate or move; also *sensory partial* – those whose awareness is exclusively constellated around a particular sensation.

Zaverts – Others who actively avoid all contact, total isolationist. When approached they send "Zavert!" which is the signal to back-off immediately.

Quasi-Others

Singers – appearing with an elongated shape, Singers only exist in the strongest currents of The Flow. Together they produce a tonal 'song' that is both beautiful and alluring. No-one has ever communicated with them; it is believed they share a group mind and have only fleeting, intermittent periods of existence.

Hummers – appearing as a transparent Other, with very low consciousness and an extremely faint *esse*; other than making a constant low humming noise, they don't (or won't) communicate with Others and rarely move or change location.

Common creatures within and around The Flow:

Bandy-legged side walker – crabs; also *Skulker, or* just *Side Walker*

Bank diggers – earthworms; also *Wrigglers*

Crawlers – water beetles, all varieties

Creepers – snails; all varieties including 'knobbed' and 'pitted'.

Dangler – a *two-legged*/human who fishes from the bank, surface vessel, or bridge

Flappers/flyers – birds; also *Winged ones*

Fur Faces – land animals; also *Four-leggeds*. Some with *Lapper-dappers* (tongues).

Flasher – fish, any type

Four-legged builder – beaver; also *Tree-chewer, Tail-slapper*

Gibbler – mud fish

Grey grippers – mussels, clams; also *Spiny Clots*

Leapers – frogs

Paddle-flappers – water fowl, including ducks, geese

Quarn – crawdad or crayfish; also *Flippin Quarn, Foam Crawler,*

Rippling Gibbit – water snake

Segmented curler - shrimp

Skimmers – water bugs

Sneaky Log – gator

Two-legged, Thinker-doer, Determiner – general terms for humankind; Also *Tender* – human gardener.

Ven – small water bugs; *moss vens*

Features within and around The Flow:

Aft bank – the left bank when facing downstream

Big Blue – the sky; atmosphere; also the non-Flow

Bloated floater – a dead animal

Bottom resters – water-logged debris, branches, leaves

Deluge – hard rain, storm

Divide – when one river or stream branches-off or divides into two

Freezes – 2 types: a *great freeze* solidifies an entire river, creek, etc. A *rough freeze* only freezes part of a body of water – usually the edges and/or surface.

Hither bank – the right bank when facing downstream
Khoots – objects originally from beyond The Flow (discarded items, human litter, refuse); includes *Crystal khoots* – glass objects/bottles found in The Flow; *Floppy Khoots* – paper, especially cardboard; and *Tin khoots* – metal items.
Merge – confluence of two rivers, streams
Occurrence – a catastrophic event; most often a pollution event
Orb – the moon
Penetrating Flow – an underground river
Sharp-flash - lightening
Sol – the sun
Span or Bank-spanner – a bridge
Still run – an area of calm beneath the current; usually along the bottom of rivers, streams
Surface floaters – floating debris, branches, leaves
Surface vessels – boats, rafts, kayaks, inner tubes

The seasons:
Winter – called by several names, including the Long Night Season, the Stormy Season, and the Barren or State-Change Season.
Early Spring – commonly referred to as the Thawing Season or the Flooding Season.
Spring – commonly referred to as the Growing or Blooming Season.
Summer – commonly referred to as the Long Light or Bearing Season.
Early Autumn - commonly referred to as Leaf-Fall.
Autumn – called by many names, including the Turning Season, the Season of Reversal, the Homing Season, or just the Passage.

About the Author

Photo by Gineve Lynnara

Ishara Kassirer has studied human nature, meditation, and diverse spiritual traditions since her early twenties. After graduating with a Bachelor of Arts degree in Communication Theory, she relocated to the east coast of Scotland, where she lived and worked for three years in the world renowned Findhorn Community. This experience broadened her understanding of human potential and introduced her to the concept of other realms, both embedded in and overlighting our own. After returning to the US, she felt called to pursue depth psychology. She received her Master's Degree in Counseling Psychology from the Institute of Transpersonal Psychology in Palo Alto, California, and has continued to study various healing traditions including energy work and classical homeopathy. She works now as a psychotherapist, is a dedicated student of *A Course in Miracles*, and lives with her husband in the beautiful Pacific Northwest. She is co-author of the spiritual holiday book, *Angelic Inspirations*. The *Droplet's Journey* books are her first works of fiction.